Luminous

THE LOST HEIRESS

Written and illustrated by K.D. Willow

For B

Wishing you joy and peace in the days to come.

KD Willow

Cover illustration by Tanya of @thomssbird_art

Printed in the United States of America

First printing, 2019

ISBN 978-1-0960-9586-6

TABLE OF CONTENTS

Thank you to all who helped make this book possible.

An extra special thanks to Mr. Charlie.

PROLOGUE

A wail echoed throughout the house and reached the ears of those passing by in the street. The pain was great. However, the promise of new life filled all who heard with excitement, for there was a much beloved couple in this kingdom who were expecting their first child. Every citizen was ecstatic when they first received the news. Many even rushed to purchase extravagant novelties for the new heir. The wife glowed in her pregnancy. Her sad eyes sparkled whenever she spoke of the precious bundle within her. The husband always seemed to be smiling, no matter how demanding she became.

All the land was abuzz the day of delivery. The parents-to-be had decided on a natural childbirth, without the aid of magic, in the comfort of a humble cottage. They also wished to keep the gender of the child a secret until birth. Of course, the mother knew exactly what she'd be having and even had a name chosen. Yet, when anyone asked, her lips remained sealed. Townsfolk, both young and old, often gathered to make their guesses on the name and gender. Some hoped for a boy to follow in his father's footsteps and become a strong leader; others preferred a girl to have the same grace and understanding as her mother. Still, there were some who had no preference. They simply wanted to know to end the suspense. People awaiting the announcement mingled near the door and in the street. The night sky was lit by the heavenly body in all its fullness accompanied by countless stars that illuminated the ecstatic faces below. The new mother's cries were all but drowned out by the crowd's idle chatter and the chirping of insects.

The children present grew restless, and one tugged at his father's coat, longing to escape the apprehension. A few onlookers shifted nervously, praying the pain was not too unbearable. All at once, the world became silent. The wailing ceased. The crowd inched forward eagerly in effort to hear the infant's first cry…but none came. Mother nature herself had reached a standstill as many held their breaths.

A man stepped forward slowly and reached for the door just before it flew open. The healer who had been assisting in the delivery bolted from the house and pushed through the crowd of worried faces. In his hurry, he failed to see the small stone protruding from the earth, causing him to trip and fall. His medical tools flew from his bag as it hit the ground with a thud. An impatient child stared up at him with wide eyes and saw the terror etched across the mender's face. The man scrambled to his feet and fled whatever horrors had befallen the cottage. As the confused onlookers turned back to the home, the silence was finally broken by sobbing. It was soft at first, but steadily rose in volume. Before anyone could move toward the door, the sky became dark as though a blanket had been thrown over the celestial lights. Parents quickly brought their children close and many in the crowd created lights in magical lanterns. Some panicked and returned to the safety of their homes. Those who had come from far off lands scurried to their ships, including the impatient young boy who was scooped up by his father.

The mother's sister, who had obediently waited outside with the others, ran into the house as soon as she made enough light to see. The sobbing had escalated to two voices. She stumbled down the dark hall to the room of delivery. Her mind raced with questions and fears. When she reached the bedroom door, she saw a hellish light glowing from its edges. She warily swung the door open and was greeted by an uncanny sight. The mother laid haggard and pale on the blood covered bed. Her husband was at her feet bound by enchanted ropes, powerless. No infant was in sight.

The woman called out to her sister and hurried to her side. She then attempted to unbind the man to no avail. "What on earth happened?" Neither were able to reply, for they had frozen in fear. The sister slowly followed their gaze to the opposite side of the room. She saw nothing at first, then a dark figure emerged from the shadows.

"You! What have you done?" she accused. Her eyes darted about the room and she asked, "Where are they?" The figure only smiled, a most sinister grin. His face was unclear in the limited lighting, yet there was no mistaking his identity. She gasped as a low chuckle escaped his lips. The sound made her skin crawl and all goodness seemed to fade from the world in his presence. He glided toward the three cowering on the bed and stopped inches from the sister's face. She found herself paralyzed with fear and a tear escaped the corner of her eye. Satisfied by their terror, he turned toward her light and blew it out.

The three were left, shaken, in utter darkness.

CHAPTER I

Special Delivery

My dreams were often frequented by a recurring image. I'd find myself lying in a small meadow surrounded by trees. The air and ground are cool, and a warm breeze makes my skin tingle as my hairs stand on end. The sun acts as a soft blanket, warding off all worries and troubles. The wind blowing through the leaves resembles voices of the trees, whispering secrets far too sacred for my ears to understand. I breathe in deeply the crisp fragrance of the forest and the wildflowers. Here I find peace. Clouds drift lazily overhead and I watch intently as their shapes twist and curl in slow motion. Leaves and branches brush against one another. Birds and insects chirp both near and far. All is well until darkness slowly creeps in. An evil entity emerges from where they lurk in the shadows, and tendrils of darkness slither and writhe toward the center of the clearing where I lay. My breathing hastens. Finally, the inky tentacles consume me, and I am left in arrant darkness until I wake.

My dreams slowly faded as I felt the sun caress my face. I clung to sleep as long as I could, for my alarm had not yet sounded. My mind wandered back to that meadow. I no longer woke in terror after seeing such things; rather my thoughts were those of curiosity. I'd long given up trying to make sense of the dream and attributed it to no more than simply the stresses of life. Still, in the corners of my mind, I couldn't help but wonder if it held some deeper meaning.

My alarm tore me from my thoughts, and I rolled out of bed. I drew the curtains from my window and let the sunlight flood into my small apartment bedroom. I'd been living on my own for almost a year while I tried to figure out what to do with my life. Memories of that day interrupted my train of thought; the last day I had seen my mother alive. She was always so strong while raising me and I couldn't help being taken aback when I saw her fragile form barely disturbing the thin sheets of the hospital bed. We didn't speak as I sat beside her, her frail hand in mine. Even then, she refused to let her pain show. I, however, was not so strong. She wiped the tears from my face and pushed a small brown envelope into my hands. I didn't get the chance to look at it with her when the doctors rushed me out of the room. My eyes locked on hers until the door separated us for good.

Since that day, I strived to be more than the shell I had become. Working helped me stay motivated, though I often felt stuck going through the motions. I closed my eyes and tried to imagine where I would be if Mom were still with me.

The thing I loved most about her was her sense of adventure. She and I were always traveling and trying new things. My lips formed a small smile as I glanced along my shelves of colorful souvenirs. Images of each place we visited flickered in my mind like the dim flame of a candle. My eyes traced the line of trinkets and lingered on the envelope. It was the last thing she had ever given me. The pouch was made of rough parchment complete with a shiny wax seal which concealed her final words of encouragement to me. Mom always had a passion for the unconventional, a quirk she inevitably passed to me.

When I finally brought myself to read the letter, her words became ingrained in my heart, *"My dearest Taylor, have faith and be strong. Life is an adventure, and like all journeys, it is not the destination that is most important. What truly matters are the lives you touch and the inner growth you experience. I am thankful for the great journey you gave me, and I pray you understand how proud I am of you. I am confident that you will accomplish great things. Everyday, I thank my lucky stars that you were placed in my life. Now, my journey has come to an end but there is still much in store for you. Go, find yourself, and live your life to the fullest."*

At times, I felt she would be disappointed to see where I was; a year out of high school and nothing but a boring little apartment, a boring job, not even a pet for company, and no adventures of any kind. Sighing, I closed the curtains and dressed for work. I arrived at Mr. Charlie's Antique Shoppe at 8:05 and started preparations for another busy day of dusting artifacts. We rarely received any customers, especially in the early hours of the day. Yet, despite my objections, I was given the opening shift. Jay and I were the only employees and his grandfather, Mr. Charlie, owned the store. My routine began with glancing around the shelves and making sure everything was in its place.

The books were sorted neatly along a tall shelf, and many were bound in beautiful vintage covers. Some even bore designs etched into their surfaces in gold and silver leaf. Most of the books contained captivating stories, others told of historical moments and legends, and a select few held names of ancestors long forgotten by their families. The shop was made up of four main rooms overflowing with vintage furniture, toys, décor, dishes; you name it.

I took special care of the wide array of small boxes. I used to imagine what priceless wonders they may have held before they ended up in the shop. One in particular had a latch with a golden dragon wrapped around the hilt of a sword. It was made with incredible detail, right down to the shiny teeth of the tiny dragon. Whoever crafted it put great care and patience into its design. That's what I liked most about it.

Once I was sure nothing was out of place, I commenced the exhilarating task of watching the artifacts collect dust until lunchtime. I read to help me pass the time. As I lost myself in the velvety pages, I fidgeted with the silver butterfly whose wings stretched around my right index finger. Three diamonds made up its body and silver swirls spiraled outward, giving the wings their intricate design. My mother gave it to me for my high school graduation, and I immediately fell in love with her gift.

"This is to keep you strong as you spread your wings and begin your flight into the next chapter of your life," mom said.

I smiled at her use of such cliché. Her words echoed in my mind often, but some memories were too painful. I snapped from my reminiscing and returned to my book. Soon, I was lost in a world of fantasy, my preferred state of mind.

I jumped from my chair when the doorbell sounded. *Odd, I wasn't expecting a customer so early.* No one had entered, so I made my way to the door. I was completely alone in the shop, but I caught a glimpse of someone rushing away from the window. I reached for the door when my foot hit something. Whoever was there left a grimy package directly in the doorway. It wasn't uncommon for the shop to receive mysterious gifts. They were often oddities donated to his collection by Charlie's friends. I lifted the parcel and carried it to the counter, careful not to get any of the dirt on my clothes. I sliced it open with a box opener and found it full of crumpled paper. Whatever it held inside must have been extremely fragile.

Tenderly, I removed the wrappings to reveal a round ornamental box that fit perfectly in the palm of my hand. It

looked ancient. It bore minuscule golden patterns on its deep violet surface and stood on three matching pegs. It was clear the same care had gone into its detail as the dragon box on the shelf. My hand hovered over the lid and I moved to lift it when the door flew open.

"Hey, Tater-tot! Whatcha got there?" Mr. Charlie strode into the shop on his morning rounds. He carried two large cardboard boxes, no doubt full of more antiques for me to organize. The flaps of the top one bounced up and down as he walked toward me. It was overflowing with what looked like toys including a goofy faced turtle. I stifled a giggle when I caught sight of it.

"I wish you wouldn't call me that; somebody might hear you," I said with sarcasm. He chuckled and stepped up to the counter.

"Oh, I'm too old for this," he sighed as he lifted the boxes to the desk. I removed the top one and took a closer look at its contents. It was full of colorful tin toys, from spinning tops to cheerful animals and everything in between. He asked again about what I was holding, and I retrieved the spherical box from the counter.

"Someone left this at the door; I didn't see who though. They must know how much you love a mystery," I joked.
His eyes lit up with excitement as he dusted off his hands, picked up the delicate item I held and began to inspect its sparkling designs. I watched his curiosity grow with each passing second.

Despite being a man nearing his sixties, Mr. Charlie possessed the heart and wonder of a child; a fact I knew would never change. His height of just over six feet gave him an air of intimidation, but within moments of meeting him all that remains was a giant teddy bear.

"This is incredible!" he exclaimed. "Are you sure you didn't notice who left it?"

I had no time to answer before he slid behind the counter and rummaged through drawers in search of something.

"Ah-ha!" He gripped a magnifying glass and examined the bottom of the tiny box, which looked even tinier in his immense hands. "There is an inscription here, take a look."

He thrust the glass and box into my hands. I chose to humor him and inspected the text myself. A coin-sized sun lay fastened in the center of the three prongs at the bottom of the box with microscopic writing in strange letters. Something about the markings seemed familiar to me, but I couldn't place where I'd seen them before.

"What does it say?" I asked, handing the box back to him, "Do you recognize the words?"

He pondered and said, "I have no idea. I've never seen anything like it. It must be a very old- maybe even extinct language." His voice bore a frustrated tone. "Let's see if we can open it. Perhaps there are answers inside." He gripped the lid, but nothing happened. We searched for a lock or latch or button or something to let us in but found none.

"Maybe the hinge is rusty?" I suggested, though we could both clearly see the whole box was well polished and shiny.

Mr. Charlie shook his head and said, "I'll ask around. I'm sure one of my colleagues knows where it came from and how we can open it. In the meantime, I brought some antique toys I want you to go through." He slid his load toward me.

"More toys?" I asked in mock bewilderment, "That shelf is almost full! You'll need a whole other building before summer at this rate."

"Hey, business isn't that bad. There are tons of people who love antiques, we just need to advertise. Speaking of, I want the nicer toys to go in the front window. Maybe we can get some kids interested in the wonderful world of vintage memorabilia. Then we'll make some profit!"

He untaped the other box and tossed me a towel to dust the contents with.

"Oh and let me know when Jay gets here. I had a talk with him about workmanship. Again."

We shared a laugh before he went to the back room where he worked on finances and fixing up worn out stock. Straight away, I got to work cleaning and organizing little dolls, cars and various other children's joys and arranged the ones in good shape in the window. I lined up fourteen tin soldiers in the front and placed a miniature dollhouse behind them. I enjoyed thinking about the past lives of the toys and wondered who might have played with them. Each antique had its own story. Some even had many different stories.

As I finished, I sensed movement outside and was overcome by an uneasy feeling. A spindly tree stood outside the window and its sparse leaves cast dancing shadows on my arms. Through its branches I saw a small figure, like that of a child, watching me from across the street. I looked closer and saw it was a girl in some kind of gypsy costume. Upon realizing I had seen her, she panicked and darted into a nearby alley. I pushed the odd occurrence from my mind and busied myself with arranging the finishing touches. As soon as my shift ended, I left to pick up some lunch for Mr. Charlie and myself.

Our meal of choice came from a downtown deli that always gave fellow shop owners a discount. Without fail, Samuel was the one behind the counter when I went in for lunch every weekday. I always felt awkward when giving him my order. We talked for a few weeks and though I had a huge crush on him, we never seemed to connect. Still, we remained pretty good friends, and he was one of the few people I felt I could talk to.

"Hey, Taylor," Sam greeted me as I walked in, "The usual?" I smiled and nodded before inspecting their dessert display.

It took all my willpower not to add a slice of their famous chocolate pie. He saw my hesitation and added two gourmet cookies to my bag before handing it to me.

He waved my protest and said, "It's on the house. Everyone needs to satisfy their sweet tooth."

"Thanks, Sam," I replied, hoping my embarrassment didn't show.

"Anything for my favorite customer," he said grinning. I laughed nervously and waved goodbye before leaving.

On my way back to the store, I saw the girl again. This time she was hiding behind a large truck. She ducked out of sight each time our eyes met. As I looked closer, I realized she was a bit older than I first anticipated. Her short stature paired with the youthful freckles sprinkled across her dark skin made her appear younger, not to mention the fact she was dressed like a trick or treater. I called out to her but received no response as she disappeared in the busy street. I had a sudden urge to find her until I remembered the food that was slowly losing its warmth. With a sigh, I wrapped my jacket tighter around me as a strong autumn breeze cut through.

I intended to arrive back at the store before my coworker decided to show up. Jay was on the afternoon shift but never arrived on time or alone. He either came in with a group of boisterous friends or his girlfriend, Casey, which made it difficult, if not impossible, to keep him focused on doing his job. That guy was always getting into trouble when left alone in the store; thus Mr. Charlie and I did our best to be present whenever Jay was around. This time, however, was different. By the time I arrived back at the shop, Jay was already there with Casey on his arm and his grandfather was nowhere in sight.

"Hey, Kida! It's so great to see you!" Casey ran to me and knocked me off balance with her embrace. I nearly dropped the food before she finally let go. "Mr. Charlie just left. He said he had some very important business to take care of and asked if you wouldn't mind helping with the afternoon shift while he's gone. I don't know when he'll be back, but he said I could stay and help this time. Won't that be fun?"

I stood bombarded by the flow of information. Casey was the only person who referred to me by my birth name since the day I let it slip that Taylor was the name my mother chose when she adopted me as an infant. Once Casey gets hold of personal information, she never forgets it. She gave me one final squeeze before dragging me over to the counter where a stack of pamphlets lay strewn about.

"Jay and I were just discussing a couple's Halloween costume. Our friends are having a party in a few weeks. We can't decide if we want to be more cute or scary. Of course, Jay prefers scary, but I just love these medieval dresses."

She showed me a Halloween magazine and pointed out her favorite costumes. All I could think about, though, was the strangeness of the situation. It wasn't at all like Mr. Charlie to leave so suddenly, let alone allow Casey to stay. While, she is a wonderful person, her perky attitude and talkativeness however tend to destroy productivity, not to mention the fact that all Jay can see is her when they are together. Anyone our age would be jealous of how close they were.

"Kida! You should totally come to the party with us!" Casey exclaimed suddenly. She knew I was uncomfortable in crowds, but she was always determined to get me involved in their circle.

"I'll think about it, Casey. Maybe I'll go if I find a good costume," I replied reluctantly.

Her eyes lit up and she said, "We could go shopping together! Jay and I are going this weekend, we can pick you up." Her excitement was contagious, and my nerves faded. She really had a way of making anyone feel more comfortable. I smiled at her and looked through the magazine.

"Did your granddad happen to mention where he was going, or why he left in such a hurry?" I asked Jay while I thumbed through the glossy pages.

"Nah, he did mention you'd be bringing sandwiches though." It was then I noticed he had already taken the bag and was rummaging through the food. "You did get ham, right?"

"Oh, good! I'm starving," Casey chimed in.

"Hey, slow down! One of those is for me," I exclaimed and quickly grabbed my sandwich before Jay could devour it. Luckily, Mr. Charlie usually ordered two. I decided it wasn't worth haggling over the cookies and let the lovebirds have them.

"Actually; come to think of it…" Jay mumbled through a mouthful of food, "Dad did say something about a strange delivery. He seemed pretty worked up about it."

Of course, I had forgotten about the box. I looked around the shop but couldn't find it anywhere. He must have taken it with him to find answers. I returned to the counter and tried to get the box out of my mind, but the whole ordeal made me feel very unsettled. My boss was an easy going, fun loving man, and not much could upset him. As I finished eating, I pushed all troubling thoughts aside and focused on keeping my coworkers on task. Casey proved helpful and loved admiring the old jewelry while color coordinating each piece for "proper presentation." A few customers visited, most only looked around. However, one couple bought a few toys for their grandkids. As the shift came to a close, Jay fidgeted anxiously.

I rolled my eyes at his nervous energy, "You two can leave if you want. I'll close up for the night."

Relieved, Jay replied, "Great, I really hate being cooped up for so long." He grabbed Casey's hand and they headed out the door.

Before they left, she turned back to me, "Thanks for letting me help; I had a lot of fun. All this old stuff is so exciting!"

She grinned and with that the pair was gone. I smiled to myself. As sickening as their romance was, I enjoyed their company. Casey had a way of making me feel less like a third wheel and more like a friend.

As I finished straightening up, something caught my eye. The door in the back stood slightly ajar. Mr. Charlie did leave in a hurry if he didn't bother locking the back room. It was as messy as ever with papers scattered on the desk and boxes littered about the floor full of random odds and ends for fixing rare artifacts. I hesitated before entering. Did he leave our mysterious gift? All I found were broken thingamabobs and paperwork. I returned to the counter in disappointment. After retrieving my purse and jacket, I locked the door and headed home.

As I walked, my mind was intruded with thoughts of the bizarre girl. I kept glancing around the street expecting to see her head poking out from behind something. By the time I reached my apartment, I was fully convinced someone was watching me. Maybe I was being paranoid, but I could not shake the eerie feeling. My purse hit the countertop with a light thud, and I tossed my jacket onto the couch. I removed my hairpins and braided my hair loosely to ease my throbbing headache. Heaving a sigh, I prepared herbal tea in attempt to relax; a remedy my mother taught when I felt nervous before a performance. Despite my timidity, being on stage was like second nature to me. Whether dancing, singing, or acting, it was the one place I could be myself and feel free to be whoever I wanted to be at the same time. Even so, things were never the same without mom to cheer me on.

Ding. I removed the teabag from the mug. It more closely resembled a giant teacup with colorful sneakers carefully painted along the rim. I added a spoonful of honey and a drop or two of mint extract to complete the calming mixture. Sinking into the couch, I slowly sipped my tea and drowned out my worries with music from my headphones. My eyelids grew heavy as the soothing liquid slid down my throat, spreading its warmth throughout my body. My breathing slowed, and the worries of the day faded away as I drifted off into shallow slumber.

Suddenly, I became alert. Movement could be heard right outside my door. By now, the remainder of my drink was cold. I arose to investigate, but there was no one there. Sighing, I closed the door. It must have been a neighbor walking by. The sun had gone down while I slept, so I felt along the wall for the light. As soon as I could see the room, I froze. There, on my countertop, was the box. Panic rose in my stomach. Someone had come into my home while I was sleeping. My eyes darted around the apartment, wondering if they were still inside. I gulped the last of my tea to rid my throat of the lump that had formed. I moved slowly to the box, listening and searching for any sign of movement. Convinced that I was alone, I grasped the peculiar little ornament.

My hands trembled so vigorously, it almost slipped from my fingers. I took a deep breath and held it closer to my eye. The clasp which held it shut was shaped like a sun, not unlike the one on the bottom. Maybe now it would open. When I touched the lid, it flew open and released a blindingly bright light that illuminated the entire room. Gasping, I tried to close it, but the white glow captivated me and refused to let me go. All at once, the light faded as did the world around me. I sank to the floor and the outline of a figure loomed above me.

CHAPTER II

Rude Awakening

I awoke with a start to the sound of muffled voices. I rubbed the sleep from my eyes until the blurriness faded and tried to make sense of what I heard.

"That was too close. Why are you incapable of following the simplest directions," scolded a gruff woman's voice, "If anyone had seen you…"

"Hey," said another, much younger voice, "it's not my fault the old man decided to take it. I did the best I could!" the other person huffed, and the faint ruffling of papers met my ears. I strained to hear more, but their tones became too hushed. The room in which I lay had very limited lighting, still I could see an empty bookcase and a dusty table a few feet away. It wasn't a door that blocked my view of the next room, rather a thick curtain. I examined the cot they had placed me on and found no restraints. Something didn't quite add up. These people had kidnapped me, but didn't bind me to keep me from escaping, didn't gag me to prevent crying for help, and there wasn't even a door to lock. My fear slowly ebbed away as I shifted. As soon as I moved, the cot let out a loud creak. I instantly froze in terror, praying they hadn't heard me.

"She's waking up," one of them said. Cringing, I began to panic as footsteps neared the room. My heart raced as I watched a gnarled hand pull back the velvety curtain followed by a woman's wrinkled face that clearly hadn't smiled in years. Her head appeared gigantic and misshapen until I realized she wore a scarf which covered most of her hair minus a few silver strands. The scarf curled upward in the back, giving her head the semblance of a large seashell. She spoke not a word when she motioned for me to rise. With no other option, I stood warily and followed her.

A strong aroma met my nose as we entered the next room, and I pondered a moment before placing it: candle wax and mildew. A tattered cloth covered the only window in sight, but it failed to conceal a sliver of sunlight peeking through the edge. *They kept me here all night!* More empty bookcases lined the walls and a short table surrounded by pillows stood in the center of a faded rug. On the table sat a ceramic tea set. Steam rose from the teapot's spout as the woman guided me forward. The girl I had seen before drank from one of the tiny cups from her seat on one of the pillows. As we approached, she set down her cup, swiftly poured another, and placed it across from her.

"Sit," the woman grumbled as she forced me to the floor. She then hobbled off to another room, leaving the two of us sitting in thick silence. I took care to avoid eye contact as I glanced about the room. The only light shone from dozens of flickering candles scattered along the table and shelves, an obvious fire hazard. Though she was out of sight, I could hear the woman rummaging around from wherever she had disappeared. The girl cleared her throat and scooted the second cup closer to me.

I didn't move a muscle when she spoke, "I understand this is all strange to you, but our purpose is not to harm you. Mam and I are here to help. My name is Aliza, and this is a cup of tea. See? Nothing to be afraid of."

Aliza smiled at me and nodded to the cup while taking another sip from her own. Gingerly, I did as she wanted. The tea's relaxing aroma filled my nostrils and reminded me of my mother's, laced with mint and rosemary. I blew away the steam and carefully took a sip. Its familiar taste was uncanny. Slurping noisily, I took another more eager sip. Across from me, Aliza giggled. My face grew hot as I lowered my hands.

"Sorry, I shouldn't have laughed," she apologized, still smiling, "It's just, you look so uptight when you really have nothing to worry about."

Before I could defend myself, Mam returned with an armful of sheets. She dropped the cloth in my lap and ordered, "Put these on."

Aliza giggled again as I held up the garments. Upon closer inspection, I found cutouts in the fabric for my arms and head.

"What are these? What's going on? I'm done playing along with your games, I deserve an explanation!"

I leapt to my feet and stared at the odd pair. Mam stood a head shorter than Aliza, but I was taller than both.

"Why did you abduct me?" I demanded, "I've done nothing wrong!"

"Listen, hon. I get that you're a bit overwhelmed by all this, but I really need you to cooperate right now. All will be explained in due time and the sooner you trust us, the sooner we can get started." Mam faced me and grabbed the clothes from my hand.

"Get what started?" I asked. Without answering, she pulled an itchy dress over my head. It was very tight and barely fit over my not so small hips. She clearly lacked in fashion know how; she herself sported a skirt made of many clashing layers of patterned cloth.

She grunted, "You're a bit wider than I anticipated. Aliza, you'll go out and buy her something more suitable when we get back. 'Till then, lend her something of yours. Make sure it's something you won't mind letting go."

"Yes, Mam," Aliza answered obediently as she assisted me out of the makeshift gown.

"Wait, get back where? Where are you taking me?" The two of them busied themselves ignoring me as my frustration grew.

"There is much to prepare! We haven't got all day, girl," Mam huffed impatiently, though I remained unsure as to which of us she had addressed. She led me to a beat-up door on the back wall that likely led to a broom closet and ordered me to stand there out of the way until further instruction. They were both thoroughly distracted by their preparations and thoughts of escape raced through my mind as they scrambled about the tiny house. I strained to hear any noise coming from outside, like cars or animals to give me some idea of where I was. My ears were met only by silence and an occasional birdsong. The way out wasn't very far from where I stood, and I could easily reach it in a few quick steps. Once I got out, I would run as fast as possible to the nearest…anything. I'd be able to outrun the old woman, without question. Plus, Aliza seemed nice enough to let me go if given the opportunity. I watched intently as they each set down armfuls of supplies and left the room. Here's my chance!

I was in midstep when Mam called out from another room, "There is no need to plan an escape, hon. I'll be releasing you shortly. Besides, I may not have much speed left in these bones, but there is no doubt I'd catch up to you." My jaw dropped. Is she reading my mind? My fists clenched when I heard Aliza's stifled giggle. She brought me another dress, much more flattering than the first. The skirt hung mid-calf, though it was meant to reach the ankles.

"Please, tell me what's going on. Why did you abduct me? And how is it you know what I'm thinking?" Neither answered as they adjusted my new outfit. Within moments, I looked just like them, totally out of place in this world.

At last, Mam spoke, "Let's start with this; we didn't, as you put it, abduct you," I stared skeptically as she continued, "we had no choice but to bring you here."

"Believe me," Aliza added, "better you wake here than the state you were in when you passed out." Mam shot her a glare and Aliza clammed up.

"It's time you knew the truth," Mam sighed, "sit down, dear." She guided me to an old stuffed chair. A cloud of dust floated up around me as I plopped down into it and stifled a cough. She crouched onto a matching ottoman directly in front of me. Her eyes were squinted so tightly the irises were hidden, but as we faced one another they widened just enough for me to see what her lids concealed. What were once bright blue eyes had long since clouded over holding a closer resemblance to the steam from the teapot than eyes. I gasped, and my eyes darted away, not wanting to offend her by staring. She grunted and grasped my hands in hers. Mam's hands were warm and soft. I looked to Aliza for some clue, but she was sitting off to the side with her eyes closed, utterly oblivious and therefore unhelpful.

"Close your eyes," I heard her speak, but her mouth didn't move. At a loss, I did as she asked. We sat in silence for a few moments, and, just as all patience left me, she spoke. Her voice was distant and powerful.

"Cleanse your mind of things of this world and listen carefully. Long ago, in the land of Ordenia, malice blossomed in the hearts of many. Provinces and kingdoms pitted against one another, leaving few untouched by promise of war. Lambart, the crowned jewel of eastern Ordenia, was one of the last to be struck by the rising turmoil of the land. A child was stolen from her Lambartian family on the very day she was born." As she spoke, her words came alive in my mind and my vision flooded with images unlike anything I had seen before.

"The child was cast into darkness as she was forced from her realm. Years passed before she was found in Warren, a realm much different from hers. It was the Great Voyager, Mamanea who located the child, but by then the girl had found a place in this world, a home. Mamanea kept the child safe until the day she would return to her world and destroy the evil that had taken root there. Her powers were filtered into a vessel, not to be released until they were called upon." The images left as instantly as they had come, and my eyes flew open.

Then, I burst out laughing, "This is a joke, right? This is crazy talk! Are you saying I'm some magic wizard person destined to save my 'real world' from some bad guy? That's insane!"

My jaw hung open incredulously as I stared back and forth between them; searching for some sign of set up or surprise. They looked back at me with grave expressions.

Aliza stood suddenly and glared at me, "This is no joke! It's actually very serious!" She stormed out of the room, indignant, as I rolled my eyes and turned back to Mam.

"I suppose you're the 'Great Mamanea', huh?" I asked, my voice thick with sarcasm. Not only were my kidnappers clearly incompetent, but they actually seemed to believe in this nonsense.

Mam only stared at me with her squinty eyes. The images from her story were unexplainable, and awfully real. Still, I couldn't believe it was true; stuff like that just doesn't happen in reality.

Sighing I said, "Look, I would love to help you; really I would. I mean, I love an adventure as much as the next person. You just can't expect me to believe that I came from a completely different world and somehow have magical abilities. It makes no sense. And another thing, you kidnapped me. That's not the best way to make friends."

She grunted and retrieved an object from her pocket. It was the box. "When you opened this, what did you see?" She asked, completely avoiding my accusation.

"What does that have to do with anything?" She thrusted it forward and insisted I answer. "I-I only remember seeing…"

"Light," she cut me off and finished my thought, "That is what you will bring back to Ordenia."

"How can you know all of this? It's impossible; why should I believe you?"

"All I ask is that you have faith. You do not need to understand everything now," she said, placing the box in my hands, "I may be blind physically, but my sight far exceeds that of any other. In the same way, you are more than the poor standard you credit yourself with."

I gaped at her as she stood, with much strain. "Come now, we must complete our preparations for the journey home."

Bewildered, I asked, "How are we supposed to travel to a different world? In a spaceship?" Without answering, she led me to the estranged door.

"I am not at liberty to train you; therefore, you must learn as you go. Trust your instincts."

With no more explanation, she placed her hands on my shoulders and squared them toward the door. I glanced nervously at Aliza as she came back into the room as cheerful as ever. A large duffel bag hung on her back. "Let the box remind you of the feeling you received upon opening it for the first time."

I cupped the box in both hands and traced its curves with my thumb, all the while staring ahead at the door. Whatever they wanted me to do, wasn't happening. I became disappointed, despite the obvious ridiculousness of the situation. Did I really think there could be more out there? Am I not doomed to live a simple monotonous life after all? As crazy as it all seemed, the more I thought about it, the more I longed for it to be true; the more I believed it could be. I felt insane, but I closed my eyes and, with a deep breath, envisioned the moment I first experienced the unnatural power of the box. Suddenly, a bright light flooded my vision. I shut my eyes more tightly, but I couldn't dim the red glow of my eyelids. A warm sensation coursed through my body and left my fingertips tingling. I gasped and stepped back as the once brilliant light faded.

"She did it! She actually opened the portal!" Aliza shouted as she jumped up and down.

A throaty chuckle escaped Mam's throat, "Did you ever doubt she would?"

Aliza shook her head, "I just didn't think it would happen so soon."

They continued chatting as I stood dumbfounded between them. My eyes adjusted as I blinked away the glare from the light. The edges of the tattered doorframe were now glowing so brightly, the entire wall resembled a softly burning flame. I remained speechless as I glanced around the room at the once empty shelves, now overflowing with books and parchment. In seconds, the once dreary place had become warm and inviting.

Mam snapped to get my attention and addressed Aliza and me, "Heed my words, children. Be wary as we enter this world. Aliza, things are not as they were when you left. A war waged in confusion has infected the land. Keep your intentions from untrustworthy ears. As for you, Kida, forget all you once knew. You will soon be returning home."

Her mystical words filled me with nervousness and excitement. Mam then gestured for me to open the door and Aliza hummed excitedly behind me. My hand trembled as I reached for the glowing handle. I slowly turned it and opened the door. To my amazement, I was met by a busy street full of people dressed as strangely as us. Carts piled high with goods rumbled amongst the crowd and shoppers haggled left and right with countless market vendors.

"What is this place?" I whispered when I finally found my voice. My brain struggled to process how anyone could have set up a hoax so elaborate. The walls could have been sound proof, someone could have turned on a flood light behind the door, maybe the bookshelves were trapdoors, or maybe it was all nothing more than a dream.

Whatever the case, I stayed frozen in awe as Aliza answered, "Welcome to Ordenia, our home."

My hand still clutched the box when Mam gently took it and placed it into a small satchel. I gave no response when she patted my shoulder and said, "The two of you go on ahead. Take Kida to your tailor friend to be fitted. I spoke with his family years ago, he should have exactly what you need. You can stay with him while in the market. I've left instructions in here for you as well as the necessary funds for your journey."

She shooed us out the door, but Aliza turned back frantically saying, "Mam, wait! Aren't you coming with us? My training isn't even near completion."

"You are more than ready for your task. Besides, I have other preparations to take care of here before I see you again. Now go and remain cautious."

Mam nodded to us then closed the door to her small wooden cottage. Seeing it from the outside was slightly disorienting. I stared in wonder until I realized Aliza had walked away, and I hurried to catch up to her.

"Where are we going?" I asked.

"You heard Mam. I'm taking you to my old friend, Xomax. His family used to own a clothing booth and, if I'm correct, he recently took over the business," she answered patiently.

"How do you know that?"

She glanced at me sideways before sighing, "Because I'm a voyager. Apprentice voyager actually, but I have become quite skilled."

"And that means…you travel a lot?" If she was annoyed by my ignorance, she didn't show it. I couldn't stand being so clueless, though. She explained that voyagers are one of the many groups of people who can use magic. Her abilities allowed her to travel mentally through time to see the past, present, or future of anyone.

"It's the most difficult form of magic to master. Most voyagers only see small glimpses of time and are left to decipher what they mean." She went on to explain how Mam was the greatest of all voyagers because she had given up her physical sight to broaden her powers. I listened intently until a sweltering wave of heat broke my concentration. When I discovered the source, I froze in my tracks. There, a mere eight feet away, was a dragon. It blew mesmerizing flames into a gigantic furnace, rattling the chain around its neck as it did. A thick leather strap stretched around its back holding its wings closed. Its dark green scales glistened with each fiery breath. A hefty blacksmith lumbered out from behind the creature and began hammering a piece of metal on an anvil just as Aliza yanked my arm.

"Do not make eye contact! Those beasts are as dangerous as they come," she warned frantically. I glanced back time and again as we continued. I had seen the dragon's eyes, and they had seen mine. They stared into the deepest part of me. There was something about the intriguing creature that refused to leave my mind. It may have been his state of entrapment that appeared cruel and unnecessary. Maybe my inner child was simply having a field day. Or perhaps it was the sense that he, like me, did not truly belong here.

Nevertheless, we walked farther along the path until we reached a booth with fabric strewn and hung all about it. I failed to see anything that resembled clothing, however. The booth seemed abandoned with a heaping pile of textiles where the vendor should have stood. To my amazement, the pile began to move as soon as we reached the counter. A white-haired man emerged from the slew of patters with three pairs of spectacles propped upon his head and another with huge lenses on his nose. His frizzy hair jutted out in all directions as if he had spent too much time around static electricity. Aliza and I both jumped back at his sudden appearance. She grinned and waved at the man until recognition flashed in his eyes. He held up a finger and rummaged through the many stacks of cloth, eventually acquiring what he so adamantly searched for. He handed me a patched satchel and shooed us away, refusing payment.

"What was that all about? Was that your friend?" I asked as I cast a glance over my shoulder. The estranged man had disappeared; no doubt back into his pile.

She shook her head and said, "He's an old craftsman. He's got booths all over this market and pops up whenever he is needed. That'll be your new satchel, a roomy one from the looks of it. I'm surprised he didn't charge us for it." As she spoke, she transferred the box from her bag to mine while explaining the importance of keeping track of my new belongings.

After a few moments, she added, "You can call me Liza, by the way. It's what my friends called me growing up."

For the first time, it occurred to me that I had never introduced myself. It must have slipped my mind in all the excitement of the abduction and introduction to a new world. I assumed they knew who I was since they seemed to know everything else. As if reading my thought, she nodded.

"You're Taylor, but I'd prefer to call you Kida, if that's acceptable to you. It is your birth name, after all," she said with a smile. I forced a smile in return. Being addressed by my real name made home seem so far away, even though I had only been gone for a short time. Still, if this world knew me as Kida, I may as well embrace it. A sudden realization flashed in my mind.

"Hey," I started, "I heard you mention an old man earlier. That was Mr. Charlie wasn't it? What did you do to him?"

"Your old boss?" she answered without meeting my gaze. "I didn't *do* anything to him. I only snuck the box away from him and gave you an alibi for disappearing."

"Alibi?" I should have known it would look suspicious if I failed to show up for my shift that morning. She used an object called a yad to create somewhat of an alternate reality without me and left it in the shop. My worries eased knowing he was safe, though I clung to the hope things would go back to normal.

"Liza?" I asked, nervously. She slowed her pace and looked at me, and I inhaled deeply, "When are you going to let me go back?"

Confusion flashed in her eyes, "I thought you wanted to help us? No one is forcing you to be here…but it is your destiny. We need you, Kida."

"But I have no idea what I'm supposed to do," I answered defensively.

"Neither do I, but we can figure it out. We have Mam. And I'm sure she'll let you go back once we've taken care of things here. That is, if you still want to."

I sighed and clamped my mouth shut. Mam made it seem like I had to stop a war, but the market we were in seemed peaceful enough. Besides, according to Liza, everything back home was just waiting for my return. Maybe a fairytale adventure wouldn't be so bad after all. And if things got too bad, I could always go back the way I came. With a plan intact, I followed her farther into the thickening crowd.

We passed dozens of booths before she stopped and looked around, her face drawn in frustration. She muttered something under her breath and pulled me to the side. I asked if we were lost and her face gave me all the answer I needed. Panic rose in my chest again. "Don't worry," she assured me, "I know where to find a map. It's by the docks, not far."

It became increasingly difficult to keep up with her petite height as she wove nimbly between the people bartering and trading amongst the vendors. I lost sight of her on multiple occasions only to catch a glimpse of the brightly colored hairband that kept her hair from her face bobbing up and down within the sea of market goers. I pushed and shoved my way through the crowd in effort to keep up with her. I felt rude in doing so, but the people paid no attention to me. My mind wandered as I admired the astonishing array of garb. It was as though I had traveled back centuries in time. While deep in thought, I lost track of Liza, yet again. I searched frantically for her until someone grabbed my arm and forced me from the condensed throng. I panicked until I met a familiar face.

"I knew you'd get lost in there. I didn't see it or anything, but I knew it was bound to happen," Liza said cheerfully as she let me go.

I rubbed my arm in embarrassment; I wasn't used to depending on others, let alone strangers. Once we were free of the massive horde of body odor, I smelled the saltiness of the sea. We finally reached the docks. My shoulders felt lighter as I took a deep breath of the refreshing air and followed Liza to a man tying up his fishing boat. While she procured a map, I stepped to the edge of the dock and peered into the distance.

A mass of land sat on the horizon and gulls screeched overhead. Ships dotted the water's surface; most were of modest size, likely used for fishing. The ones that weren't resembled those found in glass bottles at souvenir shops with impressive sails and skilled craftsmanship. The beautiful water changed color with each passing wave; from blue to green and everywhere in between. Its hypnotic motion captivated me until a figure tumbled from the side of a nearby ship. It wasn't until a splash of water sprayed my face that I looked up. Someone had just been thrown overboard and was now thrashing furiously in the ocean. My eyes darted around frantically, but no one else seemed to notice. Whoever it was clearly need help.

Without a second thought, I plunged in after him. My body shuddered as it met the icy water, but I kept moving. He was still splashing like a madman when I reached him and only panicked more with each moment. It wasn't until I touched his arm that he calmed down enough for me to help. He kept his eyes tightly closed while I spoke to him. He was quite a bit larger than I and could have easily dragged us both down. I instantly regretted coming on my own as I swallowed a gulp of seawater.

As I pushed to keep my head above the water, I felt my ring loosen from my finger. Before I could grip it, the man pulled me under again and my ring slipped from my hand. I didn't have time to mourn as I kicked with all my might to keep from drowning. Eventually, the guy relaxed, and we swam to the docks where Liza's distraught face waited for us. My legs ached, and my lungs burned with each kick. As we reached the ladder, I felt a sharp sting on my leg. He climbed up first and Liza helped us to our feet. By this time, a small crowd had gathered at the edge of the docks. A fisherman brought us blankets and shooed the onlookers. Liza paced back and forth speaking excitedly about some omen or something as the crowd dispersed. I hadn't realized how chilly the air was until a breeze cut through my now soaked body.

I turned to the shivering man, "Are you okay?"

He nodded. "You didn't have to do that," he said somewhat defensively. He appeared a few years older than I with a well-built frame and scruffy face. His dark hair was pulled back messily, and I caught the glint of a jewel near his ear.

He scooted closer the me and stuck out his hand, "I'm Leo." I accepted his hand shake and introduced myself.

"Kida? I should have known," he answered in mock surprise.

"Do you know me, or something?" I asked in bewilderment.

He let go of my hand and smirked, "You could say that."

I had to crane my neck back slightly to examine his chiseled face and averted my eyes when they met his. He acted friendly, but there was an air of mystery in his deep brown eyes.

Who was this guy? Why was he thrown from that ship? And how on earth does he know who I am? He eyed me in a funny way, and my discomfort grew. I opened my mouth to interrogate him when Liza grabbed my shoulder.

"By the moon, Kida!" She shouted and pointed to my side. I followed her gesture and saw red streaming down my leg from my left thigh. I stood there, mesmerized by my own blood. Leo tore one of the blankets and pressed it against the wound until the bleeding stopped. He then secured it with another strip, and I flinched as he pulled it tight.

"It's not very deep; it should heal in no time," he said as he completed the knot. "You will have an impressive scar though."

He flashed me a charming grin as he handed me the remaining piece of blanket which I used to clean the rest of my leg. There was a gash in the skirt Liza loaned me and its pale green fabric would be forever tainted by my blood. I apologized to her, but she only shook her head giggling.

"I guess that's why Mam told me to give you one I wouldn't mind parting with," she said. "Come on, I've got the map. We've got a long walk ahead of us; his shop is all the way on the other side of the city."

I wanted to thank Leo for his help dressing the cut, but he slipped away without so much as an explanation. I thought I saw his long dark hair darting behind a building, but I was uncertain. Liza lead the way once again into the busy street. To my relief, the number of shoppers died down significantly. I peeked over her shoulder at the map. It showed what looked like a gigantic complicated maze of booths. There had to be thousands of vendors out there! No wonder we lost our way. I sincerely hoped she'd be able to find this friend of hers.

I made sure to stay directly behind her and avoid distractions, but a loud racket coming from a stand to my right soon demanded my attention. We were coming up to a booth with a bird cage large enough to hold a bear. Inside, hundreds of tiny creatures flew around in sporadic spirals. The fuzzy bat-like beings darted to and fro in every color under the sun. A man, no doubt the booth owner, lifted a latch to open the tiny door of the cage then stuck a child's arm inside. My breath caught in my throat as I waited for the kid to scream in pain. Rather than jump back in fear, however, the child burst into laughter when he removed his hand and one of the creatures clung to it. I stared at the cage until we passed it, and it eventually fell out of sight.

We walked for what must have been hours before Liza stopped abruptly. I nearly ran into her and followed her line of sight to a tall curly haired boy. He held a stack of clothes but dropped them as soon as he saw Liza. He ran to her and embraced her before picking her up and swinging her around; all the while the two laughed and chattered excitedly. I remained where I stood, careful not to interrupt their heartfelt reunion. I couldn't help feeling a twinge of jealousy at their display but pushed my own loneliness aside. I busied myself tightening the cloth around my leg until Liza called me over.

"Kida, this is Xomax; Xomax, Kida." She gestured between us respectively for a proper introduction. He led us to the back of his booth, and behind the counter was an entire shop of clothing I failed to notice before. He drew a curtain to conceal us in his shop.

"Wow," I said, "Are all the vendor's this huge?" Xomax only looked at me inquisitively without answering.

"Sure, they are," Liza said quickly. "Everything around here is more than meets the eye."

My embarrassment grew at my ignorance of this world. Unsure of myself, I stood silently while the other two caught up on lost time. To my amazement, Xomax rubbed his fingertips together, forming a tiny bead of light. I gawked at him as he placed the light in a nearby lamp where its glow filled the entire room. He then rummaged through a wooden chest and pulled out a bulging leather sack which he handed to me.

"Here, change into these," he said absentmindedly before directing his attention back to Liza.

I stared wide eyed at him, but he paid no attention.

He directed me to a fitting room and called to me once I was inside, "Toss your old clothes over the curtain when you're finished."

My curiosity about the light he'd made would have to wait. The bag contained a vial of ointment and fresh bandages directly on top. Did Mam know I'd be wounded and tell Xomax? If so, why didn't she just warn me? I sighed and removed the old wrappings, flinching as I did. The ointment stung at first then soothed into a warm buzz. Bubbles formed at the top of the cut, so I wiped them away and wrapped the bandages around snuggly. Next in the bag were a pair of dark pants with leather cord laced along the sides. I adjusted the lacing to fit me perfectly and loosened the area near my cut for comfort. I then donned a light blue tunic that fit like a glove, save for the sleeves which needed to be rolled twice to free my hands. The bottom of the tunic was flowy and feminine. I left my tank top on under the tunic to make up for its plunging neckline. I sifted through the remainder of the bag and found a pair of stockings, more vials and bandages, and a few items I didn't recognize. Outside the curtain were a pair of boots with a golden pattern around their rims. I hurriedly slipped them on and found Liza and Xomax in a back room speaking in hushed tones.

"You've come just in time," Xomax said cautiously, "Things are far worse now than they've ever been. Half of Ordenia is at war now, including Husun. That's right on our border, Liza. It's only a matter of time before Terak arms its forces and Tafara along with it."

"That's impossible," she retaliated, "Tafara is the largest trading city in this or any world! And it has always been peaceful." The two argued on until a floorboard revealed my presence. Xomax heaved a loud sigh and Liza called me in. I froze when I realized the three of us were not alone.

A monkey-like creature with a long tail and triangular nose sat on a table while Xomax fastened a scroll to its neck. Its bulging golden eyes peered up at me, its face framed by ears much too big for its little head and its long boney fingers gripping the edge of the table. Its unblinking gaze held mine, and Liza piped up, "Before you freak out, Kida, there is nothing to be afraid of."

I snapped back to attention and insisted, "I'm not afraid; just curious."

My eyes darted to the creature as it vanished in a cloud of blueish-grey smoke, making me jump back in surprise. Xomax smirked, though he tried to hide it. "Where did it go?"

"I sent it to my family to let them know you were here," Xomax answered, returning to his more serious state. Puzzled, I glanced between him and Liza.

She clarified, "That was a malak; they're used to send important messages. They're incredibly rare and difficult to train…"

"Which is why we are extremely lucky to have one. My parents gave it to me for this very occasion," Xomax said, finishing Liza's thought. I nodded in mock surprise as Liza inspected my new getup.

"Not bad, but something is missing," Liza said as she sifted through my bag. She removed what looked like a very thick belt and exploded with laughter.

"What's so funny? What is it?" I hated being so clueless and grew tired of all the embarrassment.

"Come on, even Warren had corsets. Just stand up," she instructed. She wrapped it around my waist and tightened the thick string.

"I thought corsets were supposed to go under the clothing," I said between gasps. My struggle only made her laugh more as she finished the adjustments.

"Fashion is different here, Kida, as I'm sure you've noticed. Besides, something this beautiful shouldn't be hidden." She admired my full ensemble and nodded in approval, "In fact, I dare say this is what classy people around here wear."

"I wouldn't go that far," Xomax chimed in, "however, they are quite nice, if I do say so myself."

Their words brought little comfort, but I did feel a bit less like a fish out of water. I stared at my new garb. The corset truly was beautiful and added a touch of silky elegance to my apparel. The tunic itself was made of soft, cozy material and the pants were tough and durable. I moved a thick strand of hair from my face and decided it was time to take out my braid. There was no telling how messy it must've looked after a day or so left unattended. It was still damp in some places from our trip to the docks.

I asked Liza for a brush, and she retrieved one from her tiny satchel. I held it for a moment glancing from the brush to the bag. There was no way it could have fit in such a small pouch. I then recalled what Liza told me about my own satchel. 'Roomy' must mean they could hold more than they appeared. The concept reminded me of a character from my childhood as I sat and combed through my badly tangled hair. It reached all the way down to my waist in long brown waves.

While I brushed, Xomax left the shop and Liza skimmed over the list Mam had given her. She then took my satchel and packed it with items "essential to our journey" as she put it. With each new entry, the bag never changed in appearance. It was as though it could never reach full capacity. I finished detangling and prepared to braid the frizzy locks when Liza stopped me.

"Let me do it," she offered. "You'll fit in more if you have a hairstyle to match your look."

I relinquished the brush and let her fix my hair. It was very relaxing to have someone else do it for a change. I thought again of my mother and how she used to mess with my hair. She'd run her fingers through it to help me relax on stormy nights. Before I learned to do it on my own, I never trusted anyone to braid my hair except for her. Her fingers were so nimble, I'd often fall asleep as she did. Tears welled up in my eyes, and I forced the memories away.

Xomax returned with food from a nearby cart as Liza finished taming my mane. She led me to a mirror, and I marveled at her work. She'd made three braids from the top and plaited them into one big one at the back where she twisted them into a bun that rested at the base of my neck.

I thanked her, and Xomax beckoned us to the table for dinner. My stomach growled audibly as I sat. "I figured you'd want to start with a more familiar meal," Xomax said handing me my plate, "Liza said you'd like this." The plate held a leafy salad full of plump vegetables and bread crumbs with even a small block of cheese on the side. Mine contrasted with theirs in every way. Their meal consisted of large cuts of meat smothered in some sort of runny sauce.

"Oh, it's been ages since I've tasted dragon fillet," Liza said as she sank her teeth into the dripping meat. I dropped my forkful of food and stared, gaping at her.

"Relax," Xomax muttered to me through a mouthful of food, "it's not really dragon meat. They make it from harmless lizards found in the forest."

Lizards; like that's any better. I struggled to wrap my mind around it, but I was too hungry to be disgusted. I focused on my own plate and took another bite, but not before sifting through its leaves to make sure there was nothing questionable concealed in its deliciousness. The greens were fresh, and the cheese was rich and creamy. When we finished eating, Xomax hung hammocks in three corners of the shop. The lights dimmed outside as the sun disappeared behind the horizon of the great market.

"Hey, Liza, how long are we going to be here?" I asked, nervous about what kind of answer I'd get. What if we never returned? Would I never see my friends again?

She yawned and climbed into her hammock before answering, "I'll tell you the plan in the morning. Just be patient."

I wasn't pleased with the answer, but I didn't push the matter further. I grabbed two pillows and a cover before entering my own hammock. The noises of the market continued into the late hours of the night. Eventually, I drifted off to sleep with the idea that all would be well tomorrow and the events of the day were no more than a dream.

A boney hand emerged from the shadows and gripped a cube of quartz. Black smoke writhed and squirmed within the precisely cut prism. Her skin was as thin as paper and blue veins could be seen snaking around each bone before they disappeared into her sleeve. The meat on her bones was sparse, but she appeared neither hideous nor beautiful. She leaned forward in her throne and beckoned her beloved.

"It seems our long-lost heroes have returned," she said in a sultry voice. Her lips spread over her ivory teeth in a sinister smile. She clutched the crystal before taking the hand of Sanguent. "I think it's time we pay a visit to our old friend."

The man nodded and bowed to plant a hard kiss on her ghostly hand before leaving. The woman was once again left in the silent confines of darkness. Her surroundings were peaceful but hidden inside was a chaotic torment that had been building up for years. Her eyes rolled back in her head at the thought of the taste. The taste of her victories, the taste of their fear, and the oh so sweet taste of their blood. She breathed in deeply as she fell deeper into the black Abyss.

CHAPTER III

Warm Welcome

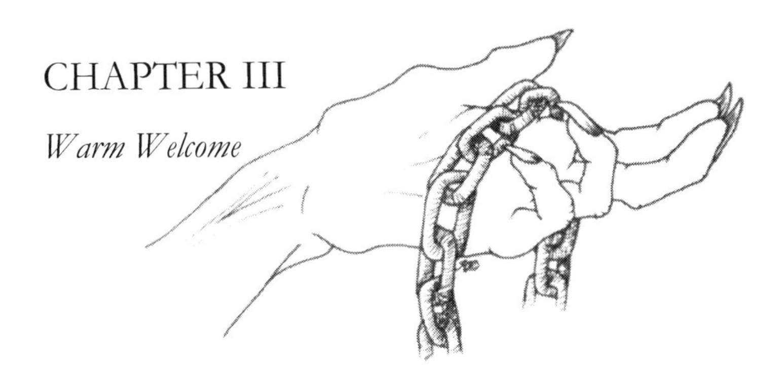

I awoke the next morning ready to begin another day of work only to find I was not in my apartment. Bizarre memories flooded my mind leaving me in a disoriented daze. So, it wasn't a dream. My feet hit the floor and the hammock wobbled as I moved. I stared aimlessly at the room. Xomax voice reached my ears from the front of his booth; he must have been working. Liza wasn't in her hammock. I massaged my temple in attempt to subdue the dizziness that plagued my head and tried to find Liza.

She sat at the table in the next room and chewed a piece of dried meat while she read Mam's list. She greeted me briefly as I took the seat across from her. She was real. All of it was real. My brain struggled to process it all. Liza looked up from her list and said my name a few times before I acknowledged her.

"Kida, are you okay?" I held her gaze for a moment then nodded slowly. She seemed unconvinced and placed a fruit into my hand. "You should eat something. We've got a lot to do today."

The fruit resembled a lumpy apple and I turned it over in my hand before forcing myself to take a bite. It wasn't half bad, and I finished it slowly then cleared my throat, "So, what's the plan?"

She swallowed and said, "It's been so long since I've been here, I don't really know where to start. I'd hoped Mam would be here by now."

"How long have you been gone?"

She sighed and set the paper on the table, "I haven't been home in eleven years. Mam took me to Warren after my parents were killed by…" She turned away without completing her sentence. My heart immediately went out to her.

Trying to change the subject, I asked, "Is Warren…?"

"Where we just came from? Yes," she answered quickly, wiping away a tear before it could fall. "I'm sorry, I shouldn't be so emotional. We have a job to do." She handed me the list and I read the instructions carefully.

- See Auster for satchel
- Find Xomax
- Purchase equipment and food
- Meet council in Dorac
- Find Kida's parents

There was more listed, but I stopped at the fifth line. My parents? I'd often dreamed of finding my real parents as a child until I realized they must not have wanted me. Could it be possible they were here, alive, and searching for me all this time? Liza noticed my hesitation and slowly took the page from my hands. I wasn't aware of how tightly I held it until the corner tore off between my fingers.

"Mam says they love you very much and always have. When you were taken, things got really bad here. War broke out in three of the twelve Ordenian provinces, including Lambart where you're from. It became far too dangerous to bring you back, so Mam let you stay in Warren for safekeeping. It's a realm that can only be reached by a portal of which only one exists, so she knew you wouldn't be traced," she explained. "That was the day she lost her sight."

I wrung my hands nervously as I processed what she said. Too much was happening too fast. "Why did they go to war?" I asked.

"There are many theories," Liza started, "but we believe one person is to blame."

"Who?"

She hesitated, "Mam should be the one telling you this. I'm only her apprentice." She stood abruptly and slung a bulky bag over her shoulder, "Let's not sit around and talk the day away. There's still more we can do before we head out."

We left the tailor stand and joined a once again busy street. The air was thicker than before, and a slight mist hung in the air as we pushed our way through the crowd. The cloudy sky threatened to rain at any moment. The first stand we visited sold tools for all kinds of 'pesky predicaments', according to the vendor. We shopped for hours until at last, Liza was satisfied. As we started back to meet Xomax, I recognized the booth with the giant birdcage. I pointed it out to Liza, but she shook her head.

"Mam gave us money to buy the necessities. You don't need a wyrm," she said. I lingered by the booth and watched the creatures swarm within the golden cage. With a closer look, I could tell they were tiny dragons, or wyrms as Liza called them, of every color imaginable. Liza thumbed through her satchel as I admired them. The man running the booth saw my interest and informed me about the fascinating creatures.

"Most of them have what we call a third wing. It protrudes from their spines and folds down when they aren't in flight. That's what makes them the most agile creatures to ever grace our skies," the man said as my interest piqued. "As soon as you make the bond, the little buggers will be at your side for eternity." The more I heard, the more I wanted one. I turned back to Liza and started to ask again when she held up her hand.

"Hold on a minute. It looks like Mam gave us just enough extra to get you a wyrm," she sighed as she glanced sideways at the cage, "although, I don't see why you'd want one."

"Really?" I asked in disbelief, "this is so exciting!" She laughed at my exclamation as the wyrm man led me to the cage. My heart pounded louder in my chest with each step. He lifted the gate and thrust my hand into the colorful vortex. I forced my eyes open, expecting something to happen. The wyrms shifted to the far side of the cage and avoided my hand entirely. My disappointment grew as I stretched my fingers toward the tiny beasts.

"No worries, little lady. Wyrms aren't for everyone," the man said as he instructed me to step back. Before I could move, the swarm suddenly burst to my side of the cage. The puffs of air from their flapping wings tickled my arm and made the hairs stand on end. I then felt the poke of tiny talons gripping into my hand.

"I'll be… you got one!" The man helped me remove my arm slowly, so not to startle my new friend. "And a pearl no less; one of the smallest."

The wyrm clung to my hand and stared at me with its beady eyes. Her pearlescent scales glistened in the sunlight and reflected every color of the rainbow as she moved. Her wings were soft to the touch, like a puppy's ear. The fuzz I'd seen before were miniscule hairs that lined her underside. Her arms were attached to her wings like a bat and the tip of her tail resembled a sharp arrowhead. She examined the big world around her before burrowing into my sleeve and popping her

head out of my collar. Her claws tickled my skin and I couldn't stop myself from laughing.

"Heh heh, she like ya," the man said and handed me a sack of food. "Fun fact about these wee beasties, they fly almost immediately after birth and never stop until they've made their bond. Oh, and keep a sharp eye out for thievery. Those buggers like shiny things."

I thanked the man and decided the name Pearl suited my new friend perfectly. She perched on my shoulder as we left the booth. Liza walked by my side while guiding me along the street and told me stories of her childhood. She loved growing up here a dreamed of returning since the day she left. Apparently, she and Xomax were quite the troublemakers as kids. She pointed out some of their old hangouts and amused me with tales of their mischievous adventures. The old man we met on the first day was their favorite target because of his magic tunnels that connected each of his booths. They would pose as customers in front of his stands until just before he popped up. Then they'd run to another and send him on a wild goose chase. It sounded like a twisted version of ding-dong ditching. We were both laughing when we reached our final stop.

Liza bought a new, much more expensive map that depicted all Ordenia. It was much larger than I anticipated. How are we supposed to find my parents? I found Lambart on the southeastern coast and my heart sank. We were on the total opposite side of the map; it could take months to reach them.

Liza told me that no one had seen them in years. If the war was so bad, they may not even be alive. She did her best to encourage me and insisted they were alive, for she herself had seen them. She refused to explain further when I asked how she saw my parents and I guessed it had to do with her voyaging. I clung to the hope that, someday, I wouldn't be so clueless.

We walked on and I noticed Liza wore a necklace with a crescent moon pendant. I assumed it was a gift from Xomax since she didn't have it until today. I complimented her on it and, though she turned away, I saw the blood rush to her face. She told me her parents had given it to her when she was young, but she'd lost it shortly before leaving. Xomax ended up finding it and kept it safe until her return. It didn't take long for me to warm up to her as we spoke. My nerves eased at the thought of new friendships and the possibility of reuniting with my family. Maybe this world isn't so bad, I thought.

Mam had yet to show when Liza and I grew hungry. For lunch, we met Xomax at an orchard near the edge of Tafara. He'd set up a picnic for us with a vast variety of fruits; a few of which were familiar to me. There was also a plate of meat and cheese. Liza reassured me the meat came from a small bird that tasted like chicken; not a forest lizard. The mist dissipated, and a ray of sunlight managed to break through the thinning clouds. By the time we finished eating, not a cloud remained in the sky. We sat and let our food settle as the sun brightened the earth and covered us in a blanket of warmth. Liza rested her head on

Xomax's shoulder and let her eyes droop closed. Pearl buzzed around the trees before landing on my head. She nipped at my hair until I took out her food and fed her tiny berries. When she was satisfied, she curled around my neck and slept. I leaned against a tree and watched a bird peck at some fruit a few yards away.

Liza appeared to be asleep and Xomax concentrated on something behind me. The concern in his eyes made me turn to follow his gaze. A stream of smoke rose from the treetops in the direction of the market. The smoke thickened and, soon, countless more grey pillars rose upward above Tafara. Before I knew what was happening, Xomax jumped to his feet and ran toward the market. Liza and I struggled to keep up with his long stride. As we neared the vendors, the usual crowd of happy shoppers turned into a frenzy of people escaping flames which engulfed many of the stands. In all the commotion, we lost sight of Xomax. Men and women shoved past us, nearly knocking me to the ground. My eyes squinted in the ever-thickening smog and I clung to Liza's arm to keep from losing her. When we located Xomax, he knelt in front of what used to be his tailor stand. His entire shop now laid in a heap of crackling embers. He was covered in soot and carried two bulky bags strapped over his shoulders.

"You didn't go in there, did you?" Liza shouted above the noise as she rushed to his side. She held his face in her hands and searched for any damage.

He stood and said, as if in a daze, "Half of Tafara is now in flames. Martana has finally made her strike."

His words hit me like a heavy stone and forced me to take a step back. Something about that name haunted me and filled me with fear. His face froze in an emotionless stare as he watched his home crumble to the ground. He then turned to me accusingly and my eyes darted to my feet. Liza grew pale and, without warning, she took off into the crowd. Xomax dragged me after her in the direction of Mam's house. Before it even came into view, I saw the smoke. My eyes darted around frantically, but Liza was nowhere to be seen. I hid Pearl in my pouch and started to enter the condemned house. Xomax held me back, saying it would be too dangerous. He gave me no chance to argue as he tied a damp cloth around his mouth and nose and dove into the house just as the doorway collapsed.

I clenched my fists and paced outside, willing them to come out any second. The once cool air grew stifling and beads of sweat formed on my forehead. The crowd disappeared with unnatural haste and, to my horror, I became aware of the few people who hadn't made it out and never would. The world blurred, and a rush of sickness overtook me. I buckled over and retched until nothing remained in my stomach. My eyes watered, but I could sense a shadow come over me. A loud thud shook the ground not far from where I stood. Something swung and knocked me off my already unsteady feet. My breath caught as inhaled a cloud of dust from the road. Someone yanked me too my feet as a loud roar rattled my eardrums. My back met a hard surface; a wall that was shockingly still standing. When at last I found my bearings, I came face to face with Leo. He'd wedged me between the wall and himself and refused to let me budge.

"What do you think you're doing?" I asked forcefully. He covered my mouth with his hand to silence me and the ground moved again. I peered over his shoulder and saw a giant scaly beast thud past us. My eyes grew wide and Leo's hand muffled my scream. My heart pounded so loudly, I feared the dragon would surely hear. As soon as it was out of sight, I pushed Leo away. I started to speak, but a fit of coughs overtook me. Leo patted my back and dusted me off.

"I never trust dragons," he said gruffly, "I don't understand why the fools would keep one in such a populated place." Pieces of the wall began to fall on top of us and we were forced from our hiding place. He held me back as I tried to leave and glanced around to make sure the coast was clear.

"Let me go," I demanded. "I need to find my friends!" He started to protest then gave in and led me to Mam's cottage. Ashes were all that remained, and tears welled up in my eyes. I was too late. Suddenly, Leo shoved me to the ground.

"Stay down," he hissed as he drew a sword from his side. The dragon slowly rounded a corner and headed straight for us. Its eyes were as red as the embers that littered the street. Leo made the first move and lashed out at the beast. The dragon let out an earsplitting roar as sword met scaly flesh. They fought on and I inched away discreetly. I heard movement behind me and saw a figure emerging from the ashes.

As my vision cleared, I realized it was Xomax carrying Liza. I ran to meet them but tripped and face planted into the dirt. I failed to notice the long tail that blocked my escape. Leo rushed to my aid, but he too was knocked down by the angry beast. The dragon spread its vast wings and prepared to take off. With each flap, we were met by a powerful gust of wind that stirred up clouds of ash and dust. Through the thick tendrils, I saw a body clutched in the dragon's colossal hand, though I couldn't tell who it was due to the smoky air which made vision nearly impossible.

"Come on, we need to get out of here," Leo said. He draped my arm around his shoulders and guided me away from the smoldering carnage. Xomax followed us; Liza still in his arms. It took an eternity to escape the smog and smell of sulfur. Other stragglers made their way to the outskirts of the market with us. Most of the flames died down leaving nothing but ash and mourning in their wake. Many gathered in groups and tended to the wounded. The air was clear where we sat but I still found it difficult to breathe in light of the terrors I'd experienced. The dragon shrank in the distance as it fled the smoldering city. I'd never witnessed such a massacre.

Movement came from inside my satchel and I quickly opened it to release Pearl. She emerged and stretched her wings by fluttering around my head. We settled next to a stump to collect ourselves. Leo sat beside me and offered me a handkerchief to wipe the soot from my face.

"How's your leg?" he asked gently. I hadn't paid much attention to it; I didn't even feel it any more. That ointment was extremely helpful. I told him it was fine and watched Liza. She'd lost consciousness in the fire, but her chest rose and fell steadily. I relaxed a bit more knowing she was safe. She held a small wooden chest in her lap as she leaned against Xomax. He was visibly exhausted and sat with his eyes closed. My own eyes grew heavy as the sky darkened above.

My dreams were haunted by the nightmarish images of the day and I soon couldn't take any more. I awoke to a starry sky by Leo's side. Pearl slept on his forehead and I stifled a snicker to keep from waking him. I shifted to my back to watch the sky. The smoke had cleared completely and made way for the stars which illuminated the night. I searched for the moon and found a small sliver of it peering down at me. Noting felt real. The horrors of the day seemed so far away in the serene setting until my ears were met by the soft crackling of Tafara's remaining embers.

I stared at the stars and tried to find shapes in the array of shinning dots. I lost myself in their beauty as the nightmares slowly faded. Pearl stirred and climbed down to my stomach where she curled into a ball and returned to slumber. I turned my head to Leo. He had come out of nowhere and saved my life. I thought of the moment we first met; a mere day ago. It felt like we'd known each other longer with all we'd been though. Part of me felt indebted to him. His face was so peaceful under the starlight and my eyes traced the edge of his unshaven jawline. A wave of warmth flooded within me and I averted my eyes quickly. This was no time to think of romance. I hardly knew him, after all.

Lights flickering in the distance caught my eye. A swarm of fireflies buzzed over the grass and one floated closer to us and landed on my nose. As I moved to flick it off, Pearl leapt forward and gulped it down. I flinched as her tiny jaws snapped shut around the insect. Leo rustled until he faced me. I shushed Pearl and told her to go back to sleep. She only stared at me with her glistening eyes. I sighed and brought out her food, but she turned away and chased the other fireflies that dared come near us. I smiled and rolled to my side to watch her. She danced through the sky and her graceful movements lulled me back to sleep.

When I awoke the next morning, Leo was nowhere to be found and Pearl had somehow nestled herself underneath my neck. Liza still slept on Xomax's lap with the box held snuggly to her chest. I sat up slowly and Leo's coat slid from my arms. It smelled of oaky wood salted by the sea. I wondered where he'd acquired his new garb since the first time I saw him he wore tattered rags. Pearl rose and scrambled up my arm to her spot on my shoulder as I inspected our little camp. Not many survivors remained, and many others packed up and started down the dusty roads. Broken carts laid abandoned at the edge of the city; some of which may have held useful supplies. I spotted Leo making his way toward us with a large sack in hand. He crouched beside me and handed me an apple.

"Most of the orchard survived the fire. I managed to get there before all the good fruit was cleared out," he said before biting into an especially juicy plumb. Liza stirred and sat up as we ate. She refused the fruit I offered and clung more tightly to the odd little chest. She and Xomax were now covered in bandages.

"What's with the box?" Leo asked, causing Liza to look up suddenly. I too was curious, but something about her demeanor made me hesitate to bombard her with questions.

Tears cascaded down her face and she blubbered the words, "Mam is dead."

My jaw dropped. Her words sounded so final and the devastation on her face told me it must be true. I knew exactly how it felt to lose someone that close and wouldn't wish it on anyone. My own eyes burned but I choked back the tears before they grew heavy enough to fall. I scooted closer to her and tried to comfort her to the best of my ability. Xomax placed his arm around her and pulled her to his chest while I held her trembling hand. As she cried, she muttered about how Mam had taken her in and raised her since she was a little girl. She mentioned Mam using something called a filter before she died, which had to do with the box. I couldn't make sense of all she said, but she made it clear she wanted to get moving as soon as possible.

"I have to get to the Lunar Isle. It's mine and Mam's native land. She would want me to…" she trailed off and gazed forlornly at the last thing she had left of her mentor. I couldn't help but feel responsible. I mean, I'm supposed to be here to help people, right? The true weight of my situation came crashing down on me all at once. This was becoming all too real. I thought this would be some magical adventure; I never imagined lives would be at stake; though I suppose I should have. They did tell me this was war. If I was going to master some powerful magic, I'd rather it be sooner than later. Leo must have sensed my uneasiness, for he beckoned me to him.

"Let's walk," he said offering me his arm. I hesitated before taking it and walking with him to one of the fallen carts. He picked through its contents and found a sturdy tangle of ropes, which he wound up and placed in his tote. "None of this is your fault, you know," he said while he worked. "If you ask me, I'd say you've way more weight on your shoulders than you deserve." He flushed as he spoke.

"How is it you know so much about me, anyway?" I asked. He shrugged and busied himself scavenging for more supplies. When I demanded an answer, he wouldn't look me in the eye.

I pried for more information and at last he turned to me and said, "Because I've been waiting for you, okay? Lots of people have. There aren't many who don't know the prophecy of Lambart's lost heir. I'll admit, you're not what I expected, but I have faith that you're capable of more than what you give yourself credit for."

I was taken aback by what he said, and it was my turn to flush. His words were meant to bring comfort, and I guess they did in some respects. However, a whole new burden was thrust upon me at the thought of hundreds, maybe thousands of people counting on me and awaiting my arrival. He stopped what he was doing and said, "I apologize if I made things worse."

"No, it's okay," I insisted. I then pondered for a moment and asked, "What did you mean by heir? I'm not royalty, am I?"

"I've heard you are of royal descent, but hierarchy is different within your kingdom. No one truly understands it; in fact, Lambart has been without a leader for quite some time now." Without a leader? Was he talking about my parents? "Regardless, I want to help. I haven't been able to get you out of my mind since the day you saved me from drowning." He shot me a charming smile which I couldn't resist smiling back to.

"Speaking of that, why were you thrown from that ship?" I asked, deterring from the topic of my lineage.

He raised one eyebrow and answered, "Let's just say, the cap'n and I didn't see eye to eye and leave it at that."

"Okay, okay. I can take a hint. It's kinda odd though, that a sailor of your physique can't swim."

His head shot up, "It's not that strange, is it?" I shrugged and nodded.

"Hey," he defended, "lots of strapping sailors can't swim. The way I see it, there's no point if you can float." I added an empty canteen to our supplies and shook my head smiling. His gaze was unwavering when our eyes met, and my face grew hot.

He laughed, "I expect it would be a handy thing to learn sometime, huh?" I agreed, and we sifted through another cart until the other two joined us.

"It's time to go," Liza said. Her voice was sturdier than before and she carried two large duffel bags in addition to her satchel.

Xomax sighed and rolled his eyes, "She wouldn't let me carry them." He then explained our plan of action. We would go find his family in Dorac which was also the meeting place of the council. From there we'd sail directly across the Xeros Channel to the Lunar Isle. Xomax had only been in Tafara to await our arrival and assist us in our journey. Many of the original market families, including Xomax's, long since moved westward in effort to avoid the spreading war, leaving behind temporary shopkeepers in their stead. After my meeting the council, we'd cross to the crescent shaped island where Liza would visit Mam's old house to say her final goodbyes before beginning our quest to find my parents. The plan seemed simple enough, though I remained leery of what 'meeting the council' entailed. Nevertheless, I felt a bit of excitement as we left the once great market city and began our journey.

The first few hours of which, were spent arguing the best route. Both men were partial to the idea of following along the coast to stay furthest away from potential battlegrounds. They also wished to avoid the vast forest that stood directly in the path leading straight to our destination. That's the path Liza wanted to take. Through the woods would be quickest, but much more dangerous than traveling along the coast. I tried to find a way to compromise but failed miserably. Both paths held merit, but we could find no middle ground. It seemed time was of more importance than safety. Eventually, the guys gave in to Liza's determination and we headed in the direction of Zole woods.

Martana's meditation was interrupted by the incessant pounding of footsteps nearing her chamber. She subdued her instinct to lash out and slaughter the cause of such a disturbance when remembered who it was. Her beloved, Sanguent, entered bringing the glad tidings of their latest victory. He burst through the door and exclaimed, "We've got her!"

He held open the door as a giant scaly hand tossed a wrinkled body through that rolled across the floor and stopped at Martana's feet. The dimly lit room was soon filled with maniacal laughter that echoed off the walls and reverberated back creating a choir of lunatics. At last, her waiting was reaching its end. The Great Mamanea was conquered and her abilities were now in the hands of the most powerful being in all Ordenia. Martana unsheathed a long dagger and motioned upward with her hand. Mam's haggard form floated into the air inches from the dark figure. She held the dagger directly in front of her and began the ritual of absorbing the voyager's powers. A wispy glow formed around Mam's body and slowly drifted toward the dagger. Before it reached the sharp blade, however, it vanished. Martana's eyes flew open and she cursed. She slashed and jabbed at the woman before her, but no blood came from the open wounds. In a fit of rage, she hurled the blade across the room where it embedded itself in the splintered frame of her throne. She paced back and forth as Sanguent attempted to comfort her. His loyalty was a marvel to behold. He always stayed by her side and was the one thing in this world she didn't loathe entirely, perhaps even loved.

"Maybe she's been dead for too long?" he offered but was silenced by a deathly stare as Martana continued pacing.

"No, it didn't work because the old hag has already filtered her powers; I should have known," she answered in a frustrated tone. She despised changing her plans and that voyager had always been one step ahead. But no more. She glanced at Mam's still suspended body and cast it into flames.

"I will possess her powers, one way or another. We shan't give up hope, my love," she said while she gathered the ashes as the fell. There was one thing she knew for certain; magic doesn't simply disappear. She'd have to wait; another thing she hated. Anger welled up inside her until she could bear no more. Sanguent saw her rage radiating from her eyes and made himself scarce to avoid being caught in the crossfire. Martana strode from the room in search of her favorite pawn; the dragon. She found him in the barren courtyard standing stiffly awaiting his next task. She hurled an electrifying blast that struck his side and caused him to topple over. As if in a trance, he slowly regained his posture.

"You disgusting beast," she growled as she dished out another blow. "You were too late!" She struck him repeatedly, with one burst after another, until he writhed and seized on the ground and could no longer stand. When at last she stopped, his chest lay still for a few moments before rising weakly. Tears streamed down her face as she heaved heavy breaths and stared at the chain she'd placed around his muscular neck. It bound them together and made the once proud creature her puppet in bringing forth her release. She thrust out her ghostly hand and more chains shot forth from her fingertips and snaked around the fallen dragon. She glided to him, gripping one of the heavy links. She'd keep him alive for now. He may yet prove useful to her. She then tossed the chain and returned to her chamber to formulate her next move. The iron links clattered as they met the heard cobblestones, causing the prisoner to flinch and tremble.

CHAPTER IV

Road Trip

We walked for days before I insisted we find some other form of transportation. Other travelers passed us on horses and carts, but none were willing to offer their services. I stared longingly at each one as they passed. We stopped at the edge of a village and rested underneath an abandoned hut with a missing wall; likely worn away by years of neglect. Xomax continued into the village in search of a cart for sale. Liza brought out an odd fruit called a marac and divided its three sections between us. It was shaped similarly to a banana with rough dark skin that easily peeled away to reveal light pink meat. The sweet yet tangy taste reminded me of kiwi.

We enjoyed our picnic while Leo determined our position. He informed us that we were a week away from the forest. Liza had worsening migraines since we set out. She assured us they were nothing but her powers acting up. There were often moments when she held a far-off look in her eyes and I supposed they were visions of another time. After each episode, she scribbled furiously in a leather-bound notebook which we were forbidden to read.

I experimented with my own powers under Liza's supervision. She taught me certain abilities that anyone would master, such as the light Xomax made before. There were also forms of magic only specific people could perform, like voyaging. My form was called illumination, according to Liza, and was so rare that only members of my family practiced it. It was, by far, the most powerful and most complicated skillset and I was on my own figuring it out until we could find my parents. Thus far, all I could do was make sparks fly from my fingertips when I attempted to make a light. Pearl fluttered restlessly as I fiddled with my hands. Frustrated, I took a break and watched Pearl as she chased ants along the ground. Impatience grew within each of us 'til at last we saw Xomax's curly hair bobbing toward us. He'd found a buggy lead by a dapple-grey mule named Thunder. It even held crates of extra food and supplies in the back. We climbed aboard the rickety contraption and enjoyed the ride. The climate became warmer as we made our way southward.

Liza spoke incessantly of things of this world and I listened as intently as I could, though most of the information only confused me further. Pearl entertained herself by bouncing from person to person before landing on Leo's head and curling up for a nap. A giggle escaped my lips at the tiny creature and her new-found friend. He passed the time by whittling a small piece of wood. When I inquired as to what he carved, he refused to show me insisting I wait until it was finished.

Days came and went, and my attention often slipped into the rhythmic rumble of the wheels on the bumpy road. We traveled only in the daylight and paused every few hours to let Thunder rest. My mind wandered to the many road trips my mother and I took growing up and I longed for home once again. I snapped to focus when Liza mentioned my real parents. She assured me that it was absolutely necessary to reach her island if we were to find them. All the best voyagers resided there. She fell silent as though her words brought back painful memories. I invited her to fix my hair again in hope of distracting her from her loss.

She said nothing as she fingered though the braids until they were all undone. My hair fell into soft waves on my back. Liza twisted the hairs which framed my face and tied them back, leaving most of the waves free to bounce and sway as I moved. I sat silently as she finished.

She sighed and said softly, "I was young when I saw my first vision of you." I glanced back at her as she continued, "I knew instantly we'd become close friends. For some reason, your hair stood out to me and I wanted to style it. I still lived in Elara, my home town, at the time and had lots of fellow apprentices with long hair to practice on whenever we had breaks."

I smiled, "What's Elara like?"

"It's…exciting," she said pondering. A look of nostalgia crossed her thoughtful face, "it's not very big, but that never stopped it from having some of the greatest Moonlit festivals of all time." Her face lit up as she described the joyous events of her people until, suddenly, her voice cut off. She dropped the hair she'd been holding, and her eyes grew wide and out of focus. Her hand moved back and forth as though she were writing in the air.

"Xomax, what's happening to her?" I asked frantically. He glanced over his shoulder and tightened the reigns when he caught sight of Liza. He leapt to the back of the cart and searched through her satchel for her book and something to write with. He placed it in her hands and she immediately wrote hastily on the paper. I looked at him questioningly, but it was Leo who answered.

"She's voyaging," he whispered in awe. "I've never seen it in person before." He edged closer to see what she was writing, but Xomax held him back. Her hand moved across the page in a form of shorthand I was unable to decipher. She seemed to be in a trance as she scribbled fervently what she saw. We sat in anticipation for what felt like an eternity before her hand finally slowed and her eyes returned to focus. She slumped back against the cart and took multiple deep breaths.

"I did it," she said once, barely above a whisper and then again with more enthusiasm. "I did it! I've never had such a successful voyage."

"What did you see?" Xomax asked excitedly, his pride for her clearly showing. She studied her page full of markings and explained to us the time she'd experienced. Her mind had traveled to one of Mam's memories from when she still lived on the Lunar Isle. She didn't tell us everything, but she assured us she would when we arrived. The voyage lifted her spirits greatly. Perhaps it provided evidence that she still had a piece of Mam living on within her.

We got moving again with Leo at the reigns. Eventually, we heard a commotion coming from further down the road behind a large hill. Liza gasped, "It's happening." I looked to her inquisitively, but she concentrated on whatever laid ahead. As we topped the hill, we found the cause of all the noise. A group of about twenty people were strewn along the road; none of them stirred. Their crates had been destroyed and their supplies littered the ground. It was then I heard an all too familiar sound; a dragon's roar. The beast hadn't noticed us when it bounded across the earth and scooped up three of the bodies. It took a moment, but I soon recognized this was the same dragon that attacked Tafara.

It prepared to take off when an arrow flew from behind me and struck the beast. I spun around to see Liza holding a bow and prepping another arrow. The dragon set his eyes on us, his chain clinking around his vast neck. Our donkey brayed in fear as the dragon growled.

"What are you doing?" Leo asked angrily. "Now he's after us!" Liza paid no attention to him as she leapt from the cart and raced toward the now furious creature. Her sudden burst of fury astounded me. Without a second thought, I ran after her. She'd already loosed three more arrows by the time I caught up with her; she was too ready for this. Her excellent shot was no match for the dragon's thick scales and he was easily protected from any serious damage. With each step, the dragon shook the earth. My brave friend continued to pull and fire arrows from her satchel. She must have stuffed hundreds of them in there. A couple of them embedded in their target, but he kept coming.

In a few short steps, he was only a few feet away from us. I thought for certain we'd soon be burned to a crisp when he reared his head back and shot fire into the air. The heat radiating from his massive throat made sweat stream down my neck. He then reached forward to grab Liza.

"Watch out!" I shouted and ran to her; right into the beast's sharp talons. Next thing I knew, I was lifted into the air. Liza screamed my name, but she sounded so far away. The dragon's strong hand gripped me so tightly I could barely breathe. He held me up to his eye and examined his prey. A blast of hot air hit my face with each breath he took. He gazed into me the same way he had when I first saw him at the blacksmith. Black clouds wisped across his iris and I lost myself in his

hypnotic gaze. The world grew dark around me as I slipped back into my nightmare. The feeling was so familiar as the darkness consumed me. Reality came flooding back when the dragon let out a roar that made my very bones rattle. Leo had stabbed him in the leg which caused him to thrash about wildly. As he did, his grip loosened, and I gasped in deeper breaths.

The end of the dragon's chain swung much to close for comfort and I realized it seemed to be throbbing. Evil coursed through each link. I tried to grab it, but he held me too far away. I peered down just in time to see the dragon knock my friends to their backs with one swoop of his tail. Adrenaline burst within me and I reached again for the thick black chain. I was still too far, but I stretched on. The more I strained, the more determined I became. My friends struggled below me, and I closed my eyes tightly. All the built-up tension exploded from my hands in a blinding light that struck the chain and shattered it into hundreds of pieces. Awestruck, I watched as the light dimmed, and the chain fell. To my dismay, I soon fell with it.

The dragon had lost his grip on me, leaving me to plummet to the ground. I couldn't scream; I couldn't even think. All I could do was pray. My eyes clamped shut and I braced for impact, but my body came to a sudden halt inches from the surface. My eyes darted around frantically, and I found Leo's face. His eyes were full of worry as he helped me up and brought me to his chest. I never wanted to leave that warm embrace.

Liza ran to me and grabbed my arm saying, "I am so sorry, Kida. I don't know what I was thinking putting you in danger like that. I should have known better! I'm so sorry." Tears streamed down her face as she spoke. I tried to reassure her that I was fine, but she refused to hear it. Xomax joined us and directed our attention to the dragon. He seemed disoriented and confused and different from before. His monstrous appearance had softened and become slightly more approachable. I moved toward him, but Leo stopped me.

"That thing just tried to kill you," he said as he stepped in front of me with his sword drawn.

"You don't need that," I replied frantically, "he was being controlled by that chain. I think he's safe now."

Leo stared at me, "It doesn't matter who's in control; a dragon will always be a monster." With that, he strode to the creature and prepared to dish out the final blow. I ran after him to stop him, but we both froze when the dragon began to change. His body shrank and warped until he became unrecognizable. In moments, nothing remained of the dragon who'd attacked us except for a haggard young man. He fell to his knees and was unable to stand on his own feet. I hurried to him and draped his arm around my shoulder. The others stood staring as I helped the one who nearly killed us twice now. Xomax was the one who came to me and took his other arm. We led him to the cart and gave him water. His strength returned slowly as he sat and drank. His hair stood in one line along his head like a mohawk and his hooded tunic was torn at the sleeves revealing bulging muscles that lined his arms. Intrigued, I had to force myself to stop staring.

Liza guided me away and whispered, "Why are we giving him our water? He just attacked us, and he killed Mam!" I tried to explain to her that he wasn't acting on his own; that he had no control over what he did. No matter what I said, she refused to trust him. Still, there was no question of his innocence in my mind, though I didn't know why. She and I stopped walking, and, for the first time, I took in the horrendous scene laid before us. A total of nineteen bodies littered the road. I choked back the urge to vomit and swallowed the bile at the back of my throat.

"We can't just leave them like this," Liza said forlornly. I looked at her nervously.

"What are you suggesting?"

She bent down near one and her face distorted in pain, "These were my people; voyagers. They must have been on their way to the isle as well," she looked up at me, "we must give them a proper burial."

I stepped back, gaping. She and Xomax retrieved shovels from the back of the cart; shovels I didn't even know we had. They then marked the ground, nineteen marks for the nineteen bodies, and began to dig the shallow graves. I joined them eventually to quicken the process while Leo remained by the cart to keep guard. He, too, had trouble trusting our guest. We worked in silent mourning for hours until our makeshift cemetery was finished. All the while, I did my best to avoid looking directly at the bodies. I never considered myself squeamish, but I couldn't deny the sick feeling that frequented my gut. The smell of blood and death was overwhelming. Liza relieved me of my duties and told me to stand back as they took care of the burial.

She explained that, in this land, magic flows through everyone; some can use it and others can't. When we die, the magic becomes unstable and must be released from the body. Those that use magic may filter their powers into an object like a box or a book to be used by a family member in time of need. They may also choose to do nothing and allow their magic to return to the earth through a burial ritual.

Parched, I returned to the cart where the dragon-boy still sat in search of water. I took a drink and asked his name. He answered, Qoal, but refused to speak any further. He watched the others work and I wondered who had been controlling him. He stood up beside me and clutched his arm in pain. I told him to relax, but he ignored my warnings. We'd caused serious damage to him when he was in dragon form. He bled from cuts on both of his arms and one of his legs, had multiple bruises and scratches on his face, and I'm sure there were many more wounds that remained unseen. I dug through my satchel and found the vial of medicine and bandages. He moved away when I offered to help but eventually gave in and let me clean his wounds. As I did, my friends called me over. I handed him the bandages, so he could finish on his own and his eyes met mine.

They were now dark forest green and I had to tear my gaze from his when Liza called to me impatiently. I hurried obediently to my friends, ignoring their disapproval of my helping Qoal.

"Kida," Liza started, "there is a ritual that must be performed to release their magic into the ground." The others looked at me expectantly and dread took hold of me. Liza saw the panic on my face and faced me, "Please, Kida. You are the only one here powerful enough to do it."

"We know you can do it," Xomax said.

"Aye," Leo chimed in, "We all saw you defeat that dragon with your powers."

"But I didn't even defeat him! All I did was break a chain and I don't even know how I managed that."

"That chain was laced with dark magic. Only a Sparky like you could have destroyed something like that," Xomax assured me. Leo nodded as he placed his hand on my back.

Skeptical, I asked Liza, "What do I have to do?" She explained everything in detail and assured me she'd be by my side the entire time. I knelt and placed my hands on the ground, per her instructions. Breathing deeply, my eyes closed, and I focused my thoughts on the task at hand. I remembered the first moment I'd felt magic course through my body when I opened my box. I remembered all I'd learned in my time here. I reminded myself that magic was not only real, but it flowed within me. A light came from my hands, dimly at first, then grew in intensity. I closed my eyes again and thought of the people who now rested beneath the earth. As my mind reached them, their magic released itself from their bodies and flowed into the ground. Liza inhaled beside me and I lifted my head. I did it. As if in conformation to my work, a tiny sprout sprung up from each of the mounds.

"Incredible," Xomax said softly.

"What are those?"

Liza wiped her face before answering, "Those are your signatures. They look like tree sprouts." I watched her inquisitively and she shook her head, "I won't even pretend to understand it. That's something your parents will have to explain when we find them."

We returned to the cart where the guys were loading the shovels; Qoal was gone. "Did either of you see where he went?" I asked earnestly. He was in no condition to walk on his own.

Xomax shrugged and Leo answered, "Good thing he left. One more minute and my mercy would run dry. Next time I see 'em, I'll end his life before he can end any others."

I glared at him, "That's not fair; he wasn't acting in his own will. It's not his fault!"

"Regardless of who's fault it is, we can't just let him tag along without proving himself trustworthy," Xomax said as he took the reins.

"Surely the fact that he left without stealing anything is proof enough," I argued.

Liza scoffed, "I beg to differ…"

"I'm with the voyager," Leo added.

"Then we have to find him and give him a chance to prove himself. Maybe he can tell us who was controlling him."

"I know exactly who was controlling him," Liza fiddled with her necklace as she spoke, "it was Martana. Trust me, we're better off not associating with anyone she's gotten ahold of."

The cart jolted into motion and I pressed on, "Is that not why you brought me here in the first place? To help people and put an end to Martana's war? He could help us defeat her!" The others knew I was right, but their prejudice kept them silent. I folded my arms and watched the road. Pearl squirmed from my satchel and played in my hair. In no time, I spotted Qoal. He limped ahead of us, leaving a trail of blood behind him. Even from a distance, I saw his sickly pallor.

"He's losing too much blood, we have to bring him with us," I insisted as we pulled up next to him.

"She's right," Xomax agreed albeit reluctantly. Leo objected as we helped in climb onto the cart. Qoal mumbled a thank you and fell asleep as I adjusted his bandages. Leo took Xomax's place at the reins as night fell.

"Thanks for letting me help him," I said to Xomax. Liza had fallen asleep wrapped in a thick blanket, despite her best efforts to keep an eye on our new guest.

"It was the right thing to do. I don't blame him for what happened." We sat in silence and I stroked Pearl, trying to ignore his implication. He sighed, "I don't blame you either."

My eyes darted up, relieved, "Don't you miss your shop?"

He chuckled, "I never liked that ol' shack. Tafara was getting too crowded for me anyway. The thought of seeing her again was the only thing that kept me going." He watched Liza sleep for a few moments before his own eyes drifted closed. He needed as much sleep as possible before his next shift driving the cart, but there was one question I simply couldn't get out of my head.

"Hey, Xomax. How did I stop before hitting the ground?"

His eyes remained closed as he answered, "I stopped you. I'm a bit of an amateur when it comes to magic, but I'm from a family of Tellies." He drifted to sleep without explaining more and I added more questions to my list to ask in the morning. I detangled Pearl from my hair and picked up a blanket that covered one of the crates and nearly screamed when I saw a small face peering up at me. The others stayed asleep as the girl whimpered within the crate.

She looked just as startled as me and I spoke softly to her, "Don't be afraid; I'm sorry I frightened you." She watched me timidly through a tangled mess of curly hair. "What's your name?" I asked holding out my hand.

She gingerly placed her tiny hand in mine and whispered, "Evelyn." When I asked why she was in our cart, she hesitated a moment and answered, "My mommy told me to hide, so I did.

But my hiding spot got on fire, so I found a new one. I didn't mean to…are you mad at me?"

"Mad? Of course not! You're not hurt, are you? Let me see." She shook her head sniffling as I inspected her arms and face. It was dark, but from what I saw she was unscathed. Her sniffing turned to whimpering as she cried for her mother. I pulled her into my lap and tried to soothe her before she woke the others. Leo glanced back briefly then returned his gaze to the road. He hadn't seen the trembling girl in my arms. She seemed to be about three or four years old and clung to my collar as I calmed her crying down to quite sobs. I wrapped her in one of our spare covers and coaxed her to sleep by running my fingers through her dark ringlets. Our little cart seemed to be getting more and more crowded. There were now six of us rumbling along the bumpy road; seven counting Pearl who refused to be left out as she flew in circles around my head.

I only knew I'd slept when I awoke to the sun rising on my right. Xomax now sat at the reins and Leo snored in the corner to my left. My eyes drifted to Qoal and met his before darting away. When I looked back, he busied himself adjusting his bandages. His color had returned in the night and appeared much healthier in the sunlight. I suddenly realized the girl was no longer in my lap and I searched for her in alarm. She'd moved to the end of the cart and dangled her legs over the edge. She must have introduced herself to the others while I slept, for she seemed more at ease than she did the previous night. I plopped down beside her to make sure she didn't fall as we rumbled along. Now closer to Qoal, I asked how he felt.

"I'm fine," he said without looking up. He contemplated his next words before asking, "I didn't hurt you, did I?"

"No, of course not," I assured him. He thanked me for the bandages and turned away. It may have been the sunrise reflecting off his cheeks, but he appeared to be blushing. He clearly felt guilty about attacking those people, but it was obvious he had no control or clear memory of what exactly took place.

"How did Martana capture you?" He flinched when I uttered her name and I immediately regretted being so forward.

"She didn't," was his only reply and my concern grew. He refused to give me any other information, so I returned to entertaining Evelyn. Liza's voice caught my ear as she whispered something to Xomax. I moved closer to them and she let me in on their not-so-private conversation.

"I think I've got him figured out," she said in hushed tones. "He must be part of the nomadic clans that illegally experimented with shifting."

"What's wrong with shifting?"

"It's an evil thing, to take the shape of another," she turned to me. "To do so, they have to destroy the other being; they can't just create their own new shape. At least, that's what I've heard. Anything that can shapeshift is malicious."

I strained to hear Xomax's reply, "That's one way of doing it. It's Martana's way. But years ago, a group of nomads came through Tafara and explained that what they did was different. Shifting is a legitimate form of magic that can be used for good."

"If you say so, but their magic is the main reason Martana has gained so much power."

"It isn't their fault she took something they created and uses it for evil." Liza pursed her lips and dropped the issue. Evelyn had taken a liking to her and climbed into her lap. We decided then to find the girl a home when we arrived at the Lunar Isle. Surely, she would have some distant relatives or friends willing to take her in.

"Good morning," Leo said with a stretch. I returned his greeting and sat next to him. "I see our fire breathing friend is still with us."

"His name is Qoal and he's still in bad shape."

"Ah, how appropriate."

"What's that supposed to mean?"

"Nothing, nothing at all," Leo said laughing. "It's a befitting name for such a hardhearted creature." I shushed him and hit his arm watching Qoal nervously. If he'd heard, he didn't show it.

"You've a strong arm," Leo said rubbing the spot I'd hit. "Sorry if I offended you." He looked me over and muttered about the scrapes and bruises that covered me from head to toe. "I really need to get better at protecting you."

"You don't have to protect me." I leaned away from him and his face fell.

"I know, you're more powerful than I could ever hope to be. I just want to be useful." His voice softened, and my heart grew light as his face drew closer to mine. I thought for certain he would kiss me until a voice piped up.

"Of course, you're more powerful than a magicless pirate."

Leo glared at Qoal, "No one asked your opinion, monster."

Qoal ignored his scowl and continued, "Dragons have extremely keen senses and there are two things you reek of; piracy and lies."

"Shut your trap," Leo's anger rose visibly, "whaddaye know, anyway?"

"I know you're lacking traces of the one thing everyone has been exposed to; magic." The two glared at one another and the tension between them thickened to the point of bursting.

"At least I know who I'm fighting for and not killing the innocent!"

"You two, stop it! You're behaving like children!" Evelyn giggled at my comparison and Leo gestured to her.

"That poor child doesn't even know we're harboring the very beast that killed her family." My eyes widened, and I stared at him in disbelief.

"I said stop it! That was uncalled for." Thankfully, Liza had distracted the girl from the argument and turned to us. My voice had risen in volume and I wanted nothing more than to separate myself from the crowded cart of discontent.

"Everyone take a deep breath," Liza's gentle tone calmed me, and I followed her advice, "We can't have all this squabbling if we're going to work together." I nodded in agreement as Leo took the reins from Xomax to cool off. I couldn't understand why the two of them disliked one another so. I thought back to the revelation of Leo's lack of powers. I'd never considered it until then, but he was the only one of us who'd never shown any magical ability. The thing was, he never needed to. He was exceptional in other ways including navigation, fighting, and his great strength. I then remembered the battle with Qoal and how he was not the only one fighting.

"Liza," she scooted closer to me and Evelyn followed, "Why did you really want to come this way?"

She avoided my eye, "I think you know why. And before you ask; yes. I know it was foolish. I placed you all in danger."

"That's not what I was going to say," I struggled to find the right words to console her. She'd lost something precious to her and had every right to be upset, but revenge wouldn't change any of that. Even still, I couldn't bear to see her in that state. "Think of it this way, Liz. If we hadn't followed you, Evelyn would be all alone out there. Not to mention I wouldn't have discovered your hidden talent with a bow!"

She laughed softly, "I knew that would come in handy."

"So, when do you start giving me lessons?" I asked. She laughed again, this time letting a sliver of her old cheerful self shine through. "Ha! Seriously though…"

"Fine, fine," she smiled, "I'll train you on our breaks. Maybe we can get you a bow from the isle. It just so happens to be the home of the grandest bowmaker alive." She told me more about her brief time growing up on the island. Evelyn listened intently and chimed in occasionally. She'd never been to the island, but we were correct in thinking its where she and her family were traveling. Liza recanted stories of the all the wonderous things on the island, some of which were fantasies to get the girl's mind racing.

The two bonded in the coming days and Evelyn never left her side. Even Pearl enjoyed playing with the little girl by hiding and finding one another in the various crates we carried with us. One evening, Evelyn crawled into Liza's lap and played with her necklace. I laughed to myself as she held it to the sky like it was the real moon. Her innocence despite all she'd been through struck me. I sincerely hoped she'd hidden before witnessing the death of her family, and a large part of me believed she did.

The next morning Leo climbed into the driver's seat and I leaned over the rail behind him. I asked him about his time at sea and his face instantly lit up. From where I sat, his eyes held a golden glow in the sunlight and captivated me. "I practically grew up on the water; it's the only home I've ever had. Ah, how I miss it," he paused smiling and a look of nostalgia filled his essence. "I've sailed all over this world ever since my younger years. Ha, the crew always tasked me with the meticulous work; what like crawling through cramped spaces or climbing up rickety heights. They never much cared when I got stuck or fell either. Aye no, 'tis not for the faint of heart. That's what the cap'n always said."

He went on spilling tales of adventures with storms, mutinies, sea creatures and growing up on the sea. His voice found a somber tone whenever he mentioned his captain, only to return to cheeriness as he recited the tale. Pirate or not, his stories fascinated me, and I eagerly listened to each one. As he finished, he yanked back on the reins. The mule snorted and obeyed. The cart slowed to a halt as we came upon hundreds of thousands of towering trees that loomed over us haughtily; Zole Woods.

Sanguent landed with a thud on the hard floor of Martana's throne room. She'd hurled him at the wall when he first gave her the news. Her beast had not only failed his mission to bring her the traveling voyagers, but he was now free from her grasp. All because of the impotent offspring of that sniveling couple. She inhaled deeply and forced herself to think clearly. This would be but a minor setback.

"I apologize, dearest, for lashing out. I only wish you'd bring me more encouraging news. But no matter; we shall be victorious, for what is victory without overcoming obstacles"

"I understand," he answered timidly and Martana hurried to him. She knelt and helped him to his feet. Blood trickled from a gash in his temple and she gently placed her hand over it and healed it.

"I give you my word; I'll not take my anger out on you again." He grimaced when she removed her hand and kissed it. He trusted her genuinely for she always stayed true to her word. She then brought him to his throne and they sat side by side while she waved her hand over the floor. Immediately, the area in front of them opened revealing two captive dragons. They moaned and thrashed about in their chains filling the chamber with their clanging racket. Martana once again unsheathed her dagger, raised her arms above her head and lifted her chin to the ceiling as Sanguent followed suit.

"There, my king," she purred. "It's time for an integration."

CHAPTER V

None Unscathed

"Are you sure we can't just go around the woods?" Leo asked Liza who shook her head. "Too many people who go in there never make it out."

"That'll take ages. We've already made it this far and we have a straight shot to Dorac through those woods."

The foreboding trees before us validated Leo's apprehension. Qoal, too, expressed objections to entering, which was met by Leo blatantly informing him he didn't have to accompany us. The tree line stretched for miles in both directions and I questioned the logic of wandering into such an eerie place. My imagination ran wild with thoughts of what might be lurking behind each trunk, just waiting for us to enter their domain. Xomax assured us we had nothing to worry about as long as we stayed on the path. Still, we used extreme caution as we entered.

The thickness of the trees forced us to leave the cart behind, much to our dismay. Thunder carried as much of the supplies as he could handle and we each took our own share of the load. The path we followed was so narrow and overgrown, I thought for sure we'd stray from it. An occasional group of pebbles peeking through the ground was our only confirmation that we were headed the right way. Everyone fell silent as we treaded deeper into the dense forest. The mule's heavy footsteps were muffled by the soft earth, and his breath hit my neck whenever he snorted. The musty air filled my senses. I lost my footing and caught myself on a nearby tree covered in moss and cool to the touch. An insect crawled across my fingers and I yanked my hand back to brush it off. Qoal stepped close from behind me and motioned for me to continue without saying a word. The serene atmosphere brought me more uneasiness than peace. Nerves tingled through my body and I felt as though I were caught between wake and sleep.

"Everyone stay alert and keep to the path," Xomax instructed. "These trees are known to warp people's minds." As if on que, the world grew fuzzy as I shuffled along. The air, thick with moisture, caught in my throat with each breath. The humidity forced us to lose a few layers. I removed my tunic and twisted my hair up to keep it off my neck. Leo eyed me as he stuffed his coat into a bag and rolled up his sleeves revealing a tattoo on his right forearm. It depicted a ship's helm with a knot of rope in the center. I strained to catch another glimpse before we started walking again, but it soon slipped my mind. We arrived at a fork in the road and paused to examine our map. My eyes widened as I peered over Xomax's shoulder. He waved his hand over the map in swift circular motions then hovered it over where the Zole Wood sat on the parchment. To my amazement, the map zoomed into that area until we saw where we stood. I didn't know what to make of it, but the others soon started down a path.

"I wouldn't go that way if I were you," Qoal said softly. Leo shot him a glare and instructed us to follow. "I mean it, that's the wrong way," Qoal insisted more adamantly.

"What do you know, dragon?" Hatred dripped from the last word and Leo continued, "We didn't ask for your help. We didn't even ask you to tag along. If you know what's good for you, you'll keep your trap shut or we'll leave you to rot in this forest. For all we know, he could be trying to lead us astray."

"Leo!" The harshness of his words astounded me, "He's only trying to help! And there's no way we'd abandon anyone, especially in this place." Leo glanced at his feet, whether in shame or frustration, I didn't care.

"I trust Xo's judgement; he knows what he's talking about," Liza broke the silence, "not to mention, Leo is a navigator. We go on." Though her words were meant for Qoal, she wouldn't look at him directly. I understood their leeriness of Qoal, and yet, in my mind there was no question to his innocence. His eyes held nothing but remorse and sincerity. Even still, he was a stranger and avoided many of our questions when asked about his affiliation with Martana. We followed the others, albeit reluctantly. After trekking for hours, our path met an abrupt end. A giant stone stood wedged between two colossal trees and wouldn't budge when we pressed against it. Its surface was oddly smooth and much too slick to climb over.

"What could have put this here?" Liza asked under her breath. Panic gripped my chest as I pushed the thought from my mind.

Xomax sighed, not hearing Liza's remark, "We'll rest here for the night and I'll think of something by morning."

"Can we not just go around it?" There was no way I'd be able to sleep knowing we were in the presence of something capable of moving that huge boulder. We could easily walk along the side of the stone and trees and return to the path on the other side.

"Not a chance; once you leave the path, you're at the mercy of the woods."

"What, can the trees move or something?" They nodded at me and I gulped. We set up camp and tied Thunder to a sturdy tree, careful to keep him on the path. As we settled down, Pearl slowly emerged from my pouch where she'd hidden since we first entered the forest. The confines of the trees made her skittish and I didn't blame her. Evelyn played with the tiny wyrm and soon Pearl was back to her usual energetic self. Leo brought me a fresh canteen and sat beside me.

"How are you feeling?" I took the water and shrugged.

"Have you been here before?"

He scoffed shaking his head, "I've only heard the stories. They say of you stray from the path the trees will shift so that you never find it again. According to legend, thousands of people have been lost to these woods simply because they left the path and couldn't find their way out."

"Woah…what are we gonna do then?" If we couldn't find a way around the boulder, we'd be trapped here forever or forced to retrace our steps and go around the woods all together. That would add another week to our travels; at the very least. Perhaps we should have listened to Qoal after all.

"Relax, Kida. We'll think of something." His words brought little comfort. The sky was completely concealed by the thick canopy overhead, but our bodies could tell it was time to sleep. We agreed to rest in shifts and I offered to keep first watch. My body ached all over from all the walking and riding and sleeping on the ground. Despite my exhaustion, my mind was wide awake and alert. Liza stayed up as well to keep me company and help me practice magic. I managed to make a soft bead of light from my fingertips and quickly mastered the technique. She showed me how to place it in a lantern that kept it from extinguishing. While we sat, she told me more about Ordenia. She spent much of her childhood on the Lunar Isle and in Tafara where she met Xomax. Before the market city was destroyed, it was home to portals, similar to the one we used, which linked cities and kingdoms all over Ordenia, including the Lunar Isle. My disappointment showed and Liza smiled apologetically. We could have avoided this long dreary journey and simply walked through a door. Our voices trailed off as the others fell asleep. All the sounds of the forest slowly died away as well. I remained still as the silence crept toward us. My heart beat quickened and I broke the quiet.

"Liza?" She looked at me wearily. "There's something I don't get. If Martana's evil is spreading, why did Mam wait so long to bring me here? Couldn't so much of this have been avoided?"

She pondered before replying, "There are many factors that come into play when voyaging through time. Even I saw the tragic outcomes of certain timelines, though I was unable to pinpoint what went wrong. All I can say is we must trust Mam's timing. It's almost always perfect." Tree branches scraped against each other like hungry claws scratching the earth. "We should sing."

Her whispered statement caught me off guard and I turned to her, "What do you mean?"

She shrugged, "I thought it would help, seeing as how freaky this place is. Besides, it won't disturb them as much as talking." She removed something from her vest pocket and handed me a crinkled piece of paper. I unfolded it to reveal notes and lyrics scribbled in ink on its creased surface. "I tore it from my mother's song book when I was little. She was cross at first;

then she taught me how to sing it. After that, it became our nightly ritual."

She smiled sadly as I studied the page, hoping I wouldn't ruin something she held so dear. As I grew more confident in the melody, she harmonized with me. Our voices blended together perfectly and created a peaceful lull that lost itself in the twisting branches of the trees. Her pure voice soothed my anxious nerves. When we finished, she wiped her face.

"Are you crying?"

"No, no," she whispered, "That was beautiful. Thank you for that. You never told me you could sing; though I suppose I should have known."

"It's nothing really. And what about you? You're chock full of hidden talents." She laughed softly. I didn't want to tell her how much I used to love singing. I dreamed of performing when I was younger, but I always lacked in self-confidence. I could never rid myself of my crippling stage fright without my mom there to cheer me on. Since her passing, I'd fallen out of practice. Liza taught me another song or two before Xomax woke to relieve us. She insisted I keep the page from her mother's song book, saying she already knew it by heart. I felt honored at her entrustment of something so personal. I made a pallet next to Evelyn and drowsiness overtook me as I thought of the words to Liza's song:

The rain whispers a lullaby

In the midst of a stormy night

To the thirsty plants

That reach for the light.

"Hush," it says to the weary trees,

"Peace to all the trembling leaves."

The lightning cracks

And the thunder rolls

But none can stop the lulling flow.

The wind joins in harmony

To whisk the tears away

From the lovely petals

Until the break of day.

I felt movement beside me as my dreams faded. I convinced myself it was Evelyn shifting and closed my eyes tighter. My eyelids were met by the dim glow from the lantern. I wondered who was keeping watch as the movement continued. Something rubbed against my leg and I jerked upright. My eyes adjusted slowly to the limited lighting. I held up the lantern and observed my leg. I let out the breath I'd been holding when I saw Evelyn sleeping peacefully next to me, her foot inches from my leg. I prepared to lie back down when I realized something wasn't right. I swung the lantern around and was shocked to find our surroundings had completely changed. Worse than that; we were alone.

The lantern's metal ring slipped in my sweaty grip as I searched for anything familiar; anything at all. We were no longer on the path, our friends were gone, the supplies were gone,

Thunder was gone, even the giant immovable boulder was gone. Pearl trembled inside my boot where she'd slept then dove into the safeness of my satchel. I struggled to comprehend our predicament. A small hand gripped my arm and jolted me from my manic thoughts. Evelyn woke and rubbed the sleep from her eyes.

"What's going on?"

"I'm trying to figure that out, Evelyn." I tried to keep my voice steady to avoid frightening the girl. I watched her eyes grow wide as she glanced around. Before I could console her, tears escaped her eyes.

"Where did everybody go? They didn't leave us, did they?"

"Of course not, they would nev…" The sound of movement silenced us. Evelyn scurried into my lap and I held her tightly to my chest. We sat in helpless terror facing the direction of the noise. The faint thud of footsteps made their way to us on the padded ground. I held the lantern close as if it's meager glow would ward off any danger. The footsteps drew nearer and Evelyn whimpered. My heart pounded in my throat so loudly I was certain the very trees could hear. The sounds were only a few feet away and I prepared myself to attack anything that tried to harm us. I set Evelyn on her blanket and wrapped mine around her before handing her the lantern.

"Whatever happens, don't be afraid. I'll take care of this." My forced confidence almost fooled myself. Almost. Inside, I was just as frightened as the little girl shaking in front of me; if not more so. The sound stopped as I turned. The darkness concealed all but the circle of ground we occupied. I held my hand out to grasp the lantern but froze when a tall figure emerged from the shadows. My fear instantly became a wave of adrenaline and I tackled the figure while screaming like a lunatic. The figure shouted in surprise, but didn't budge.

"Qoal? It's you!" I threw my arms around his neck as relief flooded my lungs with laughter. He returned my embrace before pulling away. He held me at arm's distance and inspected me.

"You're real?" he whispered before drawing me close to him again.

"Of course, I'm real, why wouldn't I be?" I asked him where the others were and he quickly let go of me and spotted the lantern.

"That's it," he said to himself. "You lit the lantern, didn't you? That's why they haven't found you."

"Wait, who hasn't found me? The others?"

He shook his head and with a grave expression said, "Scaiths." He shushed me before I could ask what a scaith was. "They know we're here, but as long as we stick close to your light, they won't bother us." He helped Evelyn climb onto his back and grabbed my hand before leading us away.

"Qoal, what is going on? Where is everyone?" I asked, struggling to keep up with his swift stride.

"I don't know, but we have to find them before they're pulled in too far." He then stopped and looked directly at me. "Listen, this is very important. If you see a light that does not come from this lantern, look away immediately and don't turn back." As soon as he uttered the words, I got the eerie feeling we were being watched.

"What happens if I look at it?"

"You get pulled in." He said no more and pushed me silently ahead. His fingertips remained between my shoulder blades as we moved and I forced my attention to our self-made path. It took all my willpower to refrain from glancing in the direction of every noise that met my ear. I soon became aware of the many shadows darting around us. The scaiths Qoal mentioned were mischievous shapeshifters. They appear as harmless shadows upon first glance until they reveal their true nature. By then, however, it's too late and you've been drug into their game. They had been imprisoned in the Zole Woods because of the inescapable trees. Scaiths once roamed all of Ordenia as Martana's henchmen until they were banished and bound to the very trees in which we stood. Now they preyed on innocent travelers foolish enough to wander into their domain.

"Why'd we even come here, then? If I'd known, I never would've agreed to come this way." My voice shook despite my best efforts to keep it steady.

"It's become a game to them, Kida. The scaiths' one rule is to stay off the path. They aren't even physically able to touch it, thanks to the people who put them here. We'd have been perfectly safe, but you all refused to listen. They must have created that split in the road to get us off the real path."

"How did you know the right way?" He shushed me without answering and moved in front of me. I peered around him. We'd come upon a clearing and in the center, lying on her back, was Liza. Her wide eyes stared blankly ahead and I pushed past Qoal to run to her. He grasped my arm to hold me back. I then noticed the dark mass that loomed above her.

"Is that a…" He nodded.

"We must be very precise," he said in hushed tones. "That scaith has your friend trapped under its gaze. You have to destroy it."

"Destr- I can't do that!"

"Yes, you can. Just do what you did to my chain."

"But I don't know what I did to your chain, it just happened."

"If you want to see your friends make it out of here alive, you will make it happen again." His voice grew forceful and I choked back my tears. I couldn't muster up the courage to try; even as I watched the scaith draw nearer to Liza's face. I felt as trapped and helpless as her. More shadows broke into the clearing and crept towards us; their tiny eyes flickering like matches. I became enthralled by their haunting glow and was unable to tear my eyes from their mesmerizing gaze. They were drawing me in, just as Qoal warned. Feelings of fear and serenity spiraled inside me and my eyes rolled back in my head. My knees buckled as the contradicting emotions consumed me. Qoal caught me as I fell back and leaned me against a tree. A flash of light streaked across my vision, breaking the scaith's hold.

"Kida! Look at me." Qoal's face came into focus. "I told you not to make eye contact. Are you okay?"

I rubbed my head and tried to shake the lingering effects of the scaith. "I'm fine. Where's Liza?" She hadn't moved from where she laid in the middle of the clearing, but the dark cloud that'd hovered above her was gone. "What did you do?"

Qoal gave a slight smile, "Shifting isn't all I can do, though it'd have been better if you'd done it. I only scared them off; they'll be back." He helped me to my feet and I rushed to Liza's side.

"What do we do now?"

He joined me and set Evelyn down, all the while glancing around to ensure our safety. "There's nothing I can do, Kida." My heart sank as all hope seemed to fade away. I couldn't lose her.

"It's up to me, isn't it?" He nodded and I drew a deep breath. My head throbbed. I couldn't allow myself to freeze up again simply from being too afraid to try. I clasped my hands and massaged my forehead in attempt to think of some way I could help. The only magic I'd mastered was lighting a lantern; what good is that? My head ached from the rubbing and I let my hands fall limply into my lap in frustration. When I separated them, a tiny bead of light rested in my palm. I stared in wonder. It wasn't like the one in the lantern; it wasn't even bright. Warmth radiated from its dim glow. My eyes shifted from Liza's terrified face to my hands and back again. Without thinking, I held the light above her illuminating her facial features. I then released my fingers and it floated to her lips where it disappeared in her mouth. Qoal and I exchanged nervous glances. She then shifted and her once dull eyes brightened.

"Wh-where am I?" she asked groggily as she moved her head back and forth. Qoal rose to his feet abruptly before I could express my relief at her recovery.

"Still in Zole Woods," he answered and held out a canteen. She grabbed it and swallowed three gulps before I helped her to her feet. "Hurry, we have to find the others."

As we set off, I touched his arm, "How did you find her?"

"Instinct," he replied with a shy grin. He revealed no more and my curiosity grew with each moment I spent by his side.

"Can you tell where they are?" Liza asked, her voice full of concern. She wrung her hands nervously, no doubt worrying for Xomax. It was obvious the two of them cared for one another. My own stomach grew sick with suspense. A piece of me was missing when we weren't all together.

"I am sensing someone, but they're moving sporadically; it's difficult to keep track of." He turned to silence us and moved more cautiously. We obeyed his instruction and followed noiselessly behind. We paused, and he leaned against a mossy trunk.

"Stay here, I'll be right back."

I reached out for him, "Wait, you can't leave us alone out here! What if those things come back?"

He stared at my hand on his arm and I gingerly released my grip. "You have the lantern. The scaiths won't come near enough to harm you as long as you stay close to the light. I won't be long."

With that, he took off into the trees leaving behind three mortified faces in his wake. We slumped against the large tree. Evelyn buried her face in Liza's chest and sniffled as she stroked her hair. I sifted through my satchel in search of Pearl but I hadn't yet gotten the hang of the magic bag. Eventually I found her and removed my hand with my wyrm clinging to it. She blinked multiple times as though I'd disturbed her slumber. She hopped onto the lantern and stared at me from her perch. I found her berries and held out my hand. She refused to eat until I tossed them to her one by one. She caught each one and I shook my head wondering how it must feel to be so carefree in the midst of such peril. Liza stared at the ground before her as she absentmindedly fingered through Evelyn's curls.

"Hey, are you alright?"

Her head bolted up with a start, "I think so." She paused before continuing, "I've never been through anything like that before."

"What did that thing do to you?" I didn't really want to know the answer, but she explained that a scaith's sole purpose is to multiply when not carrying out Martana's bidding. They ensnare their victims until they waste away to nothing but their shadow. Sometimes they trap you in a situation you fear most until you let go of any hope for escape. Other times they hold you in their gaze until you fall into a trance and lose all mobility.

"That's what they did to me. I was paralyzed and couldn't even blink." She shuddered at the thought.

"So, scaiths are just people who are trapped in the forest?"

"No," she sighed. "They're no longer people. Whoever they used to be is long gone and there is no way to bring them back. That's why it's imperative we find the others before they suffer the same fate."

My stomach churned. I found myself willing Qoal to be quick about finding Leo and Xomax. They could be anywhere and the longer it takes to find them, the further gone they will be. I twiddled my fingers anxiously and kept my eyes trained on Pearl flitting in the glow of the lantern. Her shadow bounced along the gnarly roots. Leaves rustled in the wind and twigs snapped in all directions. We refrained from looking towards the sounds for fear of spotting another scaith. A chill ran down my spine as I relived the moment I was drug into its gaze. Something about the occurrence held and air of familiarity. I strained to recall a similar predicament to no avail. Then it hit me; my dream. The trees seemed to be whispering here just as they had all those nights in my sleep. I shuddered at the implication.

Our thoughts were interrupted by an ear-splitting scream that rang through the trees. We both jumped at the sound; startling Evelyn who let out a yelp of her own. I scrambled to my feet and held up the lantern, hoping our friends would be drawn to its light. I stepped forward before lowering the lantern to Liza's side. I didn't want it to be too far from them in case the scaiths returned. Heavy footsteps advanced toward us from the direction of the scream and I squinted into the dark branches. Each footstep thudded in rhythm with my throbbing heart.

Another shout met our ears, "Stay away from me! I won't look, I won't look!" The voice was familiar and full of horror. My relief was short lived upon the realization he must be running from something, meaning he and his pursuer were headed straight for us. Liza grasped Evelyn's hand and scurried behind the tree. I tried to join them, but someone collided into me and knocked me off my feet.

"Xomax!" Liza shouted as she ran to him. She helped him stand and wrapped her arms around him. "I was so worried I'd lost you."

He placed his hand on her head and glanced over his shoulder. Whatever chased him wouldn't be far behind. We stood awaiting the inevitable doom when Qoal stepped forward. I heaved a sigh of relief at the sight of his friendly face.

"You- why were you chasing me?" Xomax demanded, breathlessly.

I brushed the soil from my hands, "He was trying to help you. He's been finding everyone and bringing us together."

"You wouldn't uncover your eyes, so I chased you to safety," Qoal added. I rubbed my elbow where a new bruise had begun to form and rolled my eyes at Xomax's blunder. He clung to Liza and I forced my annoyance to the side; we still had one more person to find. I'm ashamed to admit my disappointment at Xomax's arrival and scolded myself for wishing it'd been Leo instead. Remorse flooded my heart as I watched Liza wipe the grime from his face. I shook the thoughts from my mind and focused on the task at hand. I met Qoal's gaze and he nodded to me. We each gathered our bearings and set out yet again. Luckily, Xomax had been carrying two large satchels so we regained most of our supplies.

"Everyone keep your eyes on the person ahead of you. We're nearing the heart of the forest."

"The heart? You can't be serious," Xomax uttered in disbelief. He stopped in his tracks and started to turn back.

"We have no choice; that's where the pirate is," Qoal replied. "It seems the scaiths have taken a particular interest in him and brought him to their castle."

"How would you know? No one has ever even seen their castle. No one still living, that is." Liza shushed him and insisted we wouldn't leave anyone behind, no matter how dangerous things became. I nodded in agreement. We'd come too far to turn back now and give up on our friend. Though she may have denied it, I could tell Liza we beginning to trust Qoal and there was no hiding my approval.

We heard shouting in the distance and quickened our pace. I knew it must be Leo and my spirits instantly lifted as his voice became clearer. As we neared the heart of the forest, the air grew chilly and dense. I placed a light in our three remaining lanterns for the others as we came upon a ghastly horde of scaiths blocking our path. The swarm spiraled around the heart of the forest, shielding it from view. Stray scaiths freed themselves from the wall to lash out at us, only to be frightened away by the light.

"I didn't know they could fly." My stomach churned while I watched the dizzying display.

"Of course, they can," Xomax choked back his own fear, "They can take any shape they desire to wreak their havoc."

"Are you sure Leo's in there?" I asked incredulously. There was not an ounce of doubt in Qoal's expression and my heart sank.

"How are we supposed to get inside?" Liza asked pensively. The swirling creatures emitted a blood curdling screech like a colony of bats. Without reply, Qoal stepped in front of me, lantern in hand, and edged closer to the vortex. He turned and grabbed my hand. I followed suit with Liza's hand until the five of us formed a human chain. As we neared them, the scaiths averted from the light forming an opening in their moving wall. The gap widened until we were able to pass through without touching the wretched beasts. The sight on the other side took my breath away. We emerged into a vast clearing, the center of which was occupied by a colossal tree with blackened branches twisting and turning in all directions; their castle. Shadows by the thousands darted about the clearing around the tree. Despite our intrusion, they took no interest in us; rather, their attention was drawn to something on the far side of the glade. We moved forward with haste and caution until we found the source of the uproar. There, surrounded by legions of scaiths, was Leo.

He'd drawn his sword and flung it wildly like a mad man at the immense shadow that tormented him. Its familiar shape resembled that of a dragon. None of us moved until the light dimmed drastically. I'd made the mistake of setting my lantern down to hold Evelyn with tears streaming down her small face. Scaiths from the wall swarmed around our lanterns in attempt to snuff out the light causing the others to drop theirs. Soon, the only light came from the glowing eyes of the shadows creeping toward us.

"But they're supposed to be afraid of the lanterns!" Liza cried as we huddled together.

"They are, but there are too many of them." Xomax looked at me while shielding his eyes from the onslaught of scaiths, "Three lanterns aren't nearly enough." I stared back at him in dread. He wanted me to get us out of this mess. I held more tightly to Evelyn who shrieked as a scaith latched onto her arm.

"Everyone, close your eyes!" Qoal yelled and I clamped mine shut. Tiny fingers moved across my skin, up my legs and arms until they reached my face. The scaiths tried to pry my eyes open, but I only closed them tighter. I shook my body, trying to knock them off of me. Flailing arms and legs knocked into me as my friends suffered the same fate. I stumbled over someone and landed on my backside, opening my eyes for a split second. Countless shadowy figures stared into me inches from my face. I screamed and buried my face in my hands, but the connection had been made. They filled my mind with gruesome horrors; I could no longer distinguish between dreams and reality. Fear and adrenaline battled inside until I could take no more. My eyes flew open and a blinding light burst from within me. The scaiths scattered and tried to flee, but they diminished into nothing before they got far. The light coursed throughout my body as the forest faded away.

I found myself in a warm meadow; the one of my dreams. Only, this time, I wasn't alone. A couple stood in the distance, beaconing me to them. I walked forward, but each step I took brought me no closer. They were unreachable. My pace quickened until I ran at full speed to the figures. The distance only grew as did my panic. Tears formed in my eyes making everything around me blurry and unrecognizable.

When my vision cleared, I was back in Zole woods, though it was not as I'd left it. My friends huddled together, shielding themselves from my intensity and not a single scaith remained, save for Leo's foes. I directed my attention to the shadowy beast but paused when I comprehended what was happening. Leo had stopped fighting and stared at a new figure nearby. A second scaith morphed into a person. Leo's heavy panting stopped when he recognized the figure; me. In one swift motion, the dragon clamped its jaws on the flickering version of me. Leo's sword landed with a soft thud as he fell to his knees and the scaith hovered over his face to consume him. His body began to fade, and I jumped into action. I pushed the light to the scaith with all my might and it exploded into hundreds of smaller scaiths. The scaiths evaporated one by one until there was not a monster left in sight.

My outstretched hands fell limply to my side. Heaving large breaths, I stared upwards at the millions of stars that now shined down on us accompanied by a lovely moon. The others encompassed me in an embrace and Liza laughed out of nowhere. I couldn't help but join in and soon we all giggled like children at the immense weight that'd left our shoulders. I broke from the group when I remembered Leo's absence and found him on his hands and knees a few yards away from us.

"Leo," I spoke softly as I approached, "are you alright?" I knelt beside him and placed my hand on his back. He flinched and sat up quickly. Relief flooded within me until I saw his startled expression.

"Kida," he whispered, "I thought you were dead." He placed his hands on my cheeks and searched my face to confirm that I was there, alive. He leaned in close and soon our faces were inches apart. My heart skipped a beat as his lips pressed against mine. Shock and confusion gave way to bliss. In the moment, the kiss seemed to last an eternity until he pulled away and it ended much too soon. "Forgive me, I should not have been so bold," he said quickly with a look of guilt in his eyes. I gave no reply as he helped me to my feet. Qoal called us over before I could formulate a response. They'd gathered our remaining supplies and didn't seem to take note of our intimacy. My face burned as we approached them, and Leo retrieved his sword.

"Well, now that we're all together, I say we leave this forsaken place," Xomax announced cheerily as he threw his arm around Liza. Qoal nodded and retrieved our remaining supplies before taking the lead. Careful not to lose my footing, I followed him, yet again, into the trees.

Martana wiped the blood from her lips as the beast's power surged through her veins causing her body to convulse in pain. Sanguent writhed on the dark marble floor beside her. She watched as his body slowly became unrecognizable. It worked. Her own body distorted, and she cried out in anguish. She felt her bones grind inside her as they rapidly grew, and rough barbed scales replaced her once smooth skin. Her teeth extended to sharp points that pierced her lip as she clenched her teeth in pain. Within minutes, Martana and Sanguent were no longer human. In their stead stood two fearsome wyverns with hideous bat like faces.

Their stomachs twisted with nausea and hunger as they searched for a source to replenish their energy. A line of guards stood obediently in rows on either side of her throne and didn't flee as the wyverns attacked. By the time they reached their fill, none were left alive in the room. Martana let out a triumphant roar that shook her mountainside castle and Sanguent joined in making the entire island rattle. Outside, her remaining soldiers took cover as chunks of stone broke free from the mountain and tumbled down to their posts. The pair thundered across the room and broke through the thick walls to the courtyard. They stretched their winged arms and moved them up and down. The wind from their mighty wings knocked those nearby off balance as they ascended.

Martana had never felt so alive; so free as she shot into the sky. From this height, she could see the entirety of the Fractured Isle her isolated portion of this world. The land grew ever smaller the higher she rose. Their massive shadows caressed the barren earth, casting darkness on those below.

Sanguent glided beside her and her heart fluttered at his fearsome appearance. He'd come a long way since their first meeting. He used to be so kind and soft spoken, and, though the latter remained unchanged, he'd become as malicious as his female counterpart. A toothy grin spread across Martana's gruesome face and she turned sharply back toward Mount Crimson. Her blood boiled at the thought of why she and her beloved were forced to dwell on such a desolate island, cut off from the mainland. Despite her new ability, her soul remained tethered to her isle of exile. Regardless, she was now closer than ever to breaking their hold.

When they landed, Martana quickly returned to her human form. The transformation was easier and less painful than before. She hurried past her guards who were already repairing the damage they'd caused when breaking through the walls. She reached her chamber and retrieved her quartz cube and held it to her chest. She mouthed a chant that caused a dark string of smoke to release itself from her core into the crystal. In doing this, her strength was preserved; for no mortal can withstand the sheer amount of power she exposed herself to. With each new addition, a portion of her humanity was lost. But this didn't stop her from wanting more. Her craving for justice only grew with each victim she consumed. A craving that would never be satisfied until she destroyed those who'd wronged her and plunged this world into a new era of darkness.

CHAPTER VI

Treacherous Trek

The woods changed dramatically with my sudden burst of magic. It was brighter than before, and we didn't even need our lanterns to see. Pearl fluttered about gleefully, bringing me leaves of peculiar shapes and pining for my approval. Leo walked close beside me and my face grew hot each time his arm brushed mine. I relived our moment of bliss and failed to suppress the feelings welling within me. This was happening too fast. Though we'd become close recently, our time together had been short. I wanted to talk to him about it but couldn't muster up the courage. Our trek out of the woods was short and required few breaks. The trees thinned and gave way to a dimming sky. The sun crept closer to the jagged horizon.

"The Hazy Peaks are straight ahead," Xomax announced, full of relief. "They encompass the city of Dorac, making it the safest city in all Ordenia."

"Those mountains are why portals were made to get in and out of the city," Liza added nervously, "they're called hazy for a reason."

Xomax took her hand, "Lucky for us, I'm here. Any true Doracan knows how to navigate through the fog." His confidence filled us with hope and no one brought up the mountains again. When I asked again about his powers, Xomax told me about the twelve forms of magic in Ordenia; the four elementals which were hydros, pyros, aeros, and terras, the three healers which were menders, mixers, and pathys, as well as shifters, tellies, voyagers, knights, and illuminators, or sparkies as we are often called. From there, of course, magic branched off into countless subdivisions of abilities.

"Wait, aren't knights just soldiers?"

He shook his head, "They are much more then fighters. Anyone can be trained in combat, but only knights can use magic to enhance their battle skills. They can boost their stamina and make themselves practically untouchable. Some can even enchant their weapons to make them more effective." I took mental notes as he spoke and marveled at the thought of people using magic in such wonderful ways. The sun soon disappeared, and we set up camp. I was sad to go without Thunder; he'd made our journey so much more bearable. Xomax assured us the remainder of the trip would be effortless until we reached the mountains, still, we all missed our trusty mule.

As we ate supper, Pearl inspected Qoal. It seemed she thought it her duty to approve of each member of our party. She immediately took a liking to him and crawled around his arms. His wounds healed greatly while in the forest and I sat across from him to watch Pearl. I smiled, "She really likes you."

He shrugged and watched her dangle from a loose bandage. "I suppose. It's a shame though."

"What is?"

"That a dragon could be demoted to a mere trinket for the pleasures of man."

Stuck by his tone, I replied, "She's much more than that. To me, Pearl is a companion; a friend and I would never consider her a 'trinket'."

"Have you considered setting her free?" He asked accusingly. I gulped at a loss for words. She never appeared unhappy or trapped, but the more I pondered it, the guiltier I felt.

Xomax came to my rescue, "Wyrms aren't independent creatures. From the moment they're born they search for a bond; a caregiver. They can't survive on their own outside of their swarm. Even then, it's difficult with all the competition for resources. Most can't even produce a flame to defend themselves."

"That doesn't justify keeping them as pets," Qoal argued as he stared at his food. I felt somewhat better, but I couldn't help but notice his sudden attitude change. Before I could ask what was bothering him, Leo plopped down beside me. I carefully avoided touching his arm as we ate.

"Dragons were once a proud species before humans decided to use them for their own gain," Qoal muttered while Pearl gazed at me from his shoulder. "Now there are hardly any left."

"Blimey, what is it ya have against people anyways?" Leo asked sharply.

"Humans bring nothing but pain and suffering in their wake," he replied matter-of-factly.

"Ha! The same could be said of scaly beasts like yourself."

"Don't start this, you two. We just made it out of that creepy forest. We should be celebrating, not tearing each other down," I insisted as they continued to glare at one another. They did as I asked and dropped the subject. I gazed into the sky and watched the stars appear one by one.

Leo breathed in deeply beside me, "Eight days."

"What was that?" I turned to face him.

"The moon has reached its fullness. It was only half full when we first went into Zole woods."

"You mean we were in there for more than a week? That's insane!" How could it have been so long? All the horrors we'd faced within those trees seemed to happen overnight.

"Unbelievable," Xomax said, shaking his head. "I knew scaiths disoriented their victims, but I had no idea they were that powerful."

"Talk about losing track of time," Liza cracked before growing serious. "Who knows how much damage Martana has inflicted in our absence."

"You do realize she's been in exile for years. How much trouble can she cause?"

Her eyes darted to Leo, "All her banishment has done is slow her down. We can't afford to underestimate her." He threw up his hands in defeat and the weight that had lifted upon our escape from the woods returned tenfold at the mention of her name. Martana. My fear grew with each passing moment; not only of her, but of this world. Recent events brought to light just how real and dangerous this place was.

As we settled for the night, I reminisced the safety of my simple apartment, all snug and cozy in my simple bed, without the fear of losing my life with every step I took. A drop of liquid splashed on the tip of my nose, jolting me from my daydreams. The heavens slowly opened and poured its waters heavily upon us. Though we'd made camp beneath a large tree, its crown provided little shelter from the large droplets. We fished through the bags in search of more blankets when, suddenly, I no longer felt the rain. It still poured all around us and I looked up curiously. To my amazement, Qoal had transformed and shielded us with his giant wing. He rested it on the long branches directly above us. Evelyn stared in awe at the gentle giant who kept us dry. Panic rose in my throat at her startled expression. She took a few cautious steps toward him and paused. Holding my breath, I held her hand and said, "It's okay. He's our friend, Qoal."

I lead her to him and he laid his head on the ground at her level. Our reflection stared back at us in his enormous green eyes. As we held one another's gaze, I received the same feeling of exposure as on the day we met. His eye held an unfamiliar sadness. His overwhelming guilt was evident, but I hopped the little girl that survived would lift his spirits. She reached out and tenderly placed her tiny hand on his snout. She was no longer afraid, and my muscles relaxed. She looked from me to Qoal and giggled as his eyes drifted closed. She stroked his leathery skin as she made her way to his side where she leaned against him and quickly fell asleep in his warmth. Her bravery far exceeded my own and I couldn't help smiling as I settled next to Liza. She watched Qoal for a while before turning to me. The other two spoke quietly about the fastest and safest path to Dorac.

"I still don't understand how you trusted him so quickly," she whispered softly.

I fiddled with a blade of grass before answering, "I don't understand it either. Part of me simply knew what we first saw was false."

"But he should still be held accountable for his actions; shouldn't he?" she asked, her voice full of doubt.

"You don't think being separated from your family, losing control of your own body, and being attacked and wounded is punishment enough?"

She bowed her head and clutched her necklace, "I suppose."

"Suppose?" I stopped when I noticed a small tear fall from her eye and land in her lap.

"I miss Mam." Her voice broke. "And I know it wasn't his fault, but I watched him kill her. And no matter how hard I try, I cannot bring myself to forgive. And why should I?" Speechless, I watched her shoulders rise and fall in raspy breaths. My heart ached for her loss and a lump formed in my throat. I scooted closer to her and placed my arm around her. "I'm sorry," she sniffled, "I shouldn't be burdening you with this. And I shouldn't condemn Qoal when Martana is the one at fault."

"Don't apologize. I'm your friend; please don't be afraid to talk to me," I answered. "And I know forgiveness takes time."

She nodded and wiped her face and changed the subject, "Hey, how did you wake me up? You know, after the scaith pulled me in?"

"I'm not really sure," I confessed. I explained the bead of light and how it healed her. She listened in fascination and asked me to demonstrate. Unsure of myself, I did my best to recreate the healing light. The first attempts failed, but eventually I did it.

"That's incredible, Kida! I had no idea sparkies could do that, though you are the only one I've ever known," she handed me a small glass bottle from her satchel and I placed the light into it. It was about the size of a marble and clinked against the glass when it landed. She instructed me to keep practicing that trick and save the successful results, for she refused to let anything go to waste. With newfound peace, we rested our heads. Leo and Xomax still whispered travel plans. Their muffled voices and the steady patter of rain droplets lulled me to sleep.

The grass was still damp when we awoke and packed up camp. Stray drops dripped from the leaves overhead. The beauty of the tree stopped me in my tracks. Its long, twisted limbs were dark with moister and its green leaves were at their brightest drinking in the refreshing droplets of the rain. The contrast between the two was stark and crisp and reminded me of home. I never liked the rain, but I did enjoy the effects it brought. It reminded me that no matter how dark and dreary life may become, there is always beauty that shines through in the end. I smiled at the thought and, for the first time since my arrival in Ordenia, I felt hopeful.

Water splashed my leg as Evelyn jumped into a puddle. She then found another and startled Pearl who was just waking up and peering from inside my satchel. Shocked, she sprung from the bag and shuddered the water from her face only to get soaked by another sprinkle. The two made a game of it until the water evaporated in the sunlight. I longed to once again be as carefree as they were in that moment. The mountains in the distance grew with each passing sun until at last we were close enough to fully bask in their magnificence. The jagged rocks pierced through the earth like an ancient gargantuan weapon in hundreds of streaking colors. We'd seen smoke rising from a great distance and now came across a large settlement as the base of the mountains.

"What are all these people doing here?" Liza asked.

Xomax answered, "The must be refugees fleeing the war. My guess is they don't want to risk hiking."

"Can ye blame us, though?" an elderly man piped up from his seat ahead of us. "Our childhoods are tainted with tales of the misfortune awaiting anyone who ventures into that fog." His raspy voice sent shivers down my spine. When I came to pass him, he blocked my path with his cane. "You, girl," he said, pondering, "yer Kida, aren't ye?" I gasped and nodded. He snorted and said, "Yer the spittin' image of your mother. An' there's no doubt in my mind you'll make the same mistakes as she."

"What are you talking about?" I asked in disbelief. My friends had continued without noticing my absence. However, my curiosity enticed me to stay and hear what the geezer had to say; a decision I often regret.

He smacked my legs with his cane before answering, "I don't know what ye've got goin' through yer little mind, but we're gonna need a lot more than some foreign sparky and her clueless posse to stop this war."

"You don't know what you're talking about," I defended.

"No! You don't even know what yer doin'!" He said, his voice rising. "I'll tell you one thing; I don' want to live out the last of my miserable life knowing it's in the hands of childish twits like you. As far as I'm concerned, ye and yer kin are just as much to blame as the Sorceress herself!"

With that he spat at my feet and swung his cane at me again. I managed to dodge the blow and run away before he saw the tears. The breeze dried my face as I caught up to my friends where they'd paused to gather provisions. Their faces were twisted with worry. The crowd had turned its focus on us and their eyes bored into us as we walked. They cursed at us; particularly at myself and Qoal. They seemed to know he was a shifter and credited him with the destruction of their towns. As for me, they hated me with every fiber of their being. They began throwing things at us and we quickened our pace.

"What's wrong with them?" Liza asked as a rotten fruit made contact with her dress.

"Their minds have been poisoned." Leo answered. "It's Martana's work. Her soldiers plunder every kingdom or city she conquers and whatever citizens they don't kill, they sway. She doesn't control them, but somehow they end up favoring her."

I gulped, "She can't do that to us, can she?"

"We won't let her," Qoal answered, dodging a small stone. "These people are obviously weak-minded fools who've given up hope."

Leo shot him a glare, "That's it. I'll be traveling no further with this beast. They are clearly angrier with him for his own evil deeds."

"We can't just leave him here! They'll tear him apart!"

"If they don't, I will," Leo seethed. Qoal said nothing as we escaped the rioting refugees.

"Leo, we will not abandon him, especially in this place."

"She's right." Liza chimed in, much to my surprise.

"You too, voyager? I thought, if anyone, you'd be on my side."

"We've made it this far together and we aren't about to change that now. Maybe you've forgotten, but it's Qoal who brought us safely out of Zole woods. While I may not fully trust him, I trust Kida who does." I was shocked that she stood up for Qoal and applauded her in my mind.

Leo glanced at me and took off ahead of us in defeat. We exchanged nervous glances before following after him. The earth inclined, and my calves burned as we made our ascent. Xomax took the lead into a cave on the face of the mountain where he explained the safe passage into Dorac. The Peaks were created by the four most powerful elementals to ever live in effort to protect the riches hidden within the kingdom. Dorac was the meeting place of the Ordenian council which consisted of the rulers and authorities of Ordenia's twelve provinces, including the Doracan oligarchy. The city also concealed the most precious artifacts in the land. Legend states that the elementals combined their powers to make the peaks deadly to even the wariest of travelers. They filtered their magic into the very rock we stood on; all for the protection of their people and treasures. Once on the mountains, any use of magic becomes futile and they reach so high flying is certainly out of the question. Before portals were made, however, there needed to be a way for people to travel to and from the city. So, the elementals each created a secret path littered with traps and tests to keep those with bad intentions out. Only those worthy of entering the great city find their way through.

"The paths haven't been used in centuries, but as a kid I did lots of exploring. I managed to find one when I was thirteen," Xomax explained. We secured our belongings and tied a long rope around each of our waists to keep us connected with about ten feet between each person. Xomax then gave each of us a stone. It was small and light with a deep engraving on its smooth side. The other side was very rough with colorful pebbles protruding from within. The engraving reminded me of a wispy cloud like the shapes on my box. "These rocks were created to guide travelers safely through since one's powers cannot be used in the fog. If we are separated, you can use them to find your way out."

"What does this symbol mean?" I asked.

"It's part of an ancient language that has all but died out," Qoal answered inspecting his own rock. "My people are the only remaining ones who can read it, though much is already lost."

"Do you know what this says?" I showed him my box and he smiled.

"It says, "Raising away the darkness'." He placed it back in my hand and paused when our fingers touched. I held his gaze and wondered if he wanted to tell me something. If he did, we didn't get the chance.

"Let's go!" Xomax stepped out of the cave. Leo took my hand and pulled me after him as I hid away my box. Pearl tried buzzing around our heads but soon gave up as the fog thickened. I distracted myself by talking to Liza to keep from gushing at the thought of Leo holding my hand. Evelyn rode on Qoal's back singing a childish tune and chasing the mist with her delicate fingers. Soon the path became so narrow we were forced to walk single file. We each placed our hands on the shoulder of the person in front of us when the fog grew too thick to see anything. My breath hastened as the air thinned and the incline steepened. I locked my knees with each step to keep my muscles from tiring too quickly and lost myself in the rhythm when I bumped into Liza.

"Why have we stopped?" Leo asked behind me. I shrugged my shoulders before realizing he couldn't see me.

"We've reached the first obstacle. Now, be careful. These trials were designed to hinder and are likely to cause serious injury," I heard Xomax, but was unable to see him. Suddenly, the fog parted as though swept away by invisible hands. A stone arch loomed above us with engravings that matched the stones we carried. A feeling of impending doom formed in the pit of my stomach.

"'Candid may enter, perjurers may perish'," Qoal whispered.

Xomax nodded to each of us, "If you have any secrets, you may as well spill them now." He chuckled nervously as he walked through the arch. I hoisted up Evelyn and followed Liza under the arch. The ground leveled once we made it through and a wide path stretched on before us with walls of mist on either side. Qoal came in after me and glanced back at Leo who hesitated at the stone doorway.

"Come on, Leo. We need to stay together," I urged him. He clutched something to his chest and came forward. No sooner than he did, something whizzed by my ear.

Xomax spun around and glared at Leo, "You set off the trap! Run!" I clutched Evelyn to my chest and did my best to shield her from whatever flew at us. Liza cried in pain and stumbled in front of me. Xomax knelt to help her up as pain flashed across his face. I felt a sharp sting on my arm and a small bead of blood broke through my skin. Qoal grunted and pushed me forward. No matter how fast we ran, the fog tunnel went on forever. Evelyn whimpered in my arms as we pressed on and I hoped she wasn't being hit. At last, we emerged through another archway and the blows ceased. I counted whelps all over my arms and legs, a few of which were bleeding. We'd all been hit multiple times and gasped to regain our breath.

"What were those things?" Evelyn asked rubbing her arm. She'd only been hit a couple of times, still I wished I'd shielded her better. According to Xomax, we were hit with air as we followed the aeros's path. I failed to wrap my mind around puffs of air causing that much damage.

"Wait," I glanced around, "where's Leo?" Just as the words left my mouth, he stumbled from the archway and landed on his knees. I ran to him and helped him up; he'd gotten the worst of all of us.

"Care to explain yourself, pirate?" Qoal asked angrily. Leo only glared up at him as we sat against a boulder. "We were almost destroyed because of his deception."

"What are you talking about?"

Xomax joined us, "He's right. You are the one who set off the trap, so tell us. What are you hiding?"

Leo shook his head mockingly, "Heh, nothing. You said yourself these traps are ancient and fueled by magic. I'm the only one here with no magic ability which must be what set off the trap."

He considered it and said, "Maybe. We did make it out alive, after all." With that, he joined Liza, but Qoal remained unconvinced.

"Pirate…" He started, and I looked at him pleadingly. He met my eyes reluctantly then turned away clenching his fists. I tried to go after him, but Leo held me back.

"Thank you for believing in me," he said gently and kissed my blushing cheek. "That dragon thinks he's so high and mighty. I'm certain I'm not the one only among us with something to hide."

My admiration of him faded and I heaved a sigh, "His name is Qoal, and I wish you guys would get along. Though, I understand what you mean. Everyone has their secrets."

"Really now?" he asked leaning closer. "And what is your secret, oh bright one?" I giggled as his breath tickled my ear and playfully pushed him aside. He wrapped his arm around me and pulled my head to his chest. Something squirmed between us and Pearl popped her head from my smushed satchel. She was unamused by our embrace and buzzed around our heads until the fog slowly returned. I did understand keeping some things to oneself, yet I was unable to shake the uneasy feeling about whatever Leo may have been hiding. I sat upright and tried to express my conflicting emotions but was hindered by Xomax calling to us.

"Let's get moving." We followed his voice and treaded carefully along the uneven path. A low bellowing met my ears and steadily grew louder. The sound was accompanied by various pitches of whistling that sounded like a choir of winds. Again, the fog dispersed. As it did, a strong wind gushed around me until my feet no longer touched the ground.

"What's happening?" I cried out, but the air whisked my words away and sucked the breath from my lungs. I clenched my jaw and forced my hands up to shield my face. My loose hair whipped around my head and my satchel was nearly ripped from my shoulder. Just as I was certain I'd suffocate, the wind stopped as abruptly as it started. I landed with a thud on my side and gasped for breath. I felt along the ground for some way to steady myself. My hands grasped the rope and I pulled at it, waiting for someone to respond. My vision cleared just as my fingers found the severed end of twine. I froze and glance around me. I'd landed in some sort of wind tunnel that howled with each passing breeze.

"Hello? Can anyone hear me?" I scrambled to my feet and searched the dim hall. Pearl scurried from my bag to my shirt collar. My heart leapt when I heard a reply from within the wall. It was faint, but familiar. I pressed my ear against the wall as they spoke again.

"If you can hear me, use your stone to find your way out. Keep moving!" I thought I recognized Xomax's voice and hoped the others heard him as well. Pearl vibrated with each passing breeze and burrowed further into my collar. I examined the rock skeptically and made a light to see it clearer. My brow furrowed as my fingers traced along the rock's surface until it came across an indention that ran through to the other side. Gears turned in my mind until something clicked. I raised the stone to my lips and blew softly, emitting a tone which matched the pitch of the howling around me. With no other option, I made my way through the tunnel in the direction the wind flowed. I tried the stone again only to receive the same note that bounced eerily off the walls. The sound made my skin crawl and filled my heart with sorrow. The majestic mountain became a lonely trumpet and we were trapped within its mournful ballad. Each note was a grieving sigh which could not be comforted.

I saw the end of the tunnel, and my pace quickened. Yet, when I reached it, I was met by a heart crushing sight. The mouth of the tunnel opened to a chamber with dozens of tunnel openings lining its walls like honeycombs. Each tunnel howled its own unique note. The clashing pitches and incessant bursts of wind were enough to drive anyone mad. In exasperation, I pressed my fists firmly to my ears and cried out at the top of my lungs. My entire body shook until I ran out of breath. I stood panting in the center of the chamber until I felt warmth run down my forearm. I still clutched the rock and its side of jagged pieces had pierced my palm. I frantically fished a roll of bandages from my satchel and wrapped my hand. My outburst had frightened Pearl who retreated to her usual hiding spot. I gathered my composure and trained my ears to the faint note coming from the stone as I blew. The pitch had changed, and I soon deciphered what needed to be done. I walked along the edge of the chamber, pausing occasionally when the notes seemed to match.

At last, I found a tunnel whose sound blended perfectly with mine. It sat above two others; too high for me to reach on my own. I pushed a boulder beneath it, climbed up, and realized the tunnel was too small to stand up in. I now moved against the air flow as I crawled on my hands and knees on the smooth stone surface. With each inch, the wind grew stronger. I pushed with all my might to keep moving, and even then, a strong gust forced me back from time to time. The tunnel vibrated like the inside of a brass instrument and made my heart rattle inside my ribcage. Pearl fidgeted in my satchel and the flap flew open.

"No!" I was too late to catch her when we were hit by another blast of air. She was much too light to fly in such conditions and I released my grip to go after her. The wind blew her all the way back to the chamber where she circled the entrance. I reached out to her when another gale came from behind, pushing me out of the tunnel. I managed to land on my hands and feet as she dove into my chest. I held her gently before placing her in the bag and buckling the clamp to keep from losing her again. I turned to the tunnel and halted. Something changed. I blew through my stone and shouted in frustration. The pitch changed again!

I began to wonder if I'd even chosen the correct one in the first place. With a heavy sigh, I searched for the matching note for a second time. I circled the cavity countless rounds before sitting in the center with a huff. I plugged my ears and tried to rid my head of the ringing ache it suffered. I stared blankly at nothing and prayed the others were having better luck than I. It became apparent I'd have no help from them to get out. I thought back to my independency before arriving in Ordenia. It was easy to fend for myself when there wasn't anyone counting on me to be a hero.

I'd slowly lost faith in myself since coming here. Memories of all I'd gone through in the previous weeks swam through my mind. Every danger I faced was with my friends and it was only with their help I prevailed. However, amid my pity party, I remembered that they needed me just as much as I needed them. I was not the only one lost and alone in those tunnels. I sprang to my feet and tuned my ear to the dissonant songs around me until I found my path. This time, it was large enough to walk through, though I had to crouch a bit. I double checked Pearls safety and plunged into the unrelenting wind. The further I trod, the stronger the blasts became, but I pushed on. I nearly fell forward when I reached the end of the tunnel where the wind stopped abruptly. Ahead, the path continued into the thick fog. I glanced behind me and saw six openings. I no longer heard the howling and clung to the sweet sound of silence. I wondered if I was the first to make it out and watched the openings in anticipation. Footsteps echoed off the walls of one of the tunnels and Liza soon emerged. She ran forward a few steps before catching her balance.

"Thank the heights, you made it!" she exclaimed and embraced me. I returned her squeeze as Leo tumbled from one of the tunnels. He was soon followed by Xomax and moments later, Qoal.

We enjoyed a short reunion before he asked, "Where's Evelyn?" We each stopped in our tracks at the realization of her absence.

"Who watched her last?" Leo asked.

Liza spoke softly, "I was holding her hand; she was right by my side until that wind separated us." Panic tainted her voice.

"It's not your fault, Liza," Xomax comforted her. "These mountains were not made to show mercy. Even for the young."

She glared at him and avoided is outstretched hand. "Xo, we can't give up on her!"

"She's right," I agreed. "That little girl has made it through so much already; she's a survivor. We'll just go in after her." I headed to one of the openings but Xomax stopped me.

"We can't do that," he insisted.

"Why not?"

He picked up a rock and said, "It doesn't work that way. See?" He tossed the rock through an opening and it exploded into tiny shards. I shielded my face and stared in terror. "She must find her way out on her own."

I stared into the tunnel and willed her little face to appear bobbing toward us. Leo placed his hand on my side and said softly, "She'll make it."

"Thank you," I replied. He smiled hopefully as he tied the ends of our split ropes. The others followed suit and soon we were connected once again, save for one.

Xomax checked each knot to ensure they were secure, much to Leo's annoyance, and said, "We'll wait a short while for her, but we will need to continue on shortly."

We each nodded in turn and watched the openings expectantly. Time drug slowly, and dread grew with each passing moment. Xomax rose several times, eager to get moving, but Liza convinced him each time to wait a while longer. We all felt responsible for the girl. She'd touched our hearts and made our group feel more like a family. My leg bounced nervously as my eyes darted to each of the tunnels and back again. My hand itched so I redressed it using the last of the ointment. Qoal paced back and forth, pausing every few steps to watch the openings. I sensed he felt even more responsible for her and longed to overcome his guilt by making amends. His brows furrowed causing a deep crease to form in the center of his forehead. Our eyes met for a brief second before he turned away. Something about his anguish unsettled me. Leo concentrated on carving his secret project and paid no attention when I stood.

"Qoal," I started, but the words wouldn't come. He didn't flinch when I gently placed my hand on his arm. He glanced my direction and formed a small smile. I parted my lips to speak but he shook his head and returned his gaze to the empty caverns. He placed his hand on mine and our fingers became entwined. Each other's company brought more ease than any words could. My rising hopes were soon dashed when Xomax began gathering the supplies.

"We need to get moving. Our provisions are running low and we won't be doing anyone any good if we sit up here and starve."

His stern tone startled me, and I looked at Liza who was also speechless. My heart sunk when I noticed our dwindling supplies. He was right. We prepared to leave and took one last longing glance at the wall of empty holes. No sooner than we started off, a sound escaped the mouth of a tunnel. Qoal and I rushed to the owner of the noise and peered inside. The others edged behind us and listened eagerly.

"Don't get too close! You saw what happened to that rock," Leo warned and we each took a step back just as Evelyn came into view. She skipped toward us playing her stone whistle happily as though it were no more than a harmless game. When she noticed us, she waved and hurried toward us. As soon as she was clear of the opening, we took turns embracing her while laughing with relief. Even Xomax held her close and only let go when she pulled away. With our reunion complete, Qoal secured Evelyn's rope to his own and helped her onto his back. I followed close behind as our eyes were again rendered useless by the fog.

It took longer to reach the third trial, and, despite Xomax's insistence, I doubted its existence. Qoal set Evelyn between us to keep his strength and we followed one another as closely as possible without tripping. When at last our surroundings cleared, my breath caught in my throat. Directly ahead of us, the path ended. Liza held Xomax back before he stepped over the edge into the fog filled chasm below. To our right, a narrow walkway crept along the side of a steep mountain face. We exchanged glances before we inched onto the ledge.

We shuffled along slowly, careful not to lose our footing. A low booming sound rose from the infinite abyss before us. Evelyn whimpered and tightened her grip on my hand. I glanced at Leo who concentrated on the relentless smog. Without warning, he released my hand and pressed me against the wall just as a large stone flew up from the mist. It crashed into the mountain above us and showered us with its shattered pieces. More giant boulders followed, and we spread out along the ledge to avoid being crushed. We hastened our cautious pace, ducking and shielding when necessary. I kept my eyes trained on Evelyn whose face was buried in her hands as Qoal guided her. Leo remained close behind me and halted me when a stone flew inches from my head. Pieces of the rock exploded toward me before I could cover my face. I cried out and tried to rub my eyes free of the tiny particles. Leo gripped my shoulders and guided me forward. The mountain shook with each impact causing me to stumble countless times.

As my vision cleared, I saw a colossal boulder fly up from the chasm and make contact with the rock directly below Liza. In slow motion, the path crumbled beneath her feet. Xomax screamed and ran to her only to lose his balance when the slack between them tightened. He began to fall after her but caught

himself on the far side of the crevice. Liza now hung suspended between Xomax and Qoal, her face full of terror. She attempted to climb the face of the mountain but couldn't find a good hand hold.

Evelyn pressed her back against the wall and stared wide-eyed at the receding mist. I hurried to Qoal and tried to help him pull Liza to us. Xomax had climbed back up on the other side and peered over the edge on his hands and knees. He breathed so heavily, I saw his back rise and fall from where I stood. I, too, looked in the direction they all stared. The fog was being sucked into a giant cloudy mass that resembled a hurricane. As it spun, it sucked in more large stones and hurled them toward us. The pieces of one ricocheted off the wall and hit Qoal who shield me from the blast. I didn't have time to thank him before the swirling mass climbed up the mountain. It was upon us in seconds and made the skirt of my tunic billow around me. The windy creature bore no face but struck fear into my heart nonetheless. It extended a twisted arm to Liza who continued to dangle helplessly, though we'd pulled her up a few feet.

To my horror, she drifted toward the tornado-like beast as its wind swirled around her legs. Soon she was completely horizontal, and the rope slipped in mine and Qoal's hands. Liza screamed in fear and pain as Leo joined us at the rope. Evelyn pulled at my waist, wanting to do her part. Xomax braced against the mountainside gripping his line tightly. We tugged with all our might, taking strained steps backward. The monster slowed our progress by bombarding us with rocks. My arms ached as we made one final heave and Liza's hands found the edge of the ledge. I rushed to her and helped her up. The now infuriated mass threw objects at an increasing rate and we were forced to cower down. I peered through the dust at Xomax and found he wasn't being attacked as fiercely.

"We need to get across!" I shouted above the rumbling and crashing. In conformation, Leo stood slowly and retrieved Evelyn. With a short running start, he leapt across the five-foot break in the path. When they landed, the edged crumbled, widening the crevice even more. Liza followed suit and stumbled into Xomax's arms when she reached the other side. Qoal insisted I go next and took my hand when I hesitated. He interlocked our fingers and brought the back of my hand to his forehead. He held it there until I followed his example and placed my forehead on his hand. My reluctancy remained, but his odd gesture gave me the encouragement I needed. With a deep breath, I backed up as far as I could, sprinted forward and made the leap. When I landed, I stumbled forward into Leo who held me close. The mountain shook once more, and I turned back to search for Qoal. His form was barely visible through the returning fog and I panicked. The wind monster ceased its rampage and retreated up the mountain. I lost sight of Qoal and called out to him frantically. The others eased back from the edge when they heard rumbling overhead. A smoky figure approached from within the smog, and I hurried out of the way.

Qoal came into view at last and landed with ease on his feet. Before I could express my relief, Xomax called us all forward. We weren't out of the woods quite yet. The fog reached blinding thickness and the rumbling steadily rose in volume. We moved on quickly, hugging the wall, until a great thud shook the path. Someone asked what happened and the daunting response was, "Rockslide!"

A stone the size of a sleeping lion had fallen onto the path and blocked our escape. In a panicked frenzy, we scrambled over it using the mountain's face and our voices as guides. I trembled with each impact as I helped Evelyn make it over the boulder. Each of us was breathless when at last we reached the archway. As soon as we stepped through, the air cleared, and the stones fell no more. I counted heads to ensure we all made it out. We were each badly bruised and Liza's legs were terribly scrapped from her encounter with the wind beast. I helped her clean and bandage the cuts the best I could. My head shot up when Leo let out a triumphant shout.

"We made it!" I turned to the left and was amazed by what lie before me. The range on which we stood stretched on from both sides for miles before wrapping around a magnificent city. The peaks on the far side all but disappeared in the vast distance. Emotion welled inside me at the glorious view. The mountains resembled a ridged reptile encompassing her precious unhatched offspring. The peaks eventually ended southwest of the city and gave way to a dock crowed by hundreds of ships.

Dorac was a city unlike any I'd ever seen before. The stone cottages were stacked atop one another like skyscrapers along the edge of the city. Many structures even climbed up the sides of the mountains like vines of ivy on an ancient building. In the very center stood a beautiful stone castle with multiple towers standing erect within its walls; the tallest of which reached as high and the tallest Hazy Peak.

"I told you we would," Xomax said proudly, breaking me from my awestruck daze. All we had to do was make our way down the zigzagged path to the city. We moved effortlessly without the hinderance of the fog. The ground evened as we reached the halfway point where steps were carved into the stone. When at last we arrived at the base, someone was there waiting for us.

"Greetings, travelers! I am Eric, welcome to Dorac."

Since her exile, Martana yearned for the outside world. At first, Sanguent was able and ready to carry out her orders in effort to bring about her freedom, including the kidnapping of Lambart's precious heiress. It was not long after that fateful deed that he too was captured and bound to the Fractured Isle. Forced to find a new means of escape, she acquired the scaiths. They became her eyes in Ordenia. Once unleashed, they'd sway and turn the hearts of thousands to fight for the Sorceress. Many misfortunate souls were brought by the beasts to her isle where they were either consumed for their power or given grueling training until they became ruthless murderers. They were unstoppable. That is, until her enemies managed to find and contain her scaiths, momentarily hindering the spread of her influence. It was then Martana procured another method of reaching outward Ordenia. With Sanguent's assistance, the two created a creature similar to the earlier scaiths. This shadowy beast, however, bore no light and was entirely undetectable in the dark. Not only that, but it was able to instantly sway any feeble-minded soul to do her bidding as well as pass through any barrier; natural or magical.

It was such a creature as this she now held and stroked gently while staring into the barren chamber carved into the heart of Mount Crimson. A lone arch stood at the far end of the cave. This arch provided the only means of passage between the Fractured Isle and the rest of Ordenia. Loathing boiled within her as her eyes bored into its taunting frame. Her companion squirmed in her tightening grip. She'd just received word that the child finally reached Dorac and would soon speak in front of the council. She glanced down and said, "If all goes well, I'll soon be free of this hellish prison."

In a fluid motion, she flung the shady beast through the archway and waited for her pawns to fall into place.

CHAPTER VII

Separate Ways

We glanced inquisitively at one another then at the small, slightly pudgy boy who stood before us. He led us down the winding streets of the city towards the castle. Unlike the once bustling Tafara, Dorac more closely resembled a ghost town. Aside from the occasional pale face peering from a cracked window, there was not a soul in sight. The streets were narrow, and the buildings stood tall with multiple levels as though the city was being pushed upwards by the giant stone hands of the Hazy Peaks. The paving became nicer and more polished the closer we came to the fortress and my apprehension rose. The castle loomed ahead and grew in intimidation with each step. It was made with colorful interlocking bricks that fit together so perfectly the walls could have been carved from the mountain itself.

"Where is everyone?"

Eric answered quickly, "Anyone not preparing for the gathering is in their homes for the silent hour." Xomax later explained that the silent hour took place the day before an Ordenian gathering. The Doracan people remained in their homes while the streets were purified for the coming leaders and officials. The ancient tradition held little value to date since the representatives no longer walked the streets, however, Dorac was a city of conformity, not of change. My question opened the floodgates of Eric's pent-up excitement and he spoke enthusiastically of our long-awaited arrival for the remainder of our walk.

"Ophel will be so pleased to see you at last," he began, "The Great Mamanea told him the exact day you'd arrive. Can you believe it? Many people, even councilmen, doubted but my master never did. Nor did I, for that matter." The more I heard, the more uneasy I became. His words reminded me of just how little I knew of this world and how much these people depended on me. The thought of meeting leaders of Ordenia who expected so much from me was enough to make me nauseous. I swallowed my nerves when Leo looked my way and smiled. I glanced at each of my friends and found new confidence in their company. I eased at the thought of having them there to support me.

A fountain bubbled nearby, and I lost myself in the water's graceful movements until we passed it. The fountain was decorated by carvings of a beast I'd never seen before. A small glint caught my eye from below the rippling surface of the water. There seemed to be glittering pebbles covering the bottom of the fountain. Their bright colors sparkled in the rays of the afternoon sun. Pearl buzzed excitedly around our heads, clearly enjoying the freedom from immediate danger.

We passed through the market area which was abandoned save for a handful of vendors and shoppers. Eric guided us through the gigantic steel gates that rumbled as they rose, resembling the fang filled mouth of a dragon. Above the entryway hung a metal banner which read, "Sod Castle' followed by text in the ancient language. I looked at Qoal who stared straight ahead. He seemed as nervous as I was, though I wasn't sure why. Perhaps he was unaccustomed to such a feeling of isolation the city embodied. I too experienced a feeling of entrapment inside a stone caste with towering walls surrounded by a stone city that was then encompassed by treacherous stone mountains. Evelyn also remained unusually silent when we reached the door of the keep and were led inside.

"Kida! At last we meet!" said a man with silver hair as he approached our group. He wore a pale robe lined with silver and gold tread along with an odd hat too large for his head. The hat had four triangular flaps, two of which were pinned together and stood at a point atop his head while the others hung loosely above his large droopy ears. His robes hung tightly to his protruding belly and his eyes were lined with cheery wrinkles. He extended his hand to me and placed a light kiss on mine when I accepted it. He then bowed and placed his forehead on the back of my hand. My eyes widened, and he retrieved his hand with an apology.

"Where are my manners, I forget you are not familiar with our customs. Mam warned me to be mindful, but it seems my excitement has clouded my mind," his eyes brightened as he spoke, "I trust my apprentice treated you well and didn't tire your ears with his stories?" Eric had chatted incessantly since the moment we met, but I'd been too distracted to be bothered by it. The boy blushed, but I assured him that the trip as well as the stories were quite pleasant. Ophel nodded in approval at the now beaming boy before inspecting each of us. It suddenly dawned on me how unsightly we were. My friend's clothing was tattered and torn, and their hair lay matted to their heads. I looked down at my own filthy clothes and grime covered hands and tried to hide my embarrassment. Even my satchel was falling apart; held together by only a few threads.

Ophel placed a hand on my shoulder and said, "You've been through so much these past weeks; you've nothing to be ashamed of." Once again, I felt as though I were not alone in my thoughts. Ophel chuckled and explained he was a pathy, a magical healer who could feel another's pain or emotion. I vaguely remembered Xomax mentioning them before. He led me away from the group and instructed Eric to take the others.

"Wait, why are you separating us?" I asked anxiously.

Ophel hesitated before answering, "They will be taken care of and you shall be reunited. However, in Dorac everyone has their place. In fact, one of your friends is very eager to return to his family." I'd forgotten this was Xomax's home and felt better knowing he'd be with his family again. I waved goodbye and Leo tried to come towards me but stopped when he saw the others departing. My heart ached to see him go; there was so much I needed to say, but I reassured myself that I would see them all again. Ophel seemed trustworthy and I could tell he genuinely wanted to help me. There was an air of familiarity about him that made me enjoy his company.

We passed though many fine halls used for dining, dancing, and all manners of high-end events. The entire castle was an extravagant piece of art able to make any historian giddy. I longed to take in every detail, but Ophel's quick stride forced me to jog every few steps to keep up. The keep stood at the base of the tallest tower in the center of the castle. He called it the heart of the behemoth; a fitting nickname for this impenetrable city. I followed him up a winding staircase and my breath hastened at the effort of pushing myself up countless steps despite Ophel showing no signs of wearying. My calves ached from the climbing and I vowed to never use stairs again. At long last, we stopped at a beautiful dark wooden door.

"This will be your chamber any time you find yourself in our city. Mamanea has made all the proper arrangements, I hope they suit you well," he said as he pushed something into my hand. The skeleton key looked up at me with a golden face that matched the creature I'd seen on the fountain. It was both frightening and beautiful. Ophel informed me that it was the symbol of Dorac; the mighty mountain behemoth. "I will send for you on the morrow and we can discuss more of this world. 'til then, please take this time to rest and freshen up as you see fit."

With a nod, he descended the stairway and I was left alone. I turned the key, eager for the release of privacy, and gasped at the splendor of the room. Vibrant shades of violet and gold danced across the walls and furniture. The bed was large enough for me to sprawl out as wide as I wanted, and it took all my willpower not to dive into its plush invitation. Pearl was not so hesitant as she landed with a plop on a velvety pillow. I smiled as she made herself cozy. My eyes were drawn to an expertly carved vanity with a large oddly shaped mirror. I placed my tattered satchel down and gaped at my reflection. The girl staring back at me was nearly unrecognizable with her dirt smeared face and malnourished frame. My hair hung in helpless tangles and I considered chopping it all off rather than attempting to brush through it. I tore myself away from my horrific reflection and followed a pleasant aroma coming from an open doorway near the vanity. My nose filled with the scent of aromatic herbs and wildflowers that took me back to the meadow of my dreams.

I jumped when I caught sight of two young girls waiting for me in the washroom. One of them held a heap of neatly folded cloths and the other pumped steaming water from a brass faucet into a large marble basin. They said nothing but acknowledged me with matching smiles as they busied themselves with their work. The eldest finished filling the tub and motioned me forward while the younger of the two placed the towels on a nearby stand. I asked their names and the little girl received a stern look from her companion when she attempted to answer. The two resembled one another like sisters.

"Can't you talk to me?" I asked nervously as the older girl helped me out of my tattered clothing. She shook her head and busied herself removing layers. When we reached my undergarments, I stepped away and the girl bore a look of confusion. The other girl dampened a cloth and brought it to me, ready to remove my grime.

"I can do this myself, thank you," I spoke defensively. The whole situation was uncanny. I understood they must be doing their job, but I prefer solitude to awkward silence. I accepted the cloth from the now disappointed girl and tried to apologize but she was pulled away by the other. The two bowed their heads and left the room swiftly. I tried to shake the uneasy feeling brought on by the encounter and finished undressing. With the damp cloth, I removed as much filth as I could before approaching the tub. As I scrubbed, I counted all my bruises and scrapes and winced when I discovered patches of sun burn. I then inspected the wooden stand which held glass bottles of various sizes and shapes. I grasped one and examined its contents. It was oily and made my fingers slippery. It was also the source of the flowery smell that filled the room. I continued to search the vials until I found a substance that created foamy suds and eased myself into the crystalline water.

My skin tingled as I submerged myself into the almost scalding hot water. When bearable, I plunged my head under and exhaled slowly. I felt the bubbles rise to the surface and escape into the air. The water encompassed me in an overwhelming calming sensation. I could have slept right then and there if not for my need to resurface for air. I inhaled deeply the earthy aromas and rested my head on the smooth marble. I moved in slow-motion as the warmth spread throughout my body. Using a small cloth, I lathered myself with the soapy substance. I put a bit in my hair and scrubbed until certain all the dandruff and dirt were gone. Satisfied with my cleanliness, I leaned back and found slumber.

My dreams didn't last long, for when I woke the water was still warm and a few suds remained on its surface. I rose slowly and climbed out of the now murky water. I wrapped a towel around myself and stepped cautiously to the doorway. The girls were nowhere in sight; nor were my old clothes. Though grateful for the privacy, I'd hoped for an explanation. Too many of my questions went unanswered. I found a silky cream-colored gown draped over a chair and pulled it over my head. I climbed into the cloud-like bed and, within moments, I was sound asleep.

I awoke the next morning to movement in the room. My eyes opened to an empty room and I told myself it was nothing. I rubbed the sleep from my eyes and noticed another dress on the velvety chair. It matched the colors of the bedroom with a pale blue cape attached at the back. It reminded me of something a princess would wear in the fairytales I grew up reading. To my relief, there was no tight corset. I began to dress when I again heard movement. The noise came from behind a door on the opposite side of the room. Just before I reached it, the door flew open revealing the two girls.

I jumped in surprise and the youngest giggled. The small room contained two cots pushed against the far wall and a wardrobe barely big enough for five dresses. Not much else could have fit, yet it seemed to be where the girls resided. "Is this where you sleep?" I asked, "in a room within my room?"

The eldest nodded and guided me to the vanity. She smiled as she sat me in front of the mirror and gently brushed my hair. She opened an ointment that smelled of nectar and rubbed it into my scalp before working it down to the ends with a comb. The younger girl watched her sister work, handing her the ointment when needed. They noticed my hand and rewrapped it for me, though it no longer hurt. They moved gracefully, as though caring for me was second nature. It made my skin crawl.

"Please say something," I begged when the silence became unbearable. "At least tell me your names. If you think you'll get in trouble, I promise not to tell anyone."

I searched their faces in the mirror expectantly. At last the eldest sighed, "It is quite unheard of for servants to speak to royalty, let alone burden them with what we call ourselves." Her sister nodded solemnly in agreement.

"But I'm not royalty-" I started but their expressions were unwavering. Leo had mentioned my being an heir, but I never imagined it could be true until now. I wondered why Liza hadn't told me more about my heritage, but I couldn't blame her completely. As curious as I was about my biological parents, I avoided the topic whenever possible. I still couldn't grasp why they'd give me up and abandon me in an entirely different world. Not to mention, part of me secretly yearned to return to the only home I'd ever known. I figured if I became too attached to this world, I'd never see my old friends again. I thought of Leo and shuddered. The emotions between us were obviously side effects of the excitement and adventure; nothing more. I told myself I wouldn't get any closer to him and pushed him from my thoughts.

"Regardless of who I am, your names are not a burden. Besides, I much prefer your friendship to servitude." They glanced back and forth from one another and to me. I hoped I hadn't overstepped my boundaries or insulted them and soon regretted saying anything at all.

My worries subsided when the older girl smiled and bowed her head, "Thank you for your kindness. Since you insist upon friendship, we must do so but keep it to ourselves. I am Dahlia, and this is my sister Rosette." They bowed low and placed their foreheads on the back of my hands.

"Why did you do that?" I asked as they resumed combing through my hair.

"Though we are now acquainted, we are still your servants. Placing one's head on another's hand is a symbol of trust and allegiance." Thoughts of my first encounter with Ophel entered my mind as I pieced together his gesture. I thought, too, of my friends and wondered where they were. When I asked the girls if they knew, Dahlia shook her head, "They are likely staying in the lower lodgings, but I am not certain."

"Where is that? Can you show me?" They led me from the vanity and drew back a large golden curtain which revealed a window cut into the stone wall. The sight took my breath away. We were high above the rooftops and the mountains were all but hidden behind the brilliant city. My stomach fluttered as I grasped how far above ground we were. It reminded me of staring out the window of a plane at the distant world below. Dahlia pointed to a line of columns that stood beneath a long building built into the outer wall of the castle. From this perspective, I could see the castle in its entirety and felt my excitement grow.

As a girl, I'd been enthralled by magical fairytales that described castles such as the one in Dorac. Back home, my mother filled my young mind with tales of bravery and enchantment. Her soothing voice had a way of bringing the stories to life. I never stopped believing in them; instead I kept them alive for younger generations. Mom was a pediatric nurse and invited me to story time often. The children's faces would light up each time I entered the room and within seconds I'd be surrounded by little hands offering their books. I remember clearly the wonder that filled their eyes as the knights and princesses leapt from the pages. Looking out at the city of Dorac, I felt as though my own childhood fantasies were coming true and, for a moment, I was carefree once again. The sisters left me at the window to take it all in and when they returned, they carried a bowl overflowing with delicious fruits.

"You must keep your strength for the gathering tonight," Rosette said as she offered me the bowl.

I chose a ripe fruit and asked, "What happens at the gathering? Ophel mentioned he would send for me but that's all he said of it."

"We're not permitted to know of the council's affairs," Dahlia started. She hesitated before continuing, "However, there are many servants and, though we do not speak, we cannot help but overhear…"

"Overhear what?"

Rosette looked at her sister who nodded, "The council is split in regard to you, Miss."

They saw my confusion and Dahlia tried to clarify, "I'm sure you are aware that Ordenia is at war. Nine of the twelve provinces are pitted against one another and our only hope of peace is you, Lambart's lost princess. Some waited in hope and excitement, while others waited in apprehension. Among those loyal to your family, many lost patience and therefore their faith in you and your cause has dwindled. Our city has yet to declare war, but even the Hazy Peaks have failed to keep out the Sorceress' influence."

"Wait, do you mean to tell me she has councilmen on her side?" I asked astonished.

Rosette replied, "They are but men, your highness, and there be no spirit more corruptible than man's." The wisdom of the girl alarmed me, but her words brought little comfort. Could they be meaning to harm me at this meeting? My mind raced with worse case scenarios. Seeing my worry, the girls pulled me from the window and lead me to the bed. As I sat, Pearl awoke and climbed sleepily to my shoulder where she continued to doze. Dahlia turned to the door as though she sensed something.

"We are deeply sorry to have troubled you, miss. We should say no more of the matter," she gripped her sister's hand, "Please forgive us, we must go now."

"Wait, don't leave me!" I called to them in a panic as they stepped into the stairwell.

"We shall return," Dahlia said barely above a whisper, "please rest while we are gone." The sisters closed the door softly behind them as I stared after them. My hands clutched the now bruised fruit and I tossed it into the bowl. My appetite had diminished along with the rising hope of finding my way out of this ever-complicated land. I had nothing to offer these people. I knew nothing of them or what they expected from me. Worst of all, Martana always seemed one step ahead and, though I'd never seen her, I couldn't help feeling our paths were nearing.

I shuddered at the thought of facing her. The room suddenly became less inviting and more like a cage. I stood abruptly and faced the door. Startled, Pearl fluttered from her perch and landed in the fruit bowl. I watched her gorge on the fruits for a moment before snapping back into reality. A wave of determination overtook me, and I couldn't bear the thought of being trapped inside with my worries. The last thing I needed was to psych myself out by overthinking every possible thing that could go wrong. I decided my best option was to explore and occupy my thoughts with something less dreary.

My new dress bore no pockets and I refused to use the filthy satchel, so I found a violet ribbon on the dresser and strung it through my key before hanging it around my neck. As I did, I stared at my new reflection. The haggard, grimy nobody had been replaced by a stunning princess with neatly combed hair plaited with jewels. I was no longer the same girl who kept a downtown antique shop and lived comfortably in a single bedroom apartment. I wondered if that girl would ever come back. I tucked a bit of stray hair behind my ear and hoped that with this pretty façade I'd prove myself before the council. No amount of fine clothing or diamond accents could hide the terrified girl within, but I was determined to conceal my fear. I smiled at my reflection and, with forced confidence, broke my gaze and left the room.

If I had until evening to meet with Ophel, I had plenty of time to see the castle and take my mind off troubling thoughts and maybe even find my friends. My loyal wyrm returned to my shoulder and I mentally prepared myself for the long winding decent. Music drifted upward from the lower steps and I matched my pace to the lilting notes. The journey down was much less strenuous, though I had to pause to catch my breath when I reached the bottom. There was something new and exciting to behold at every turn. At last, I could truly admire the artwork that filled the castle halls. Before reaching the courtyard, I passed through a hall filled with gorgeous tapestries made of fine thread that hung beside each window. Each fiber seemed to tell its own story, though I was unable to decipher their true meaning. Most depicted men of status, whom I supposed were councilmen. Others showed mighty warriors fighting alongside mythical creatures much like the one Ophel told me about. My interest in this recurring beast grew with each step. I wished to admire more, but the room became crowded by servants hurrying about. I met the gaze of a few of them before pulling my hood up.

I entered the wide courtyard expecting it to be as bare as before. To my surprise, it now teamed with people bustling to and fro. It was also the source of the enchanting melodies that filled the castle made by flutes and lyres. I supposed the people of Dorac saw the gathering as a cause for celebration since they themselves were not involved in the seriousness of it. Or perhaps they were aware of the weight of the situation and did their best to lighten the tension in the air with song and gaiety. Whatever the case, they were too preoccupied to notice me walking among them, much to my relief.

A genuine smile formed on my lips as I ventured about the castle. I recognized the building the sister pointed out and felt my spirits lift at the thought of visiting my friends. There were four rows of interconnected pillars which held up the lodging quarters. The arches were beautifully carved with interlocking rhombuses and between each was the ferocious face of a mountain behemoth. The longer I stared at the creature, the more fearsome its snarling teeth became until I was sure it would leap right out of the stone.

I marveled at the detail and strength of each column until I realized the vastness of the guest lodging. There was no way I could find them on my own. I searched for a door along the wall but found nothing but solid granite. Several people moved in an around the arches, but I failed to see an entrance to the structure above. A large group gathered around a small boy standing on a tall platform. He held three colorful wyrms flapping their tiny wings gleefully. I moved closer to ask for help just as he began his little show.

"Lords and ladies, never before has a single gent bonded with triplet wyrms in one setting, and yet, here I stand! Not only are these little fellas inseparable, they are also the most talented and clever of any wyrms ever born!" Pearl snorted in my ear as though to scoff at the boy's outrageous claim. I chuckled and watched him curiously. "My good people see how they dance in the sky like delicate frost pixies!" The wyrms glided effortlessly around the people's heads and created invisible shapes and swirls with their movement. The display was quite mesmerizing, though Pearl was not amused. "And now, for our final trick we will play their favorite game: hide and seek!" As soon as he uttered the words, the wyrms vanished. The crowd gasped in surprise and searched for the little creatures. "Now don't worry, folks. They haven't gone far. Just play along! All you have to do is close your eyes and count to three and they will reappear!" The child's commanding tone was both surprising and amusing. A few onlookers cast skeptical glances to one another and some left the circle. "All together now," the boy said, raising his hands to silence the doubtful murmurs, "One…two…" The people lowered their heads and closed their eyes and the boy peered into the crowd to make sure there were no peekers. I quickly lowered my head before his eyes reached mine and we all said, "THREE!"

Just as the boy promised, the wyrms instantly reappeared and flew from within the small crowd. They were each carrying something in their talons which they dropped into a small sack the boy held open. "Thank you all for being a wonderful audience," he called before hopping from the platform and pushing through the crowd towards the entrance to the castle.

"Hey! My money's gone," a large, rotund man shouted, "The little thief must have taken it while we weren't looking!" He towered above the others in the crowd and shoved them to the side to get to the boy. Others felt their own coin purses only to find empty sacks. Instantly, a riot broke out to find the sticky-fingered lad. From the edge of the gathering, I could see nothing but a throng of people badgering one another, stumbling over themselves and coming no closer to finding the culprit. This was no time to ask for directions and I started to turn around when I saw two small hands poke out from the crowd. The hands were followed by the smirking head of the cunning boy. He'd crawled right under their feet! I both pitied and admired him.

When at last he was free, he bolted forward while looking proudly at the mess he'd made. I swiftly blocked his path and he ran right into my unwavering stance. He fell back onto his rear and stared up at me in shock. I grabbed his arm just as he vanished from sight. I gasped and tightened my grip before he could scurry away and pulled him behind a pillar far from the crowd. Once hidden, he reappeared.

"Please don't hand me over to them, it's only pocket change! Ain't like they don't have plenty if they're hanging around here," the boy pleaded. I paid him no head as I snuck a glance at the dissipating crowd. "I'll give you some of my taking, please, just let me go!" I shushed him when the tall man emerged from the crowd in a fury. The rage on his face sent shivers down my spine. The only hair on his face was a long spiraling beard and eyebrows that jutted unnaturally from his forehead.

I addressed the boy, "I'm going to help you, but you have to help me too. Got it?"

"What makes you think I need your help?" I pointed to the angry crowd that now spread to the surrounding pillars searching eagerly for the boy.

"Your little trick is handy, but I could easily turn you over to those people which would be the right thing to do. That big man seems really interested in getting his hands on you, doesn't he?" He put his hands up submissively and we watched the wrathful man leave with a group who thought they'd seen the boy leave the palace.

"Tell me something, how is it you manage to bring in crowds with a magic show when this world is full of magic?"

The boy rubbed his nose on his free arm, "No one's got magic like me, lady. It got you interested, didn't it?" I looked at him inquisitively.

"That is quite a scheme you pulled, it's a wonder you haven't been caught before."

"Yeah, well, the audience isn't usually that bright, if you know what I'm sayin'. Not to mention the big guy's got it out for me," he peered around the pillar and mumbled, "I'd better lay low for a while."

I chuckled, "Yes, I can see how that would be in your best interest."

He cut his eyes toward me, "Welp, thanks a lot for the help, lady. See ya!"

"Hold on just a minute," I exclaimed, grabbing his cloak to hinder his escape, "you agreed to help me! Now, I'm not asking for much." He moaned in annoyance and rolled his eyes. "Seriously?" I asked incredulously, "Is this the thanks I get for saving your life?"

"Pah-leez lady. You did not save my life. I could have taken any one of those blundering saps."

"Oh really? Even the colossal one seething with pure hatred?" He puffed out his chest in mock bravery but flinched when someone shouted from across the courtyard. "Ha! That's what I thought." I smirked as he crossed his arms and plopped onto the ground in a huff.

"Fine. What do you want any way?"

"Let's start with something simple; what's your name?" I knelt to his level. He avoided my gaze and fiddled with one of his wyrms as it crawled around his fingers. "Come on now, the sooner you cooperate the sooner you can run off and enjoy your spoils."

He heaved a sigh, "It's Ro and I told you I got no more than pocket change. Barely enough to buy a marac."

"Well, Ro, it's nice to meet you. I'm new around here and I have friends staying in the lodging above the arches. Can you show me how to get to them?" He stared at me as though my skin had just turned some inhuman color.

"That's all?" he asked in disbelief, "You wanna get into the stilts?"

"Stilts?"

He laughed and placed the palm of his hand on his head, "You really are from out of town, aren't ya? This'll be a piece of cake!" He then led me to the far corner of the castle wall where a staircase stood hidden in the shadows. "Here we are. Go right up those steps and you'll be in the stilts where you'll find the best view of Dorac second only to the phoenix's nest of the central tower," he said mockingly as he turned to skip away.

"Oh no, you're not getting off that easy," I called after him, "I need you to help me find my friends, only then will you be off the hook." He looked at me sideways then sulked back to my side. "Perk up, little one. This won't take long."

"Don't call me that, lady. I ain't little."

It was my turn to look annoyed as we climbed into the stilts. We entered a long corridor with rustic doors lining either side. My friends could have been in any one of those rooms but there was no way I'd go knocking on a stranger's door. I wrung my hands nervously, not knowing where to start.

"Who did you say your friends were?"

Startled I answered, "I didn't…what does it matter."

"Things around here are very orderly, but don't worry, you'll get used to it. Eventually. Everybody's got their place and Dorac has a way of keeping you in it." He explained the order helped the council members keep up with who was in the city and who to look out for. I gave him a description of my friends and their magic; Aliza the voyager, Xomax the tellie, Qoal the shifter, Leo the sailor and a little girl named Evelyn.

His face lit up in excitement when I mentioned Qoal, "You know a shifter? A real shifter? I thought they were deadly and evil. Did you tame him or something?"

"No, of course not! Qoal is just like you or me, in fact, he's one of the kindest people I've met." Ro seemed mildly disappointed but became cheerful as he informed me how the Doracan sorting worked.

"Based on your time of arrival and the amount of magic your friends have, they should be roomed right about…here," he said pointing proudly to a door on our left.

"Are you absolutely sure this is their room? I don't want to disturb anyone." His look said it all; he was extremely confident in his abilities. I had my doubts, but he seemed to know what he was talking about. With a nervous sigh, I reached out and knocked on the door. We awaited a reply and when none came, I knocked again. I looked at Ro who shrugged.

"Maybe they're sleeping," he said as he grasped the handle. I moved to stop him, but he opened the door swiftly and stepped inside. My heart fell as I followed him into the empty room. "I don't get it," he said, concern sweeping across his face, "I've lived here my whole life. I know the system inside and out. They should be here!"

"You lived here? In the stilts?"

He stared solemnly at his feet, "Not exactly. My parents used to work at the castle. They oversaw room prep for the council members that came from afar. They were tasked with arranging their rooms in the most comfortable way possible…" His voice trailed off and I heard him sniffle as he turned his back to me.

"What happened to your parents?" I asked, taking a cautious step towards the trembling boy.

"That tall man you saw chasing me…he had them framed for something bad and we were thrown out of the palace. He locked my dad in the worst prison with the worst dungeon master to ever walk the earth. That's the only reason I take things from his kind. They deserve it."

"Ro," I started, "I'm really sorry that happened to your family." My heart broke for the child and his parents. I suddenly felt guilty for dragging him into my own problems. "Yniu don't have to help me anymore."

He looked up slowly and met my gaze. His face brightened, "Are you kidding? You're hopeless without me. Besides, we had a deal. I'll help you find your friends." He beamed at me with crooked teeth and I couldn't help smiling back. One of his wyrms screeched which set all the others off in turn. Pearl left my hood where she'd been hiding.

"No way! You have one too?" Ro exclaimed as he nodded in approval. "I've got two ambers and an emerald; they aren't really triplets. Yours is a pearl, am I right?" Pearl dove to the ground and picked something up which she struggled to carry to me. The object slipped from her talons and landed at Ro's feet.

"What is it?" he asked holding it up to his eye.

I gasped, "It's a button from Leo's coat!" I took it from Ro's hand to confirm what already raced through my mind. "They were here, Ro! You were right!"

We celebrated our discovery until I grasped that now they really could be anywhere in the city. The room held no other sign of my friends; all that remained were five empty cots and a creaky rocking chair. If the button was the only thing they'd left, it was highly unlikely they'd return. I sat on a cot and pondered. Ro followed suit and tried to look deep in thought. His wyrms circled Pearl who snapped at them when they came too close. Their little game ended when she nipped one of their tails.

"What's with your wyrm? They ain't done nothing wrong."

I smiled, "I guess she just likes her space." I supposed she'd grown accustomed to being the only wyrm around and didn't like the idea of returning to a swarm. It was then I remembered the most important detail about my friends. "Hey! I forgot to mention Xomax is from Dorac! Ophel even said he'd get to see his family. They must have gone to his house."

Ro jumped up and smacked his head, "Doy, I shoulda known that when you said he was a tellie. They originated in Dorac ya know."

"That should make things easier, right?"

He thought carefully before answering, "I don't think so. There are probably hundreds; no thousands of tellies around here. It would take ages to track them down. It's hopeless." His head sank as he spoke. I didn't have ages. I was supposed to meet Ophel at some point and my stomach jumped when I realized how long I'd been gone. I hoped the sisters weren't worried about me.

"It's fine, Ophel assured me we'd be reunited. I just hoped to see them a little sooner. But you got me closer than I ever could!" I lifted his chin and smiled until he returned a grin. "That's better. I guess we should go now." He nodded, and we left the stilts.

When we reached the columns, he asked me to take him as far as the fountain in the towns square, just in case the angry man showed up again. His mom usually met him there after her work in the market. I asked why he couldn't just vanish like he did before, and he explained, albeit reluctantly, that it only worked for short spurts of time. I needed to get back to my room, but I couldn't just leave the boy all alone. With a heavy sigh, I followed him to the fountain.

As we arrived, the sun neared the horizon. Ro sat at the fountain's edge and motioned for me to do the same. Once seated, I stared into the calming ripples. What I once thought to be colorful stones turned out to be trinkets of all shapes and sizes. There were coins, shards of glass, rings, brooches, and all kinds of sparkling objects.

"Where did all this come from?" I asked Ro who giggled.

"This is Klic's hideout. It's where he keeps his collection. If you lose something, it's likely to be right here in this fountain. But don't even try to get it back or you'll lose a finger too!"

My curiosity piqued, "And who is this Klic? He sounds feisty."

"Oh, he is! Watch this." Ro revealed a coin and placed it on the fountain's edge and instructed me look at it from the corner of my eye. I did as he wished and, before long, a glistening scaled hand grabbed the coin and pulled it into the water.

I nearly jumped from my seat, "What was that?"

"Ha, ha! It's a peilei; a little water dragon that steals things," he said as he fell to the ground in a fit of giggles. I couldn't help but join in and we made a game of leaving shiny objects further and further from the water's edge until the creature revealed itself completely. It was the size of a small dog with the limber build of a feline covered in blue-green scales that sparkled almost as much as his collection of relics. His four paws were webbed, and his fin-like tail curled upward. This time, I held the object in my open palm and coaxed him closer. He moved slowly toward our bait, his yellow eyes darting back and forth between us, then snatched the coin from my hand. He took a few steps back and held our gaze until a squeal sounded near us.

"Eek! It's a behemoth!" A little girl cried as she scrambled up her mother's leg.

The woman scooped up her daughter and spoke soothingly, "There are no behemoths here, darling. They live in the mountains where they keep us safe. There is nothing to worry about." She must not have seen the creature and continued her shopping despite her little one's objections. Ro and I laughed again and decided to stop pestering the peilei. I took note of the similarities between the boy and the creature and chuckled to myself. Someone called his name and I looked up to see him leap from his seat and run to his mother. Her clothes were very worn, and her eyes expressed extreme fatigue. He led her to me and told her the whole story of our little adventure. All the while, his wyrms flapped excitedly as if to act it all out.

"Ro, what have I told you about stealing? What would your father think?" His face fell as she turned to me, "I cannot thank you enough for your help. I don't have much, but is there anything I can do to repay you?"

"Please, if anything, I should pay you. Your son helped me greatly. I never would have found my way around without him." I pushed back my hood and pulled the jewels from my hair. They both stared at me dumbfounded and tried to refuse my gift.

"Take them," I insisted, "You've earned them." I pushed the jewels into Ro's hand and replaced my hood. He reached into his pocket in search of something. "You don't need to give me anythi-"

I froze when I saw what he held. Immediately, I recognized the chained pendant. When I asked where he got it, he smirked shyly. Evidently, I was not the first of my friends to witness his wyrm show. I gently placed it around my neck for safekeeping. "Did you happen to see where they went, perchance?"

He shook his head, "They disappeared in the crowd before I started my next performance. And I'm pretty sure there were only three of them." He'd assumed they returned to their room and apologized for not telling me sooner. I thanked them once more and smiled at Ro. I couldn't stay cross with him for long. He was only a child looking out for his family after all. Besides, he returned Liza's necklace.

The heartfelt moment was soon dashed by dread when I thought of what he'd said. Why only three? I'd assumed they would stick together. Once again, my brain flooded with frightening possibilities. Had they been separated? Were some of them lost? I forced in a deep breath and convinced myself they were all safe with Xomax's family and we would be together soon. When I returned to the castle, Ophel was waiting for me inside the keep. I rushed to him and apologized for the delay. I hoped I hadn't overstepped my boundaries by leaving my room. He only laughed and assured me that I'd done nothing wrong.

"In fact, Kida, I'm glad you had the chance to enjoy the beauty of Sod Castle. There are not many who truly appreciate the great effort it took to build the walls you now stand in." My spirits were lifted by his kindness. We entered the hall of tapestries and Ophel led me to the nearest one. They each told a story about Dorac's history and he explained each one as we walked by. My brain soon ached with all the new information. I recognized a tapestry with four powerful beings at the top and a mountain range at the bottom. I was not familiar, however, with what was at the center. Dark swirls infiltrated the city and Ophel explained that many dark forces tried to overtake Dorac in the past. One such attack was so fierce and unwavering that the four elementals were forced to give up their lives to protect the city and the riches within. I recalled Xomax's story of the mountains which paled in comparison to Ophel's narrative. According to Ophel, a fraction of each elemental continues to live on in one of Dorac's hidden relics. It is the most precious and highly guarded item in all Ordenia.

"Is the relic in the castle somewhere?" I asked, my curiosity getting the better of me. I had no idea Doracan history would be so fascinating and I was grateful for the distraction.

Ophel laughed, clearly enjoying my inquisition, "That's entirely possible. It was created on the day the elementals filtered their powers into stone and it cannot leave this city. If it did, we'd be more vulnerable than ever."

"What exactly is this relic?"

"That, I cannot share," Ophel answered, "but I have no doubt you will have your answer someday."

I scoffed lightly, "I was kinda hoping you'd clear things up for me. My friends and I had the intention of passing through.

We really need to reach the Lunar Isle and I'm not sure we have time for some council meeting I am in no way prepared for."

He smiled sadly and rested his hands on my shoulders, "Kida, my dear, you mustn't rush your destiny. All things happen in their due time, though I understand your apprehension. Mamanea may have been both talented and wise, but there is only so much of the future that can be seen. Come with me." He led me through winding hallways, up and down steps, through arches and doorways until my brain throbbed and I could no longer keep track of each turn. We reached what appeared to be a dead end until I took a closer look. A small door stood hidden behind a solid emerald tapestry. Ophel held back the thick cloth and beckoned me to open the door. It had engravings etched beautifully across its wooden surface including a tree whose branches stretched and twisted toward a swirling sun. My excitement rose as I reached for the handle and pushed through to the other side.

Nothing could have prepared me for what wonders the door concealed. It was almost as if we'd entered an entirely different world teeming with growth and natural aromas. The cool dark hall gave way to a warm garden of trees and plants of endless variety. Colors of every shade popped from countless hues of green. Long blades of grass brushed against my hand as I walked by. Pearl was giddy with excitement as she bounced from petal to petal, sensing their sweet fragrance. The room seemed to have no ending in any direction. Even the towering trees failed to reach the ceiling. My nose filled with smells of fresh orchids, sweet honeysuckles, rich herbs and loamy soil. In the center of it all, a single light source hovered above the tallest canopy. It resembled the sun and its warm glow filled me with joy.

"What is this place?" I whispered in awe. I basked in the soft light as I spun in circles trying to take everything in.

Ophel watched me with the same sad smile as before and said, "This is the greatest gift your ancestors have ever given. It's a burial garden. There are many in each kingdom, but this is by far the most intricate and beautiful." I stared at him startled as he continued, "Ordenia is made up of many different kingdoms, but there are strong ties between them that have withstood even the fiercest of borderlines. That is, until now. One such tie that once unified us was the burial ritual, and from what I understand, you've already had experience with this."

Realization flashed in my mind as I remembered the ritual Liza helped me perform for the travelers. I then held the garden in a new light. This was the sacred burial garden of past members of the oligarchy.

"The ritual cannot be performed by just anyone, and even then, the outcome varies. As you can see, there are many different species of plant life here. Some are large and took great quantities of power, while others are small and fragile for less power was required for their creation." He went on in detail about the ritual and its origins. As he spoke, I took note of all the different flowers, trees and bushes and noticed some recurring. I remembered the sprout I'd made, my signature, and wondered what it looked like now. We reached the center of the garden and stood directly beneath the light, its lucid rays caressing my face.

Ophel sprung me from my thoughts and gestured to the light, "Now, this signature is the greatest of all. It was placed here by the very first illuminator. As long as your family lives, its light shan't fade." He faced me with a kind expression, "I visit this place often, though few still do. Its unwavering radiance has kept me hopeful all these years."

"Ophel," I started and struggled for the right words, "You all expect so much from me…what if I let you down? What if I'm not what you've been hoping for?" I searched his face for some sort of acknowledgment, but he turned away and walked along a narrow path ever deeper into the wild growth. Concerned, I followed him while wondering why he hadn't answered. He paused at a tree shorter than most of the others with broad limbs and drooping branches.

"This is my favorite spot in this entire garden. A dear friend of mine is buried beneath this tree," he spoke over his shoulder before glancing back at me, "I also know its creator. She, too, doubted herself in many ways."

"It's beautiful," I whispered; though my words hardly did a justice for the gorgeous display of nature which stood before me. The tree seemed to draw me to it and I followed Ophel into the leafy curtain until we reached the hidden base. Its bark was dark and rough to the touch and thin vines snaked and wove around its trunk like woven armor. My hand traced the aging cracks of its surface and a surge of energy spread from my fingertips into the rest of my body. I inhaled deeply and closed my eyes, feeling the energy vibrate within the tree. For a moment, the two of us merged as the tree breathed and hummed in content. I removed my hand suddenly and met Ophel's gaze.

He chuckled, "It should come as no surprise that you felt a connection. It was created with magic very closely related to yours."

Somehow, I already knew the answer before asking, "Whose signature is this?"

He smiled, "It's your mother's, Kida."

Martana breathed in deeply until her lungs filled and forced her mind to see through the eyes of her minion. After moments of searching, she found it at last. She could now see the shadows of the earth as they provided coverage for her beast. She longed to return to the sweet embrace of Nahaliel's breeze, feel the sun caress her face on the shores of Xenoc, and rest once again in the lands of Ordenia. Though she was unable to experience it for herself, she found content in viewing it through the eyes of another.

The world flew by in a blur, past desolate towns, smoldering battlefields and scarce carefree cities not yet touched by war, until she saw the Hazy Peaks. The vibrancy of their cheerful colors made her sick, but she was determined to keep the connection. She clenched her fists and willed the beast to pass through the mountain. Once it reached the other side, she let out the breath she'd been holding. It had taken nearly twenty years of seclusion for Martana to muster up enough power to bypass the work of the four elementals, making it so no one in all Ordenia could escape her influence.

The shadow slunk cautiously through the city and at long last spotted it quarry. Grinning, Martana shuttered with glee as her target turned toward the shadow. He nodded once and didn't resist as the creature entered his core causing him to lose his balance. She'd darkened his heart many times before in preparation for this exact moment. It was time to sway the council to her will. She could hardly contain her excitement upon realizing she would soon see the lost heiress of Lambart for the first time in nineteen years.

CHAPTER VIII

On Trial

Tears welled in my eyes as I was overcome by a wave of nostalgia. I'd only been without a mother for a few years and the thought of repairing that bond ensued a whole slew of emotions. Thoughts of my apartment, the shop, the park near where I lived, and all those I'd left behind made my heart ache. I didn't want to voice what had been nagging in my mind since arriving for fear of disapproval. Even so, I had to know, "Ophel…will I ever be allowed to return home?"

"Home?" He asked and pondered a moment, "Ah right, Warren. Your realm of refuge. As I understand, the portal to reach that land was destroyed and making another is quite impossible." His sympathetic eyes glistened as his spoke. My heart already knew what his words confirmed, though I'd been in denial for some time. My heart sank into my stomach and made me queasy. Guilt seeped into my already troubled mind at the thought of abandoning my new friends and wishing to be anywhere but here. And yet, that's exactly what I wanted. To leave this place full of dangers and horrors beyond anything I could have imagined. This whole journey to save millions of people I've never met from an all-powerful murderer was simply too much. I twisted my key nervously causing the ribbon to rub against my neck.

Seeing my distress, Ophel opened his arms invitingly and I slowly laid my head against his shoulder. In the exact moment his arms encompassed me, the tears fell uncontrollably. I clung to the key as sobs escaped my lips. All the pent-up trauma and emotion spilled out in an unrelenting flood.

Ophel sighed and said soothingly, "I know your pain. You were forced to leave everything you know…twice now." My breathing slowly steadied as he spoke, "You've displayed strength for the sake of dignity, but I can see the burden of your responsibility is far too great to carry on your own." I stepped away and wiped my face, not wanting to meet his gaze. "If you wish to find your parents, defeat Martana, and fulfil your destiny, you mustn't go on alone. Your time here has been brief, but there are many who remain loyal to you and your family. Including the fine friends who entered the city with you."

I nodded then paused, "If I wish…do you mean I have a choice?"

"Everyone has a choice, Kida. You may not be able to return to Warren, but you always have the option to stay here in the safe confines of Dorac. Perhaps if you did, you'd feel better prepared to take on the task at hand."

New possibilities fluttered about in my mind. I could stay. It was a gorgeous city and my room in the tower was quite luxurious. Not to mention, my friends and I wouldn't have to fight for our lives every ten minutes. My friends; what would they think? Would they see me as cowardly? It's not cowardice to want more time…is it? If they insisted upon continuing right away, they would have to go without me. Ophel was right, this was way too much for me to handle.

"Will I still have to meet the council?"

His gaze wavered only for a moment, "You don't have to if you aren't ready." I looked at him skeptically. His demeanor told me the council would not be pleased if I failed to stand before them today. In light of the new information I'd received, I decided the least I could do was go through with the gathering. After all, if I was going to stick around, I may as well do it on good terms.

"What do I need to do?" His eyes lit up as he explained the purpose of my meeting with the Ordenian council. They met once every three years unless a time of dire need arose, like this one. Rulers and leaders from the twelve provinces of Ordenia as well as the Doracan oligarchy would gather in Sod Castle to discuss the state of the country. The Great Mamanea had instructed the council to meet on this very day for she had seen my arrival in one of her many voyages. I was to appear before them and prove my lineage and worthiness. If successful, I'd take my place as the ruler and representative of Lambart.

"But…I thought my parents were the rulers…and they're still alive, right? Why should I have a place on the council?"

"I believe your parents are still living, yes. But there are many in the council who do not." I pulled my fingers through my hair nervously. I refused to ponder the idea of my parents being dead. I mean, according to everyone I'd heard from, no one had seen them in years. Because of that, I'd received no training whatsoever in illumination. Anything I managed thus far was pure luck.

"Not to worry, Kida," Ophel said as my breathing hastened, "your greatest strength is light; therefore, your instinct is to vanquish darkness. Your friends have informed me of your wonderful feats. The council's trial will be but a simple test compared to your previous victories." I nodded in understanding, though still unsure of my capabilities. Ophel turned his head to the door and sighed, "The time had come."

I called to Pearl who slept on a branch of my mother's tree and followed Ophel out of the burial garden as she landed on my shoulder. He led me again through the maze of castle corridors until we reached a grand circular room with doors all along the wall; thirteen in all. "Where do these go?"

He answered patiently, "These are the portals that lead to each of the twelve provinces. Only the representatives can pass through. There was a similar room to this one in Tafara before the city was destroyed."

"So, what's the thirteenth for?"

He moved to the grandest of the doors and opened it, "This is the Hall of Sod, where the gathering is held." He paused and faced me, holding my shoulders. "I apologize for not giving you more guidance, for there is much I do not yet know. Whatever may come to pass inside, please know there will always be some loyal to you. I know your heart is true. This is where I must leave you."

With not a word more, he showed me inside where a room full of stern faces peered down at me from their lofty seats. I started to turn back when a pair of hands gripped my shoulders and led me to the center of the great hall where I was left standing alone. I forced myself to breathe deeply and bent my knees to keep them from locking. The enormity of the room was much more intimidating than the courtrooms of Warren. My eyes traced along the bleacher-like rows that circumference the hall about ten feet from me in every direction. I caught sight of Ophel as he slipped into a chair among fourteen others wearing garb like his, including their own weird looking hats. Every chair was filled, save for one which I assumed was intended for Lambart's representative. Once I'd made full circle, I again searched for Ophel's kind face amongst the crowd. He nodded and smiled when our eyes met, and I managed to smile nervously in return.

Even Pearl shifted uneasily and hid herself in the hood of my cape.

I became all too aware of every pair of eyes that stared in disapproval to the center of the hall where I stood. My heavy heart beat seemed to echo off the walls and each intake of air was harder than the last. I clutched my skirt to keep my palms from sweating and my eyes darted between Ophel and the door. After what felt like an eternity of tense silence, three in his section stood. The one in the middle, Remah the Elder, introduced the members of the oligarchy followed by the leaders of each province until each stood with their heads bowed. Behind each leader, a young scribe sat with a quill and scroll. Many representatives exchanged icy glances and it became evident I was not the only one feeling the tension.

"Mind you all, while the trial is in effect, we are not at war. Hold your tongue on all matters not pertaining to the task at hand or you shall be dismissed," Remah announced before she turned her attention to me and said, "Tell us who you are."

I strained to swallow the lump in my throat and choked out my name. She nodded and lifted her hands, and their heads followed her motion. As her arms rested at her side, everyone returned to their seats. The man to her right, Draz the Elder, stood and said, "Kida of Warren, you are present today that we may determine whether you are who you claim to be; Kida Saedau, the lost heir of Lambart. If you prove to be the heir, we shall further discuss your loyalty to Ordenia. If we discern that you are not as treacherous as your predecessors, you'll take your rightful place in Ordenia. Your chair in the council and your Lambartian throne shall again be yours. However, if you prove to be an imposter or a traitor, you'll be banished to the outskirts of the city where you will carry out your days among the refugees at the mercy of those you have let down."

I clenched my jaw to stop it from dropping as the blood drained from my face. I thought the stakes would be high, but I had no idea I'd face banishment. And what did he mean about my predecessors? My parents were the good guys, right? I stared at Ophel who seemed just as shocked as I. I wondered just how many had been swayed by Martana and panicked. How could I possibly defend myself if I didn't know who I was supposed to be? The third elder, Myren, spoke and tore me from my thoughts, "Tell us, Kida, how you came to be in this land."

I took a deep shaky breath and began my story. I recounted every moment to the best of my ability, from meeting Liza and Mam in Warren, opening the portal, arriving in Tafara…

"You opened a portal?" Someone interrupted, though I was uncertain as from where in the crowd the question came. Councilmen whispered amongst themselves and the scribes scribbled furiously as I continued. I told of the attack on Tafara, the journey through Zole woods, and finally how we arrived in Dorac. When I mentioned Qoal, many wore faces of surprise and distain. I'd forgotten how hostile my friends had been toward him in the beginning and wondered why the nomads bore such negative connotation. When I reached the end, I shifted nervously awaiting a reply. I opened my mouth to speak again only to clamp it shut when Remah held up her hand to silence me. Just when I thought I'd burst from the suspense, the statements began.

"As miraculous as your story is, I see no evidence of your loyalty to this land. Everything you've done in your limited time here seems to have been to save your own skin. Even these friends of yours have failed to fight for anything that wasn't in their best interest."

"I concur," said another, "since your arrival, things have only gotten worse. That attack on Tafara was utterly unexpected, in fact, next to Dorac, it was in one of the most peaceful provinces. There are many who believe you are to blame for the spontaneous attack, and I know few here would disagree." I gaped dumbfounded at this accusation.

"You seem shocked, and yet if it were not so, what could have possessed you to bring the very beast that murdered the Great Mamanea into our city?"

"I was not responsible for what happened in Tafara and neither was Qoal! I told you he was being controlled by Martana. I broke her hold on him and he is entirely his own; he'd never hurt anyone!" The council remained unconvinced and I felt myself growing faint. I gripped my hands to keep from getting sick.

"That is a likely story. Everyone knows Martana is bound to the Fractured Isle with no access to the mainland and according to your account, you destroyed the last of her influence while in Zole Woods. Are you, therefore, claiming to be more powerful that the Sorceress herself?"

I shook my head violently, "I don't claim to be more powerful than anyone. All I'm saying is I am not evil." Many shook their heads in disgrace.

Another voice chimed in, "Why has no one mentioned the child? Evelyn, correct? You endangered a helpless little girl on multiple occasions; first you failed to slaughter the monster who killed her family, you forced her to remain in his presence, you took her into the woods knowing full well the risk of death, need I go on?"

All around me, heads nodded in agreement and I found the courage to speak up, "What was I supposed to do? Leave her on the road to die? I didn't even realize she had survived the attack until she'd already snuck onto our cart!"

"So, you didn't intend for her to survive?"

"That is *not* what I said." I glared at the man who uttered the heinous claim who smirked from his comfortable seat.

Another spoke, "You very well could have taken her to one of the many small villages nearby, or at the very least, gone around the woods to avoid exposing the child to such dark forces."

"We had every intention of finding her a safe home when we got to the Lunar Isle; it's where she was headed anyway," I defended.

"From what I understand, you had plenty of opportunities to do good for that child. Lambart's people have always been held in very high esteem for their compassion and care for all living things, a quality you are clearly lacking."

My chest tightened. I could hardly take a breath, let alone defend myself between the unrelenting accusations. Voices all around pointed out my every flaw, everything I did wrong, endless reasons why I was unqualified for any place in Ordenia. It felt like no one was on my side. I found Ophel in the throng of chattering councilmen and stared pleadingly, willing him to speak up. He was deep in conversation with another member, his brow furrowed in a grave expression. My last line of defense wouldn't even look at me.

I massaged my temple and tried to process all that was being said. Their words became less and less coherent and I couldn't even tell if they were talking about me anymore. If Ordenia was at war with itself, it was evident in the Hall of Sod. It's a wonder the representatives didn't destroy one another right then and there. Maybe the claims were true. I only made things worse for everyone around me. Maybe Mam brought me back by mistake. The box could have opened for anyone, couldn't it? My so-called accomplishments were nothing but accidents. Maybe it was all too good to be true. My eyes burned and threatened to spill at any moment as the thoughts became too much to bear. Just then, someone called out from among the throng of voices, "This shifter you travel with, his second form is a dragon, correct?"

A few silenced themselves in anticipation for my answer, no doubt awaiting another opportunity to pounce my unstable argument. I nodded toward the direction of the voice and a sturdy man rose, crossing his arms. Beside him, a woman of similar build joined him in standing and said, "Dragons, as you know are native to Tiglath. While they can be extremely dangerous and quite stubborn, they are not evil beast."

"She's right. We have also had many run ins with the nomadic tribes, as they use our forests for their coming of age rituals. Let me just say, the fact that this boy was chosen by a dragon says an awful lot about his character and you are wrong to accuse him."

He directed the last bit to the council before someone across the hall argued, "I'd think you, of all people would hate his kind. They are the very reason dragons are on the brink of extinction."

"Ha!" Another scoffed, "That's rich coming from you, Tanokan. Was in not your people who hunted the dragons down for decades on account of your king having a fit?" Remah raised her hands before the argument grew out of hand and the involved parties returned to their seats begrudgingly. The murmuring softened as the other members digested this new information.

"Assuming you are being honest, none of this excuses the fact that the boy was in coalition with Martana for a time, whether against his will or not. She is not one to relinquish her grasp easily."

"It is true he hasn't shown any hostility since his arrival," said another.

A woman scoffed, "Well, of course not! He knows he doesn't stand a chance in this city!" Some chuckled with her while others pondered.

We seemed to be going in circles, but I was glad to know I wasn't entirely alone. With newfound confidence I replied, "I don't know exactly how, but I do know Qoal is not evil and it certainly wasn't easy to break that chain. I also don't regret it for a second. We made it here because of him. He is the one who got us out of Zole Woods. Not only that, he cares for Evelyn and he clearly feels great remorse for what he did while in Martana's reins."

Remah leaned forward in her seat and a thick silence fell upon the room as she spoke slowly and with great thought, "My child, are you willing to stake the souls of all Ordenia, yourself included, on that claim?" The tension thickened as the council awaited my answer. Everyone in the room seemed to be sitting on the edge of their seat.

I pondered only for a moment before replying, "Yes, I am. There is not a doubt in my mind that Qoal is good." Remah smiled and I felt the entirety of the council exhale.

A woman stood to my left and was the first to break the silence, "You suddenly seem sure of yourself, girl. Pray tell us, what exactly are your intentions here?" Once again, I was unprepared and felt like a fish out of water. My intentions? I'd never considered the *why* in what I was doing in Ordenia. I basically followed Mam and Liza to what they said was my destiny. I supposed in the end, my goal was to find my parents and discover the truth about my past; maybe even help save this world from the evil that was so clearly present. I'd grown fond of my friends and I'd do anything to ensure their safety. After that, any hope of returning home had been dashed by my talk with Ophel. Yet, even then, I couldn't help feeling like I was searching for something more. A tear escaped the corner of my eye and fell unnoticed from my chin.

"My intention…" I breathed in shakily and continued, "is to give my all. I can't go back to where I came from, therefore I should make the most of my time here. I don't know much about my lineage. I'm not even certain I am capable of the great things everyone seems to expect from me. All I know is what I've been told and seen for myself. Even if I'm not the heir you're looking for, I will still do all I can to assist in bringing peace to Ordenia."

My words rang though the air and the strength of my voice surprise both me and the council. At the time, I was unaware of the true meaning behind my words, but they felt right on my tongue. For the first time since my arrival, I believed I was where I needed to be. Whatever the verdict, I'd still have my friends and we'd refuse to give up. I met the gaze of Remah who rose from her seat. Her expression was pleasant and merciful. She then motioned for me to look down and when I did, my breath caught in my throat. The tile directly beneath my feet glowed in a swirling pattern of colors that danced around until a small sun formed. Its twelve rays then stretched from the center of the room to the edges where the leaders sat in awe.

"Kida, I must thank you for your honesty. Many have stood in your position in hopes of deceiving the council, yet none with so great a claim as you. It is now evident that you are none other than the rightful Heiress of Lambart; once lost and at long last found! I am certain your loyalty to Ordenia is unwavering." I gaped at the gathering as each and every member bowed their head in reverence toward me. Ophel caught my eye wearing an expression of pure joy and I grinned back at him. Though I was uncertain as to how I succeeded, the weight of two worlds lifted from my shoulders in that moment. Remah then turned over an hourglass. "I now ask you each to cast your vote. Should she, or should she not be given her rights as Lambart's representative?"

No one moved once she spoke. Instead, every eye trained on me. I stared at the floor to avoid their gaze and saw the tile once again fill with color. I stood in a circle encompassed by two rings that slowly filled as seconds passed. Realization struck my mind. I could see their votes! The outer ring was silver and bore the word *yes* scrawled in beautiful calligraphy at its head. The inner ring, the more popular of the two, was golden and read *no*. I shuddered as I watched the two rings compete. The gold grew so rapidly I was certain I'd fail until at last the silver caught up. The top of the hourglass was nearly empty when the last votes were cast. I looked again at my feet and heaved a sigh of great relief.

Just as I was sure I was out of the fray, a man said, "Pardon my boldness, if you will, but it seems quite obvious that this trembling child should have no place in the council. Lost heir or not, she's only been in Ordenia for a few short weeks and I am certainly not the only one facing such apprehension."

"He's not wrong," said another, "The responsibility of membership has always been granted to those deemed worthy by their loyalty *and* knowledge of Ordenia's many diverse cultures."

I looked to Remah expectantly, but it was not her that spoke up on my behalf. A different member from the Doracan section stood and I instantly recognized him as the angry man Ro was so afraid of. Whatever he had to say couldn't be good. His round face was red and puffy, and his bulbous nose whistled as he breathed. Dread sunk deep into the pit of my stomach as he cleared his throat, "Good council men and women, Remah the Elder, in all her wisdom, as well as most of you have declared this girl worthy of her chair. As stated before the hearing began, Kida now has every right to sit amongst us."

"Pirathon," the first man argued, astonished, "You understand what you are implying, do you not?" I sensed an air of hatred in his voice and immediately wondered if he was among those who'd been swayed. I also experienced shock at Pirathon's backing me up. Ro made him out to be such a cruel, wrathful man.

"It's no implication," Pirathon answered, "Now that Kida is the ruler and representative of Lambart, the chair belongs to her and no other. Not even the one who last sat there; may their soul find solace."

"As he said," Remah spoke, "we knew very well going into this gathering what was at stake. While no one is certain of the state or whereabouts of Lambart's previous representative, we can safely say the position is once again filled and our council is now complete." My stomach twisted. They must have been talking about my parents. *May their soul find solace?* The words made a chill run down my spine. What if after all this, they weren't even alive? I shook the thought from my head. Mam wouldn't have told me to find them if they were dead.

My thoughts were interrupted by a steady tone from a horn. Remah once again lifted her arms and, as if in slow motion, the entire gathering rose to their feet and placed a closed fist over their heart. In a daze, I did the same and received a face of approval from several members. The three elders spoke as one, their voices booming through the hall, "Welcome, Kida Saedau, ruler of Lambart and guardian of light, to the Ordenian council.

May you find favor with your people and wisdom in your travels. May your kingdom stand forevermore, and may your land be fruitful."

Their speech was met by a unanimous "Aye!" that shook me to my core. Once again, the floor erupted with swirling colors like those of the mountains surrounding the city. Everything following that moment happened so fast. The councilmen left their seats and congratulated me as they left the room. In the midst of the pandemonium, angry voices rang out amongst the crowd. Suddenly, a brawl broke out between several representatives and guards showed up to escort everyone through their respective portal. As I escaped the crowd, a scribe caught me unaware and guided me to a small room with nothing but a table full of dusty scrolls and a lantern. The scribe closed the door behind me, much to my confusion. I picked up the lantern to investigate the room and screamed when I spotted two giant eyes staring at me. A creature sat on the table, like the one I'd seen at Xomax's shop only much fluffier.

Its big eyes blinked at me and a voice said, "Congratulations, Kida!" I spun around a heaved a sigh of relief when I saw Ophel enter the room. "First of all, I must apologize for my lack of input in the hearing. I was specifically instructed to refrain from speaking on your behalf."

"Mam?" I asked, and he nodded smiling. "Well, I guess she knew what she was talking about. Everything seemed to work out in the end."

"I never doubted they would," he replied with a chuckle. "I see you've met your malak. He will notify you whenever you are needed at the council. The oligarchy gathers seven times annually, but you will only be required to attend the triennial gathering or in times of weighted circumstances like today." He then instructed me to bond with the malak so that it would be able to find me. Obediently, I stroked the creature causing it to squint its eyes in pleasure. A giggle escaped my lips, though I tried to suppress it. Just as I became comfortable with the creature, it bit my finger in one rapid movement. Gasping, I withdrew my hand and found the small puncture its tooth had made. "Wha- why did he do that?"

"It didn't hurt did it?" Ophel asked concerned, "They have such small teeth, bonding is usually painless." I stared wide eyed at him until realization flashed across his face. "Oh, I've done it again. I cannot apologize enough!" He rubbed his face with his hands and I tried to stop myself from laughing.

"One of these days, I won't embarrass myself by startling you," he sighed.

"Maybe one of these days, I'll actually know what's going on." At this he smiled then chuckled when his eyes met mine. I snickered and soon the two of us giggled like tickled children. Pearl tried to make friends with the malak who swatted at her attempts which only fueled our giddiness. Soon, she gave up and retreated to my hood. Our laughter died down and Ophel wiped a joyful tear off his wrinkled cheek.

I caught my breath and asked, "So what happens now? Can I finally see my friends?"

His smile widened, "Of course, my dear." He then retrieved each scroll and placed them in a new satchel which he handed to me. "I took the liberty of having your old satchel's contents transferred to this one. It was awfully worn. This one is entirely yours; only you can remove anything from it."

"Thank you," I replied, thankful to be rid of the old one, "What are the scrolls for?"

I followed him into the hall as he answered, "Those are the sacred documents of your province. Read them whenever you have time alone. It is imperative you keep them hidden from any eyes other than your own. I do not wish to overwhelm you, but council membership is no small task. I truly hope you locate your parents soon, so they can assist you with the responsibility. Until then, these documents will help you understand what it means to be a representative."

I subdued my rising panic and calmed myself. I didn't even want to think of extra responsibility. I didn't care. All I cared about was seeing my friends again. Things always seemed easier with them. Besides, I had no intention of attending another gathering anytime soon. I pushed thoughts of the scrolls from my mind and focused instead on our path through the castle.

The walls grew more familiar and less threatening with each step. We were met at the gate by Eric, who was as ecstatic as ever. Word of my trial and victory had already spread to the farthest reaches of the city. I wondered if the others had heard. I found myself giddy with excitement to be with them again; with

Leo. So much had changed. Maybe the destruction of the portal was for the best. Maybe he and I were meant to find each other on that fateful day. My stomach filled with butterflies at the thought of resting in his arms once again and my lips spread in a cheerful grin as we walked along the cobblestone streets. For once, I was confident in my purpose. As we traveled deeper into the city, the path narrowed, and the houses heightened. The crowding buildings forced us to walk single file through the maze of towering homes. Lost in thought, I bumped into Eric when he stopped in front of me.

"Here we are, your majesty," he said gleefully, "the home of the Othniel family. They reside in the fourth residence from the bottom." Perturbed, I peered around the boy at a tall ladder that reached the highest level of the building before us. My eyes scaled the rickety looking rungs and the building seemed to sway as it reached the top. I took a cautious step backward.

Ophel placed a hand on my shoulder and chuckled, "Go on, Kida. I assure you it is perfectly safe. Simply climb straight to the forth level and don't look down."

Skeptically, I glanced from him to the ladder. Eric motioned me forward impatiently and I heaved a sigh. My hand grasped a rung and I began to climb. I glanced over my shoulder and noticed the others weren't following.

"We have other matters to attend to, Kida. This is your time to rest," Ophel said. His words brought me encouragement and I was sad to see him go.

Eric looked slightly disappointed when he said, "It was an honor to meet the heir of Lambart."

"It was an honor to meet you as well, Eric." He beamed at me then at Ophel who nodded in approval. They bowed their heads before turning and made their way back to the castle. I watched after them until I could no longer see Ophel's strange hat or Eric's bounding stride.

The metal rungs were still warm from where the disappearing sun had shone and the ladder was surprisingly sturdy. A railed ledge jutted out from around each level with a gate built right into the ladder. I carefully opened the forth gate and stepped gingerly onto the balcony. I approached the door and, with a shaky breath, gave two knocks.

"They're here!" A familiar voice exclaimed. Footsteps rapidly approached, and Liza flung open the door. Surprise flashed across her face but vanished in an instant. She pulled me inside and wrapped me in a friendly embrace. "Kida, I hardly recognized you! We were so worried; I take it the gathering went well? They weren't too harsh?"

"No, no," I replied smiling, "Everything worked out."

She let go and gave me a big toothy grin and I grinned right back. Xomax greeted me with a nod from where he sat. A squeal resonated from the back of the house and four girls came running toward me. The youngest of the group peeked bashfully from above her blanket as they crowded my legs. Evelyn was among them and hugged my knees as the others watched in awe.

The eldest spoke in a hushed voice, "Are you really a princess?" Evelyn answered for me, nodding her head enthusiastically. The other girl gasped and touched my dress.

"She's so pretty!" The girls giggled and the youngest toddled over to see what all the fuss was about. I'd never felt so giddy as the girls marveled at something so simple as me.

Their excitement fueled my own until a voice scolded, "Girls! Give her highness some space to breathe!" I looked up guiltily and Liza burst out laughing. A couple came forward and gathered the girls while Xomax introduced his family. His parents, Xomax senior and Nara, and his sisters, Macelyn, Elaura, and Olivine.

"It's nice to meet you all," I said warmly. I glanced at each of them and realized someone was missing. My heart froze, and I asked Liza, "Where are Leo and Qoal?"

Pirathon retched as the scaith slithered from his body. He'd never been fond of this part, but found it was best not to resist. He coughed until his throat was clear enough to choke out her name. "Martana…" The beast shuddered, showing he'd been heard.

"Why," he breathed in gasps, "why did we speak on behalf of that illuminator?"

She suppressed her annoyance and spoke through the creature, "I don't answer to you, Doracan."

"But the only way to bring lasting peace is to destroy their kind. All Ordenian warfare throughout the centuries has had her ancestors at the center. Her parents are as good as dead making her the last one. Victory was at hand!" His voice rose as he spoke, and his strength slowly returned.

"Silence!" Martana answered, her voice distorted by the flickering beast. "You are a fool to question me. It is not them that must be destroyed, it is their power."

Pirathon opened his mouth to give a rebuttal but was cut short by the scaith as it plunged into him. Once inside, Martana twisted his mind to see the world as she did. She revealed her plan to the darkest of details. He could now see into the very depths of her soul and it filled him with terror. He wished desperately that he'd held his tongue and wanted nothing more to do with her or her cause. He waited in anguish for the scaith to leave him once again but Martana spoke.

"Keep this as a gift," her voice echoed in his skull, "and never question me again." He called out to her but received no reply. He fumbled about his room and found the mirror. To his horror, it was no longer him who stared back but a being that vaguely resembled him; aside from the dark holes where his eyes once were. He tried to scream but contorted in pain at the attempt. He was completely hers. One wrong move and his heart would be crushed within its nesting place in his chest.

CHAPTER IX

Warmer Welcome

As soon as the words left my mouth, Liza's face fell, "I'm sorry, Kida. We don't know. Shortly after we started toward Xomax's house, they were escorted away."

Xomax spoke up quickly, "You needn't worry. Everyone has a place here. I'm sure there was just a bit of confusion." His words only fueled my frustration. Dorac's categorization of people had caused nothing but trouble since our arrival. Where ever they were, I hoped they were getting along. I scoffed at my own thought.

"But we've been here nearly two days," Liza argued, "Surely they would have sorted it out by now!"

"These things take some time, dear," his mother chimed in. "There is no doubt in my mind that they will turn up in any moment; what with Kida being here and all." His father expressed his agreement, but I remained to be convinced. Where could they have been taken if not the stilts or Xomax's house? I followed Liza to a couch on the back wall. The house was small and cozy. I fiddled with the key around my neck and remembered Liza's necklace.

"Thank you," she said as she returned it to her neck, "I'm sorry we didn't do a better job sticking together. I'd hoped they'd arrive before you, so we could give you a proper welcome."

"It's not your fault. I wish I had known; I could have asked Ophel…" my voice trailed off. Did he know they wouldn't be here? My stomach sank at the thought of him withholding things from me. I pushed my doubts aside; he never once showed me any signs of ill will. He wouldn't keep something like that from me. Xomax and his parents joined us in the sitting area and his mother offered me a cup of tea. Liza then inquired about the meeting. She wanted to know every detail. I recalled all I could and they each listened intently. When I mentioned Pirathon, Xomax's parents' expressions grew grave. It seemed he was not well thought of anywhere in Dorac.

We discussed the meeting further until at last the topic was changed. The girls returned to the back room where they played noisily. Evelyn fit right in. She even resembled the family, apart from her hazel eyes. Nara, as his mother insisted I call her, spoke fondly of Evelyn, "Now, these two have explained her situation and I would be honored to keep her here when you continue your journey."

I nearly choked on my drink and swallowed a few times to prevent a coughing fit. Xomax started, "Mother…"

She held up her hand, "Now son. I won't hear another negative word from you. You couldn't find a better home for that child of it was hand delivered by the behemoth himself."

He looked to his dad for support, but he only shrugged and chuckled. Liza spoke up, "Please, Nara, we can't burden you…"

Nara cut her off as well, "That precious girl is not a burden; she is a blessing and I'll hear no more about it. She will make a fine tailor, mark me. That is, unless her majesty has any objections." I shook my head fervently. She arose with a satisfied huff and snatched my empty cup from my hand to refill it. I knew it was futile to refuse and took another small sip when she handed it back.

Xomax massaged his temple and smirked, "Why I even bother…"

"Why indeed, son," his father laughed as Nara returned to her seat. I thanked her for her offer. This truly was the safest option of Evelyn. Not only that, she was obviously happy with her new friends. I laughed to myself as Nara and her husband chattered back and forth. The rest of us sat in silence until a loud knock sounded on the door. Xomax barely left his seat to answer when Leo barged in with Qoal in tow.

I leapt to my feet and spilled tea on my hand before setting it on the table. Liza saw and rushed to find me a cloth. My heart jumped to my throat knowing we were at last all together and a wave of mixed emotions flooded my head. I started toward them but stopped when I noticed their demeanor. They were still filthy, and the clothing was in worse shape than before. Both also bore fresh wounds on their wrists and ankles that resembled burns. To top it all off, anger seethed from Leo's gaze as he glared at Qoal.

"What happened?" I asked, dreading their reply.

"What happened," Leo snapped, still cutting eyes at Qoal, "is that I was forced to spend a night in a cool dark cell with this bloody beast! It's a wonder I'm not barking mad. If I have to look at your hideous mug for one more…" He stopped himself as, what I could only assume was recognition, flashed across his dirty face. He turned to me, "Kida?"

I stared in disapproval at the quarreling pair and they stared back in disbelief. They must have been shocked. The last time they saw me, I was a grime covered mess of tangled hair and tattered clothes. Xomax's parents had left the room; conceivably in attempt to escape the tension.

"Kida," Qoal began, "allow me to explain. Shifters are not welcome in any part of Dorac; aside from the dungeons. And, much to our dismay, the guard mistakenly associated me with this pirate. We ended up in adjacent cells until we were pardoned."

"I assume our release had something to do with you," Leo piped up, his tone much more level than before. Perhaps, my induction to the council had won their freedom. I explained briefly the hearing and Nara came back into the room.

She exclaimed when she saw their grungy state, "Peaks! This won't do at all. You two look worse off than the first pair!" Without a word more, they were rushed to a different room and told to wash up. Leo went in first and Qoal was instructed not to touch anything while he waited. Nara opened a chest and called me over before I could talk to him. "Let's find them something more suitable to wear, dear."

Liza and Xomax had disappeared without my noticing, so I obediently joined her at the chest and rummaged through an endless supply of clothing. They had everything from garments of status to servant uniforms. At last we found the perfect ensemble for both of the 'unruly gentlemen'; as Nara referred to them.

She delivered the clothing as Leo finished up. A wave of warmth encompassed me when I caught sight of him leaving the washroom. He'd not yet donned his shirt and my eyes darted away what I noticed myself gawking. This was my chance. I took a deep breath; if we didn't talk now, I'd never get up the nerve. My heart skyrocketed when our eyes met, and my stomach knotted.

He glanced down guiltily and said, "I shouldn't have blown up back there. Can you forgive me?"

"I'm not the one you should be asking for forgiveness." He looked at me for a moment then nodded. I had no way of knowing what they went through in the dungeons and both refused to speak of it when I asked. Still, he needed to get over his problem with Qoal. He promised me they'd work it out then finished dressing and wrapped his arms around me. The hairs on his chin brushed against my cheek. I returned his embrace and clung to him when he began to pull away.

"Is something else wrong?" He asked, his eyes full of concern. I shook my head.

"Nothing's wrong," I hesitated before adding, "I've missed you is all." A chuckle escaped his throat as he drew me nearer. My eyes drifted closed in the security of his embrace, and he rested his chin on my head. I started to speak when we were interrupted by a wave of giggling girls. Evelyn squeezed Leo's leg and refused to let go, which caused the other girls to erupt in a fit of laughter. Neither of us could refrain our own laughter as he tried to take a step with a child attached to his boot.

"Well, hello there, little one!" he exclaimed. She remained at his side until Qoal came into the room. She gasped and ran to him with her new friends close behind. He tried to hide his smile as he picked her up and swung her around. She squealed with joy until he set her down. Once again, the girls filled the room with their joy. The next thing I knew, we were all gathered in their small living area.

"Now, this is the reunion I had in mind," Xomax's father announced. He then beckoned us all to the dining room where a table stood full of home cooked food, "We've been saving this feast for this very occasion! First, may I say, it is a great honor to meet you, Kida, and have you in our home." He took my hand and led me to a seat at the far end of the table. The girls quickly found their spots, ready to dig in. Leo took the seat to my left and smiled as he sat. Xomax's father sat at the other end directly across from me.

"Did you know we'd all be together today?" I asked, in awe of the stunning display of assorted foods. There was no way they had just prepared all of that in the short time we were present. The couple laughed. Xomax senior was a master of a form of telekinesis called preservation. He'd begun preparing the meal the moment he received Xomax's message and froze it in time until this moment.

"Each dish is as fresh as the day it was made," he said proudly as he waved his hand over the table. All at once, the room was filled with dozens of delicious aromas. Steam rose from many of the dishes and my stomach let out an audible growl.

Liza giggled at my right hand, "Looks like we are just in time!" I grinned to hide my embarrassment at my stomach's impatience. We were promptly instructed to help ourselves to the feast. I was at a loss until Liza identified each dish and helped me fix my plate. A slew of flavors danced on my taste buds when I took the first bite. Each bite was better than the last and I struggled to refrain from scarfing down every delicacy within reach. I savored every morsel and only paused to take a large gulp from my cup. To my surprise, it was not water. I choked down the hard cider and felt burning bubbles run down my throat. Luckily, my colleagues were too caught up in conversation to take note of the stifled belch that followed.

My attempt to contribute to any topic was futile. Xomax's family was deep in discussion of their business and some nuisance client of theirs. Leo and Xomax spoke in hushed tones only to burst out laughing occasionally. Liza made faces at Olivine who sat in her mother's lap sipping from her little cup. At one point, the girl's drink spewed from her nose from giggling so hard. Those of us who saw joined right in. It felt so good to laugh without holding anything back. Even Qoal snickered with his face in his hand. Our eyes met for a brief moment and his smile widened. His eyes appeared bluer than usual in this mirthful setting. He seemed more relaxed and I could tell the others were finally accepting him.

Throughout the meal, Leo and I exchanged awkward glances. Each time he passed me a plate, our fingers touched. At first, I was disappointed that our talk had been cut short. Then again, I was grateful to have some time to unwind before such an important discussion. Our closeness felt so natural, and yet, a bothersome thought would not leave my mind. With my royalty established, were we allowed to be together?

Once everyone ate their fill, we tidied up. I insisted upon helping despite Nara's objections. Olivine sat on her hip and stared at me with drooping eyelids. At last, Nara relented and took the girls to the back room for bed. Xomax's father again preserved the feast after we removed the used dishes. There was still enough food to last days maybe even weeks. Liza showed me to the room she and I would be staying.

"Xomax is letting us use his room for the night and the guys will stay in the living area," she explained.

"For the night? Are we leaving tomorrow?" She glanced sideways at me as she fluffed one of the pillows. Her demeanor suddenly pivoted.

I asked what was wrong, but she only shook her head, "It's nothing. We won't leave until you are ready." I tried to press the matter further, but she busied herself straightening up the already tidy room. She asked to be left alone and I realized prying would only make things worse. Reluctantly, I left her to her thoughts. I quietly closed the door and tiptoed to the front, careful not to wake the sleeping girls in the room next door. I found the guys chatting engagingly with Xomax's dad and started to turn back rather than interrupt them. Leo stood when he saw me, and my breath hastened as the distance between us shortened. It was now or never.

"Is there somewhere we can talk?" I asked quietly. His brow furrowed in concern as he glanced around the room. We didn't have many options. I led him to the door and we stepped outside. The balcony was wide enough for the two of us to sit comfortably. The night was cool, yet pleasant and I lost myself in the brilliance of the city. The teetering buildings seemed to breathe with the breeze and a candle lit nearly every window. Our view of the castle was blocked, but I didn't mind. I felt out of reach from duty and responsibility. I looked at Leo who seemed as enthralled as I by the magnificent city.

With a sigh, I broke the silence, "Tell me about the picture on your arm."

The question caught him off guard, but he smiled, "I wondered when you'd ask about it." I smiled shyly, knowing I was beating around the bush. Directness was against my nature. He rolled up his sleeve to reveal the image. The rope was knotted in the middle of the helm then frayed outwards in twelve sections. He explained the rope represented the unity of the twelve provinces. Each of his shipmates bore the same mark. "I'm not a pirate, you know. At least, that's not who I always was; nor is it who I want to be. When war broke out, we were forced to choose a side. Turns out, the cap'n chose the wrong one."

He kept his eyes trained on the starry sky and tugged at the stubs protruding from his chin. I joined him in admiring our view of the galaxy. He then wrapped his arm around me and pulled me to him.

"We didn't come out here to discuss my tattoo, did we?" he said with a smirk.

"No," I said finally. I lifted my head from his chest and searched his face, "Is something happening, you know…between us?" My cheeks flushed as soon as the words left my mouth. He looked at me with an unreadable expression chuckling to himself. He then removed his arm from around me slowly and fiddled with something in his pocket.

"Kida, you are so incredibly gentle, I often forget just how powerful you are." He returned his gaze to the sky, "When we first met, I knew there was nothing I wouldn't do for you. Not only did you save my life, but you gave me a purpose for living. And to top it all off, you've made me feel loved." At this, his eyes met mine. My heart melted with each word he spoke. Nothing else seemed to matter as we sat together in the serene night.

However, dread crept in as he spoke again, "But…"

His eyes fell as I asked, "But what?"

"We can no longer deny your royal status; as much as I'd like to," he replied, covering my hands with his. I'd unconsciously been wringing them in my lap and had to force myself to be still. I did have a responsibility to my kingdom, but I had no idea what that entailed. The council stated that I was now Lambart's ruler. Who's to say I couldn't change a few rules if needed? My mind reeled at the possibilities. I was torn from my thoughts when Leo opened my clenched fist and placed something in my hand.

"Whatever you decided, I will stand by you to the end of my days," he whispered softly and planted a light kiss on my forehead. He then stood and offered his hand to help me up. We stood face to face and felt my heart beating faster. We'd make it work. Our noses touched, then our lips. He held my waist and pulled me closer until our hearts beat as one. Blood rushed to my head as his hand traced my spine and rested on my neck. He stroked my cheek with his thumb before moving away. I'd wished to stay on that balcony forever, but he was already at the door holding it open for me. I blushed and clutched his gift as he followed me inside. I smiled to myself when I noticed Qoal already sound asleep on a large pile of cushions in the corner. Leo and I exchanged goodnights before I made my way to mine and Liza's room.

As I reached the hall, I examined what Leo gave me. A wooden pendant expertly carved into the shape of a curled wing hung from a thick chord. I admired the detail of each beautiful feather and placed it around my neck. I then removed the ribbon which held my key and placed it in my satchel. When I reached the door, I started for the handle but paused when I heard voices from within.

"What's your hurry, anyway?" I heard Xomax ask in a frustrated tone. "You know as well as I, whatever is in that box is likely useless. We've done everything Mam instructed us to do. Kida is on the council, Evelyn has a place with my family and the other two are out of the dungeon."

"You can't honestly be suggesting we abandon Kida now, are you? And as for the box, how dare you consider it worthless!"

"Liz, I didn't mean…"

"No," she interrupted, "just stop talking. I am going with Kida, whether you like it or not. You can stay here and cower in your mountain city while we go out and bring an end to this war."

"Aliza, please. You'll die out there," silence came from both ends for a moment until, "I can't lose you again."

I heard Liza sniff and say almost inaudibly, "That's your choice, Xo." Again, the two were silent until someone moved toward the door. I quickly stepped around the corner and almost fell into an armchair. Xomax rushed past me and stepped outside with a huff. I glanced at Leo who lay on one of the couches who looked at me questioningly. I shrugged and went back to the room. Liza was on the bed studying Mam's box and didn't flinch when I entered. I sat beside her and watched as she traced the edges with her fingers.

"Mam wouldn't have left this for me if it didn't hold some sort of purpose," she said stoically.

"I suppose…" I answered, unsure.

She kept her eyes glued to the box and asked, "How much did you hear?" I swallowed and looked at my hands guiltily. She heaved a sigh and I thought I saw her wipe away a tear, "All my life, I've had someone around to take care of me and tell me what was best for me. I'm done with being helpless." Our eyes met in understanding. She knew we needed to get to the Lunar Isle and find a way to unlock the box. She assured me she hadn't forgotten about my parents and would do everything in her power to reunite us. We made a pact, then and there, to never leave one another's side; come what may. Before lying down, I took out my own box and admired its intricacy, as I often did to relax. I fell asleep with it clutched tightly in my hand.

The following morning came much too soon for my liking. Daylight brightened the room and I felt a small arm draped over my waist. Evelyn had climbed into the bed, who knows when. Liza's authoritative voice reached my ears from another room and I sat up slowly, careful not to disturb the child. The house was all abustle when I entered. The couches were piled high with supplies and Qoal carefully placed each item in four large bags. Liza and I had agreed the previous night to leave as soon as we could have everything prepared. Clearly, she'd taken my words to heart and wasted no time in organizing our journey. She informed me that Leo was already at the docks procuring a suitable ship.

"I apologize for the rush," she said to Nara, "it is important we get moving as quickly as possible." Nara nodded with a concerned expression and silently prepared multiple containers of food. Xomax and his father were nowhere to be found. I wondered if they'd accompanied Leo. The conversation I'd overheard ran through my mind. Did Xomax really intend to

stay behind? I couldn't blame him for wanting to be with his family. Still, it would break Liza's heart. Not to mention, he was a huge help in our getting this far.

Leo returned a while after and announced everything was in order. The girls awoke to all the noise and said their farewells. Nara embraced us each in turn and Evelyn sobbed as we pried her from our side. She and the girls watched us leave with expressions of a bittersweet goodbye. We swore to visit soon and left for the ship. The moment felt surreal and awfully like leaving home. I genuinely hoped to return someday. When we arrived at the docks, Leo showed us to our vessel. The beautiful ship, or brigantine as he informed me, was significantly smaller than many of the other Doracan ships, yet it bore not less embellishment. Its figurehead was that of a behemoth covered in gold plating. When Liza asked how he'd managed to afford it, he grinned. He and Xomax's father planned to combine their funds to pay for it, however, when they mentioned my involvement, both a ship and crew were assigned to them free of charge. Liza and I exchanged excited glances as we reached the loading docks.

To my happy surprise, Ophel stood waiting for us there with Eric. He again took my hand and planted a kiss on it, "I received word of your departure this morning and wanted to see you off." He then stepped closer and whispered, "I must warn you; it may be in your best interest to keep your identity secret once you have left the safety of this city."

His request puzzled me, but I had no time to question him when the others called to me. I thanked him for all his help and, with one final goodbye, we boarded the ship. Once on board, Qoal seemed uneasy. He glanced at each of the crew men and then at us.

"Where's Xomax?" He asked nervously. I'd been wondering the same thing, but I didn't want to bring it up for Liza's sake.

"It seems he won't be joining us," was all she said, but I heard the pain in her voice. I followed her to the banister facing the city and leaned on it. We stood in silence watching the people go about their business while the crew prepared for the launch. I placed my hand on her back in a poor attempt to bring comfort. She sighed and buried her face in her hands to stifle her sobs. My mouth opened to speak, but I was unable to produce any words of encouragement. I had no idea what to say. Xomax held no real obligation to me, yet I could not deny my disappointment at his treatment of Liza. If he cared for her as much as he let on, how could he stay behind?

Liza suddenly stepped back, jolting me from my thoughts. "What is it?" I asked, but she paid no attention to my worry as she ran from the ship. I hurried after and found her wrapped in Xomax's arms. Several passersby paused at their display, some in admiration and others indignant. I, myself, was giddy with excitement for them.

Their lips met and only separated when a strong voice shouted, "Weigh anchor!" Xomax scooped up his satchel and the pair hurried aboard. A giggle escaped my throat. Leo shook Xomax's hand and patted him on the back before returning to work. We were soon underway, and Leo glowed in his element. When he found time, he showed me the ropes and gave me a tour of the ship. The Lunar Isle was but hours away and energy buzzed in my skull as we embarked on our next adventure.

After leaving her precious creature in the head of Pirathon, Martana was forced to send out a second. There was another in Dorac she was determined to see to complete her escape from her prison.

The dungeon master paced in her quarter in anticipation. The councilmen would be dispersing as of now. She grunted as she sat in her small, creaky chair. Water droplets dripped from a pipe nearby in unwavering rhythm and the tiny claws of some vile creature could be heard scurrying across the stone floors. Azazel no longer flinched at these sounds. Instead, she welcomed them as a sign she was still alive.

Fed up with the waiting, she returned to her feet with a grunt and hobbled into the hall cursing under her breath. As she passed each cell, the prisoners within cowered in the furthest corners of their cell and peered warily at her. She paid them no attention, much to their relief, for her mind was elsewhere. Her thoughts were interrupted by bickering voices as she reached the farthest cells.

"You don't deserve my trust, and so you will never have it," an angry voice hissed, "Just as you don't deserve her." It was the shifter.

His colleague answered swiftly, "It pains me to say, but you are right. I don't deserve her, but she is mine nonetheless."

"You can't claim her! She's too far above you, pirate."

"We don't know that yet," he replied, then added, "Even so, she has chosen me. I know it. She cares for me in a way she will never care for you." Their voices gave way to rattling chains and clattering thuds of stone meeting steel. Azazel reached their cell at last and could hardly contain her amusement.

Her laugh was more of a raspy cackle that escalated to a fit of coughs. When she composed herself, she snarled, "I'll not be toteratin' brawls in my dungeon, gents."

The pair gawked at her and dropped their clenched fists. She stood a head or two shorter than both due to her collapsed spine and had not a single hair on her body. Her left forearm was missing and in its stead an iron pike protruded from her elbow. She held up the piked arm and admired it as sparks danced around its polished surface. Their steely eyes wavered as she touched the cell door. Electricity shot forth from her and traveled down the connected chains until it reached her prey. The two shook and writhed in pain as the current coursed through their bodies. The dungeon master's eyes lit up at their anguish and she increased the voltage.

She was not yet satisfied when a stern voice shouted her name. She spun around to find a Doracan guard eyeing her in disapproval, "You were instructed not to touch these two until their fate was decided."

"Beggin' your pardon, sir, but these ingrates was disruptin' the inmates with their ruckus. If I ain't stepped in, they'd've done themselves in."

The guard rolled his eyes and ordered her to release them. She obeyed begrudgingly and removed the shackles from their feet and hands. Once they left the dungeon, she returned to her quarters touching each cell door as she passed with a jolt of electricity. She grumbled with each step; her fun was always spoiled by the guard.

Something waited for her when she arrived at her room. She leapt back when she caught sight of the creature. It was different than she remembered. The scaith no longer had flickering eyes. Without a word, she knew what needed to be done. She retrieved a glass vial and stepped to the far wall of her chamber. She then pulled a candelabra from the wall, revealing a hidden cell.

"It's time, *your majesty*," she said mockingly to the haggard figure that lay within. She slid into the cell and stabbed him with her piked arm. He was too weak to resist as she caught his blood in the vial. It trickled out slowly from the small puncture until the bottle was filled with his crimson tears. She sealed the vial with a cork and took it to the creature who immediately encompassed it with its shadowy form. Azazel retracted her good hand and stared expectantly at the creature.

Martana's distorted voice came forth, "Well done, Azazel. Your loyalty is most commendable. You may now do as you please with him."

"Thank you, Sorceress," she replied proudly. With that, the scaith left and she turned back to the cell. By the time she reached her prisoner, however, all remaining life had drained from him.

CHAPTER X

By the Moon

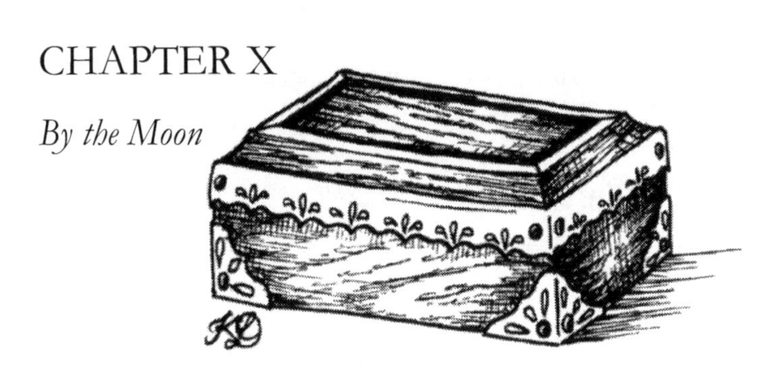

We arrived at the Lunar Isle just as the sun kissed the horizon. I inhaled the salty air. The gentle rocking of the waves against the hull calmed me and the crystalline waters of the Xeros channel captivated me with teaming colors of reef life. On more than one occasion, I caught myself searching for Evelyn. My heart would jump at her absence until I reminded myself, she stayed behind. I laughed to myself and joined my friends as they prepared to go ashore.

Liza buzzed with excitement as soon as we set foot on the island. She went on and on about her memories of growing up there; her old friends, her favorite spots, and her family. Xomax watched her with a smile on his face. I walked beside Leo with my hand in the crook of his arm. Qoal took up the rear of our party and remained as silent as he had on the ship. I asked what was bothering him, but he refused to answer plainly. He always gave a trivial excuse then dismissed it as nothing. As we left the docks, Liza's idle chatter became more concentrated on finding her way back to Mam's old house. Eventually, her confidence of the way increased, and we followed her enthusiastically.

Pearl hopped from head to head, happy to be off the ship where she'd hid away until landing. She wasn't overly fond of being surrounded by water. A group of small children caught sight of her and grabbed at the helpless wyrm. Before I could object, she dove into my collar and dug her claws into my back. Qoal snickered behind me as I struggled to free my skin from her talons. I shot him a glare before joining him in laughter. I figured hating the water was just a dragon thing as his nerves finally eased.

We were forced to huddle close together as the sun set and people filled the streets. The islanders walked about in a daze, and, more than once, someone came up and spoke like they knew me only to walk away like nothing happened. Xomax pulled his satchel closer protectively. I did the same as we pushed our way through the thickening crowd. By the time we reached the heart of the city, where the market was set up and people haggled angrily for goods, our progress had nearly slowed to a stop. Night fell, and the people raved all around us. Lanterns and torches glowed in unnatural colors, illuminating the faces in haunting hues. Had I not been holding onto Leo, I surely would have been lost in the sea of chaos. I often looked over my shoulder to ensure Qoal wasn't left behind. The crowd slowly dissolved as we neared the outskirts of the city and, after a quick headcount, we continued.

Our destination was Elara; one of the less populated inland towns. It's where Mam resided for many of her later years in Ordenia, and, according to legend, it's also where she grew up and did her training. Most of our journey entailed passing through countless towns and villages, each more worn and haunting than the last. We found difficulty finding lodging and, when we did, we rarely slept. Of all the populated places I'd visited in Ordenia, the Lunar Isle was the most unsettling. In the light of day, encounters with the islanders were rare and unpleasant. Those we came across seemed to be sleepwalking and stared expressionless when we asked for directions. When the moon hung in the sky, however, the isle and its inhabitants came to life exuberantly. Even the smaller villages put on quite a show. We only paused to rest and eat when absolutely necessary; not wanting to be sucked in to their erratic displays of gaiety. It was hard to wrap my mind around the fact Liza, my kind and mellow friend, came from such a high-strung place.

In two days' time, we arrived at last. Elara was not unlike many of the other towns we'd passed, but Liza was quick to express her concern. "This isn't how I remembered it," she muttered with her eyes downcast. I recalled her tales of the thriving city, its streets full of children at play and air full of laughter and song; neither of which matched the town in which we stood. Not a soul was in sight. Many of the homes were abandoned to the mercy if the elements and I coughed when the dust of our arrival reached my throat. Liza heaved a sigh and lead the way to a worn shack decorated with gaudy painted tiles. I knew immediately it must have been Mam's.

Liza stopped in her tracks when she saw smoke rising from the chimney pipe. The faint sound of humming came from inside and filled us each with worry. She glanced back at me and I gulped when our eyes met. Before I could utter a word, she barged into the cottage without so much as a knock. The rest of us stared after her, dumbfounded. A bout if dejavu flickered in my mind as I ran in behind her. Someone was in for a rude awakening.

We stumbled in on a woman with peppered hair who shouted in surprise. She dropped a ceramic dish upon our intrusion and muttered to herself as she found a broom. Instead of acknowledging us, she busied herself with cleaning the mess.

"Who are you?" Liza demanded, still breathing heavily.

The woman looked up and smiled at each of us. The others entered warily and inspected the filthy cottage. "Why, my dear," the woman's voice was gritty and made me cringe, "I am none other than the Great Mamanea! No doubt, you have come here to seek my counsel." My jaw dropped as did Liza's. The lady didn't even remotely resemble the Mam I knew. She shuffled over to Qoal and held his chin to inspect his face.

"Ah, yes. I've been expecting your arrival. You, young man, have greatness in store for you. And you," she said moving to Leo, "I see you are haunted by a dark past, are you not?" Leo stepped back as she edged closer and I felt my blood boil. "The Great Mamanea sees all and knows all," she cooed, "and for a small price, you can too."

At this, Liza hollered, "Imposter!" She lunged at the woman but Xomax held her back and demanded the woman identify herself. Liza spat at her from Xomax's restraining hold.

"What is the meaning of this? How dare you come into my home in such a barbaric way and accuse me of such things?" she retorted, all the while backing away slowly until she bumped into a dusty table.

"You can't be," Liza said sternly, "The Great Mamanea is dead." The woman gasped and clutched her chest in disbelief.

"No," she whispered, "no, you're lying. Martana sent you, didn't she? To dishearten me! Well, begone, evil doers! I'll not be swayed!" Her hand fumbled around the table and found a wooden ladle which she grasped and held up defensively. I stifled a chuckle at her cowering stance.

"We are not evil, and we certainly don't work for Martana," Qoal's steady voice came from behind me, both to my surprise and gratitude. Xomax took a cautious step toward her in attempt to retrieve the spoon. The woman, however, refused to be consoled until Liza removed something from her satchel. In an instant, everyone froze, and all eyes trained on Mam's box.

"So…it's true," the woman's voice broke. I flinched when the spoon fell from her laxed grip and clattered against the floor. She then cursed and kicked it across the room where it stopped at Qoal's foot. "And I suppose you must be Aliza, her apprentice."

The last word sounded like an insult as it seethed from her mouth. She huffed bitterly as she dragged her feet to the cupboard and removed a keg. It was the only item in the house without a speck of dust. She downed a swig of its contents with a disgusted face before offering it to us. We each refused, save for Leo, who matched her drink with two gulps of his own. He shrugged when he caught me watching him, and I turned away. With her drink in hand, the woman finally gave us an explanation. Her name was Petula of Mecas, a city in the province of Shamgard, just north of Dorac. She was a relative of Mam.

"She was no islander. She practically disowned us, you know. She abandoned her own son, my grandfather, claiming she was 'only protecting him and the family'. Said her calling wasn't the life she wanted for him and what not. He didn't care. He got along fine without her. We all did," Petula paused to take another swig and her eyes grew dull, "Then the letter arrived."

"What letter?" Liza asked eagerly.

Petula glared at her, "Nearly twelve years ago, I received a letter from 'her greatness' stating all kinds of hubbub about you and the oncoming days of war. Didn't believe a word of it. Not 'til things started coming true." She explained the instructions given to her and her family. In the end, Petula's doubt won out over the haste of Mam's words, thus leading to their doom. By the time they began their journey to the isle, their party was ambushed and slaughtered. None were left alive. None but Petula.

"Riddle me this, voyager. Why would she send me, of all her relatives, the letter if she didn't know the others would perish? Can you answer that? She sees everything, right?" She stared at Liza accusingly, "and another thing, why would she choose *you* over her own flesh and blood?"

"Hey," I reprimanded, my anger rising, "That's enough."

"Kida, please," Liza stopped me, "she's right. I don't know what Mam saw in me. But at least I don't have the audacity to waltz around in her home tarnishing her good name and demoting her to a mere drunken gypsy people pay for prophesies." Petula's face turned scarlet; whether with anger or embarrassment, I wasn't sure. The two had reached an impasse and all the rest of us could do was watch in silence and try not to choke on the tension.

Petula rubbed her temples with the heel of her hands and growled, "Just go." Liza's response was to take a seat at the table and stare defiantly at her. They locked eyes in a way that made me want to fade into the background. If looks could kill, they would have then. Without blinking, Liza told us to go wait outside. Xomax's objection was met by glares from both fuming women. Eventually, we complied and stepped out.

The moon was soon to rise, yet the streets remained barren. The warm island breeze wisped through my hair. We'd long since changed into garb more suitable for the climate, courtesy of Nara. I was glad to be rid of the fine gown from Dorac as we sat on the ground just outside the house. I bounced my leg mindlessly as I strained to hear what went on inside. Leo knelt beside me and placed his hand on my knee to stop the movement. I smiled at him and placed my hand on his. I happened to catch Qoal watching us nonchalantly a few feet away and found myself blushing. Xomax paced in front of the door restlessly. With a huff, he leaned against the wall briefly only to resume pacing moments later.

Despite my best effort, all I could hear were their muffled voices and an occasional song from a passing bird. The house grew silent and I rose to my feet. My hands had become sore from my wringing them. The door opened abruptly to reveal Liza's beaming face and we watched her expectantly as she beckoned us forward. Her cheery disposition surprised the lot of us. The quarrelsome pair had somehow reached an understanding and Petula agreed to help us. As it turned out, Mam had mentioned our arrival in her letter, including details about the box.

"My assumption was right," Liza stated once we entered, "before she, you know, Mam filtered her powers into this box.

This is her legacy; the sight of the greatest voyager to ever live." Her words faded to a whisper as she held the box tenderly and gazed at it in wonder.

Petula rolled her eyes, "And surprise, surprise, she wants her apprentice to have it."

"Wait, so Mam gave you her powers?" I asked in astonishment, my mind reeling.

"Well…not yet. They're still in the box," Liza replied, "and I can't open it." She looked at Petula who rolled her eyes, again.

"You cannot honestly expect me to hand over my ancestor's limitless power to a bratty child like you. It's unheard of; unthinkable…"

"It's her wish!" Liza cut in, "You are her blood; you're the only one who can fulfill her final will." Petula remained skeptical and insisted Liza wasn't ready for the responsibility. We each did our best to convince her, but she refused to comply. The night drug on and on. Her stubbornness and our own weariness forced us to camp for the night in one of the nearby unoccupied homes. As I fought to find slumber, thoughts of the day filled my mind. If the box were to open, would Liza really get all of Mam's powers? My own box crossed my train of thought. If her experience was anything like mine, possessing the power only meant as much as how well you could use it.

I tossed and turned restlessly until daylight shone through a broken window. It danced on the walls with the motion of leaves from a tree. The bright shapes faded whenever a cloud passed by only to return seconds later. The light brought me ease. Leo snored softly beside me, and I envied his state of peace. Liza had stayed with Petula hours after we'd left but was eventually forced to give up. She now laid comfortably on Xomax's lap. I saw tuffs of Qoal's brown hair from the window and carefully tiptoed out of the creaky shack to join him. He didn't acknowledge me as I stood next to him beneath the spindly tree.

"Something is bothering you," I said softly, not wanting to wake the others. His eyes darted toward me. He fiddled with a leaf he'd pulled from the tree and tore it into pieces before letting them fall from his fingers. "Whatever it is, you can tell me. We're a team, and it's not good to hide things from one another."

At this he met my gaze, "I'm not like you; quick to give my trust to those who are unworthy." His comment stung, and I looked at him incredulously. "You're going to get yourself hurt if you aren't careful."

I immediately knew he must have been talking about Leo. Was all that just jealousy? Thoroughly annoyed, I turned to go back into the shack when he took my hand and said, "I'm only trying to look out for you. To repay my debt."

"Qoal, you don't owe me anything. All I ask is that you return the trust I've already given you." I stared at his hand that still held mine and he let go.

Neither of us spoke for a while until he broke the silence, "What would you like to know?"

He and I never had much chance to get to know one another; he was always reserved when the others were around. We sat in the sparse shade of the little tree as the sun rose. I asked him about his people and how he became a shifter and his eyes lit up. His people were native to the province of Husun in northern Ordenia, right next to Tiglath. I often thought of the council members from that region and their mention of the nomads' coming of age ritual. He explained in great detail what it meant to reach maturity in his clan. The children must travel through a certain forest, the name of which he refused to give, to find their second form. The forest was filled with creatures of all shapes and sizes; from swift rabbits to strong one-eyed giants. Their quest was simple; travel as deep as you dare and wait. The further you go, the more powerful and dangerous the beasts became. It seemed easy enough. However, once inside, you were at the mercy of the woods and its inhabitants. Children would spend years training to build up their survival instincts. Their patience was tested as well. They couldn't just take the form of the first thing they saw, no. They had to be chosen by a dying creature who would then give their form to the child as they passed from this life to the next.

His story fascinated me. I sat captivated by his words until his voice trailed off. He stared past me at something in the distance and I asked about his family. He flinched and gave no reply. I started to ask again when he pointed ahead. I followed his line of sight and my eyes widened. There, walking toward us on the dusty road, was Petula. She carried a woven basket and hurried her pace when she noticed we'd spotted her.

"Is she here?" she asked wheezing. Qoal and I nodded and lead her inside. Xomax shook Liza awake when we entered, and she scrambled to her feet. "I've done a lot of thinking, girl. Maybe you're not what I had in mind when Mamanea mentioned her prodigy, but she must have seen something in you to bring you this far."

Liza still clutched the box and gaped at Petula's sudden change of heart. The rest of us looked back and forth between the pair, not wanting to spoil whatever was about to happen. Petula then took the box and held it facing Liza. The color drained from our friend's face as the weight of the situation crashed down on her. Petula saw her nervousness and retrieved her hand that hovered above the lid.

"I'm fine, I'm fine. Go ahead," Liza said hastily. Again, Petula huffed in vexation. The four of us bystanders stepped back as she opened the chest. A thin stream of smoke went forward from the box to Liza, encompassing her with a soft glow. Her eyes rolled back in her head and she stumbled backward until she hit the wall. Petula gasped and slammed the box shut as soon as the smoke dissipated. Liza gulped for air until her breathing steadied. I glanced as the others who clearly shared my initial thought; that was awfully anticlimactic. She smiled as she took a few steps and, as if in slow motion, she collapsed into Xomax's outstretched arms. He barely made it to her before she made contact with the floor.

Petula smirked, shaking her head, and headed for the door. She announced she'd be fine once she was used to the change in energy and wished us luck before leaving the way she'd come. Xomax said with a chuckle, "I guess she got what she wanted. We'll stay here until she wakes up again." Relief flooded the room and soon we were all laughing.

Liza rested peacefully as we contemplated our next move. Leo explained our previous ship was now useless since it was unable to leave the Xeros Channel. The crescent shaped island faced the mainland and, evidently, extended just below the surface of the water creating a barrier on either side. He encouraged me not to fret, stating there would be docks on the other side of the isle where we could purchase a ship. With luck, we'd be able to use my status to procure another deal.

The next morning, Liza woke somewhat dazed. When she was no longer disoriented, we set off toward the southern coast. I pestered her the whole way with questions about what she'd seen. She answered me patiently and with enthusiasm about her visions. They mainly consisted of memories from Mam and others of whom Liza held no connection. She'd pause every so often to scribble in her notebook. Late one night, she confessed to me her disappointment.

"I can tell a difference in my abilities," she admitted, "but I know I can't see *everything*."

"Maybe it doesn't work like that. You may have to give it more time," I offered. She agreed, and I left her to her scribbling. I distracted myself with feeding an irritated Pearl, yet thoughts of our next destination penetrated my mind. My heart buzzed with dread and excitement. It was time to find my parents.

Martana shuddered with glee as she held the vial up to the moonlight. Eleazar's blood glowed deliciously, but it was not for drinking. No, this man's blood was the key to her freedom. She again stood in the cave, staring triumphantly at the carved arch. Sanguent stood at her right hand and her legions of soldiers were erect along the mountainside behind them. It was time for the ritual.

She removed her dagger from its holster and Sanguent gave her his hand and took the vial. She slit her palm then his. She caught his blood as it dripped into her bleeding hand and nodded to him. He removed the cork and poured it over the cut, drenching her hand with the scarlet liquid. The pair stepped closer to the opening. She ignored the pain as she dragged her hand across the frame of the archway, leaving a ghastly red smear. When she removed her hand, her breath caught in her throat. The once empty frame came to life with swirling tones of grey until a clear image of the outside world came into focus.

She was unable to contain herself and ran with open arms through the arch that had taunted her for so many years. Sanguent followed swiftly, not wanting to be left behind. Tears welled in her eyes when they met his. She then embraced him and kissed him, both of which he returned with great passion. He picked her up and spun her around, all the while enjoying the return of her smile.

"We are home at last, my love," she whispered. Their celebration ceased as quickly as it began as Sanguent clasped her hand in his and healed their wounds.

"Very good," she cooed. "I knew it was wise to give you that healer." He grinned at her approval. She then peered around his shoulder. They were in a heavily wooded area, which itself made it clear they were no longer on the lifeless Fractured Isle. It could have been any number of Ordenia's many forests, for she was not entirely sure where her captors had hidden the portal. Unperturbed by their predicament, she turned to the arch and shouted to her army, "March! Bring justice to this war-stricken land!"

In perfect sync, the soldiers emerged from the portal and dispersed in all directions. Martana smiled gleefully. She caught Sanguent's gaze who knew immediately what was to come. Without further hesitation, the pair morphed into wyverns and took to the sky. This time, they'd prepared for the transformation by eating their fill of whatever they could find on the island. Fully energized, the bone grinding shift was much more bearable. No longer enslaved by injustice, the fearsome beasts set out in pursuit of their prey.

CHAPTER XI

Weigh Anchor

Upon our arrival to the docks, a sickening feeling filled my gut. Was I only days away from meeting my parents? What if they weren't there? What if they didn't recognize me? What should I say? My stomach churned and threatened to up my breakfast. Xomax and Leo went to the shipyard with most of our funds while the rest of us stayed in town. We used what was left to buy food and supplies.

While at a fruit stand, I pulled Liza aside and gave voice to my worry. No sooner than I did, the tears began to fall. Liza gasped and draped her arm around me. She had to stand on her tiptoes to reach my shoulders and I laughed through my crying. She scolded me for making fun of her height and burst into a fit of giggles. Qoal watched our foolishness with an expression of concern.

After unsettling the people around us, she and I composed ourselves. She wiped away her tears and said, "No matter what happens, we're here for you. So what if it's not everything you expect? Life seldom is." Qoal agreed, clearly grateful to be free of our hysterics. I couldn't have asked for better friends and I thanked them for their support.

By noon, the other two returned and spoke emphatically about the difficulties of finding an able-bodied crew and a seaworthy ship. Those they did find scoffed in their faces at the miniscule pay we offered. Not to mention, few were willing to sail further than Dorac due to the rising turmoil in the east.

"I'm confused, did you find a ship or not?" Liza asked, not withholding her frustration.

"Of course, we did, milady," Xomax answered flirtatiously and I suppressed a well warranted eyeroll.

Leo chimed in proudly, "It was no easy feat, mind you." His eyes locked on mine and my face grew hot. They led us to the ship, which was significantly larger than our previous one. Pearl took one look at it and flew around my head sporadically until I opened my satchel for her to scurry inside. We crossed the gangway with haste, as instructed by the first mate. He was a weathered old man, tanned by decades in the sun and lacking sorely in manners. His hair was bleached white and so thin that the shine of his scalp could be seen clearly when hit by the sunlight. The ship's size said nothing of its cleanliness. In fact, I was certain we were at serious risk of catching some incurable disease. Its dark wood was damp and covered with a layer of gunk and the crew was none too pleasant either.

I suddenly wished I'd told Leo about Ophel's warning. The entire crew had shifty eyes and a look of malice about them. Leo assured me their intentions were good, despite their shady appearance. After all, they were kind enough to offer their services when no one else would. I remained skeptical despite my efforts to be positive.

"Relax, I won't let any of them harm you," he said soothingly. I quickly changed the subject and asked how long the trip would take. My heart sank at his reply. With the wind on our side, our destination was a little over a week away. He led me below deck and showed me where we'd be staying. He said I looked unwell and instructed me to lie down until I gained my sea-legs. I gave a small smile when he kissed my forehead and left me to rest. The cabin reeked of fish and alcohol and I jumped at the sound of claws scurrying along the floor. My stomach churned at the thought of spending another hour on the vermin infested boat.

Several hammocks hung from the low ceiling. I chose the one with the least amount of mildew and lit a lantern on the wall beside it. I tasted bile as the ship began to move. My mind filled with worry at my sudden queasiness; I'd never had a problem with motion sickness. I told myself it was the combination of my nerves and vile surroundings. Sighing, I found a crate and used it to climb into the hammock. Once comfortable, I let Pearl out of my satchel, and she nuzzled her way under my neck. My insides settled as I let the hammock rock me to sleep.

The rest did me well and I awoke with a new sliver of confidence, ready to take on whatever life had to throw at me. The first few days of the trip were, for the most part, uneventful. The crew kept to themselves, much to my relief. One slept consistently against the mast, no matter the time or weather. I'd kick his foot whenever I walked by to make sure he was still alive, and he'd reply with a grunt. Qoal was more aloof than ever and spent most of his time in the crow's nest where he could keep an eye on everyone. Xomax and Leo busied themselves talking with the crew and helping when needed. Occasionally, Leo and I would catch a moment alone. When he and I weren't chatting, I worked on my powers with Liza.

I'd often move to the bow which was unoccupied for most of the daytime and practice. While I fiddled with light, I discovered many new tricks. I found I was able to bend light around objects, rendering them invisible if I did it just right. I also noticed a difference in the strength of my powers. It was more difficult to use them at night without the guidance of the sun. One morning, while eating a fruit, an idea sparked in my brain. I finished the fruit, leaving nothing but the seed in the palm of my hand. I focused a ray of sunlight onto the seed and waited. Just before I gave up, it happened. A tiny green sprout popped out from its shell. In my excitement, my concentration broke, but I didn't care. I had to show Liza. Memories of the burial ritual came to mind as I searched for her.

Before I could find her, however, Qoal landed directly in my path and pulled me into the cabin. He had jumped all the way down from the crow's next. It's a wonder he didn't break his legs.

"What's gotten into you?" I demanded.

He shushed me and whispered, "Something's coming." We had intruded on Liza and Xomax who came forward, slightly disheveled, when they heard us. I ignored their flushed faces. Qoal mentioned a feeling in his gut that danger was approaching that began the moment we'd boarded. Mere moments ago, his fears had been realized. Something was headed straight for us. We asked what it was, but he shook his head claiming he hadn't gotten a good look at it.

"I brought you down here because I need your help," he said intently, "I don't want to waste our provisions, but I need to eat all I can before I shift."

"Wait, you want to turn into a dragon *now*?" Liza asked with a panicked tone.

He sighed impatiently, "It's just a precaution; I want to be prepared." I nodded in understanding and we gathered all the food we could find. But we were too late. The ship quaked with impact, knocking every one of us off our feet. An armful of food flew from my grasp as I landed with a thud on the hard wooden floor and found myself unable to breathe. Qoal landed on top of me before he staggered to his feet and helped me up. No sooner than he did, we were hit by another impact. Qoal braced himself, but I fell forward onto my hands and knees. A trickle of blood made its way down Xomax's face and Liza patched it up in a flash. We suffered no other injuries aside from a bruise or two.

The cabin door flew from its hinges while we regrouped. My eyes had grown accustomed to the dim lighting and I squinted when I tried to distinguish the dark figure in the doorway. The figure stepped aside to make way for others to pass by. Several crewmen rushed into the cabin and dragged us out. It took two to subdue Xomax and three for Qoal. To my disgust, the first mate was who restrained me. He was surprisingly strong despite his withered appearance. I fought against him with all my might, but his grip only tightened. He cackled at my futile struggle, and the stench of his foul breath filled my nostrils. I leaned forward to escape the odor then jerked my head back. Bone cracked as my skull contacted his nose and he screamed in pain. He shoved me away and I fell forward into someone. Without needing to look, I knew who it was.

"My, that was impressive," Leo said as I took a step back.

"Leo? What's going on?" Fear gripped my heart when I realized he was not being held back by the ruffians. He opened his mouth to explain but stopped and peered behind me.

The color drained from his face and a woman's voice spoke up, "I would love to enlighten you." In all the commotion, I'd failed to notice our two new passengers. I didn't need to see her to tell how vile and malicious she was. Her voice was cold and breathy. The icy hand of terror gripped my spine as I turned to the speaker. What I saw didn't quite match what I heard. The woman before me had fair skin without a single blemish and hair of dark mahogany with the slightest touch of grey. Her face was not devoid of age, but it wasn't haggard either. One might even say she was beautiful. Her pleasant face gave me no inclination to fear her, but I didn't trust her either. The only unruly feature about her sat atop her head. Her crown looked as though it were made of shards of glass.

She closed the distance separating us and placed her cold hand on my cheek. "Look at you," she murmured eerily, "you've grown so much." My breaths were short as I stood captivated by her unwavering gaze. Her eyes were as dark as onyx, though I could have sworn I saw a flicker of color on her iris a time or two. No one moved as she eyed each person on the deck, aside from her accomplice who had spoken nary a word. He kept his eyes trained on the woman in admiration. His face was clean shaven, but his mousy hair hadn't been cut in years.

Once satisfied with our attention she spoke, "I trust you know who I am, and you are right to tremble."

Her voice captivated all who heard. My friends were in a trance as they watched her with wide eyes. The silence was soon broken by a gruff voice, "What's yer name, wench? And what business have ye on our ship?" All eyes shot to the source of the daring remark. It was the sleeping sailor. Why now, of all times, would he choose to wake up? I held my breath in anticipation. The woman glided effortlessly across the splintered boards until she was inches from the man's face.

"I am Martana," she replied through clenched teeth. Her answer confirmed my fears. I thought for certain the salty old sailor was done for, but she turned her eyes from him back to me and announced, "I am here for one thing and one thing only. Kida, I'd much prefer to have your cooperation."

With much effort, the words sputtered from my mouth, "You- you'll get nothing from me."

Her sigh was like a warm breeze over drought-stricken land, "I'd hoped we'd reach an agreement. We are so much alike, after all; you and I." I stared at her in confusion and she continued, "We were both forced into exile. Cut off from our families. Unwanted by our own people."

A bit of strength returned to me as I replied, "That's not true. You're the one who kidnapped me."

She chuckled and said, "I meant no harm by that. It was merely a desperate attempt to escape my prison. I had every intention of returning you to your family, but it was the Great Mamanea who banished you to Warren. Or did she skim over that detail?"

My breath caught in my throat. It couldn't be. I tried to recall Mam's words at our first meeting, but my memory failed me.

She extended her hand to me and said, "Together, you and I can right the wrong of this grieved land."

Time stood still as my eyes darted from her hands to her eyes. There was no way I could trust her, but her invitation was tempting. I began to question everything I'd come to believe. My gaze lingered on her outstretched hand before Liza caught my eye. The look of terror on each of my friends faces gave me the push I needed to refuse. I stepped back and stared defiantly at Martana. Her face fell in disappointment. Confidence welled inside my chest but was dashed in an instant.

She nodded to her friend whose hand shot out. Before I could even blink, ropes bound my arms and legs until I was completely immobile. I lost my balance as my ankles were pulled together. It was Leo who steadied me. My voice cracked as I gasped his name. I couldn't bear the thought but forced myself to ask, "Are you involved in this?" His eyes gave all the answer I needed. He pushed me against the mast where another rope wrapped around my torso.

"I can explain," he whispered, "Just give her what she wants."

He turned his head to Martana, careful to avoid direct eye contact with her. She then taunted, "Having second thoughts, are we? I gave her due chance." Her associate, I later came to know as Sanguent, tensed and glared accusingly at Leo who shook his head vigorously. He turned back to me. We stared pleadingly at one another, but there was no way I could join her. When he saw

I wouldn't budge, he reluctantly pulled something from around his neck. It was a tiny vial full of red liquid. My blood. I begged him to stop whatever he was about to do. He refused to look me in the eye as he came closer. My heart thumped painfully in my chest and my hands ached from my clenching them.

The world blurred. Tears streamed down my face as Leo obediently crushed the thin vial between his fingers, allowing his blood to mix with mine. Qoal found his voice and shouted a protest. He fought his way free of his captors and ran to me, but he was cut short by Sanguent who backhanded him so forcefully he crashed against the other side of the ship. A loud sob escaped my lips as he slumped over, unconscious. Leo hesitated before proceeding. He then placed his bleeding hand beneath my bare collar bone, drawing a scarlet line with his fingers. His touch was soft and gentle, yet I felt like he was ripping my aching heart from my chest. I was unable to move when he leaned closer to me. A shiver trembled through my body, beginning where his lips brushed against mine as he whispered, "Please, forgive me."

I didn't return his kiss and he abruptly pulled away. A tear escaped his left eye, but I gave him no pity. To my surprise, he removed my box from a large pocket of his coat and smeared what was left of the fresh blood across the top of it. I stared gaping at him as he opened it and held it toward me. Fury raged within me and rendered me speechless. Though I hadn't the slightest inkling of what was happening, I knew one thing was certain; Leo had betrayed us all. My mouth opened and closed in

frustration, unable to form the words that scrambled in my mind. He wanted to say something but was interrupted by his master.

"Ah, how romantic," she cooed in her breathy way that made me shake with rage, "I must say, dear boy, your performance was impeccable. And, Kida, my humblest apologies. I never wanted to use force. I cannot fully express my dismay at this turn of events." She tsked as she came forward, revealing a dagger held by her right hand.

"What are you going to do to me?" My voice trembled as I spoke.

"Worry not, my child. It was never my intention to harm you. Without your cooperation, my hand was forced to more unorthodox methods. There's just one more thing I need from you," she said as she admired her blade. The sunlight glinted off the knife and caught my eye. Something clicked in my mind. I shut my eyes tightly and unleashed my powers with all my might, intending to blind them and make an escape. My ears were instantly met by manic laughter. I opened my eyes and gasped in disbelief. The light from within me was being sucked into the dagger where it surged up Martana's arm and into her core. She became enveloped in light. Another stream of magic flowed from the dagger into the open box Leo still held.

My life drained slowly and soon I was unable to lift my head or even keep my jaw from hanging slack. My ears rang incessantly, and it was all I could do to keep from passing out. It became harder and harder to inhale. I had no control. The stream of light continued to flow from my chest and soon dwindled to nothing. At last, the connection broke. My head rolled to the side in effort to catch a glimpse of my opponent. Her mouth moved, but her voice sounded like she was underwater.

"...you can still change your mind," I heard at last and she gestured to my box which she took from Leo. My eyes furrowed when I saw him. His eyes were downcast when Martana placed a hand on his shoulder and whispered in his ear. He turned sharply to her and asked about the captain. Her reply was not the one he wanted.

"Deceiver! You promised he would live!"

Martana spoke in mock pity, "Foolish boy. I said I'd not kill him, and I am always true to my word. He was overcome by the siren's snare."

He stepped back in horror and gripped his hair before kicking a nearby barrel. My mind couldn't yet process what he was so worked up about as I struggled to regain my strength. Suddenly, the ropes loosened. Still weak, I leaned against the mast and slid to my knees. The edges of my vision darkened, but I fought to stay conscious. I could hear relatively clearly, though I was immobile. My friends broke free of the pirates, who appeared just as shaken as the rest of us. Martana stood at the center of our attention and addressed us, "Know this; I pity you. The lot of you. Nothing brings me greater distress than seeing children forced to finish the battles begun by the previous generation. Needless to say, many of you will not survive this encounter. Be that as it may," she paused and looked directly at me, "you will not perish by my hand." She then moved to where Qoal stirred.

"Oh, how I've missed you, dragon. You made my life so much easier. You'll be happy to know I am no longer in need if your services," she said tauntingly. She turned to Sanguent who morphed into a hideous winged monster. My shallow breathing hastened, and I gripped the ropes that had piled limply in my lap. The beast was covered in leathery skin with a thick glossy mane which framed its gruesome face. The wind from its wings knocked those standing to their rumps as it rose into the air.

Qoal's eyes widened and he cried out, "No! Where did you find them?"

"My dear, don't you remember? You led me right to them," she replied as she too began to shift.

He stared in disbelief while on his knees. My bones rattled as the creatures roared; the sound thundered and shook the entire ship. As they took off, they each snatched up unfortunate crewmen, one for each talon, and ate them. The entire ship responded with chaos. I vomited as their blood sprinkled down on us from above. The blackness spread to cover my entire line of sight as I crawled forward on my hands and knees. Someone yanked me to my feet. I caught glimpses of people running frantically but could not discern what they were fleeing. A blast of heat hit my face, and I heard the crackling of flames. "Abandon ship!" Someone shouted amidst the mayhem. Smoke filled my nostrils as the world faded completely.

The ship was in pandemonium as soon as the wyverns made their strike. The first mate was among those who'd been torn to pieces by the starved beasts and few were sad to see him go. Once they were high enough, Martana and Sanguent sent forth bursts of flames which immediately engulfed the ships sun-dried sails. The fire from their bellies scorched all it met and made their throats sore. Martana knew the sailors would likely drown, but she held onto the hope of seeing Kida once again. There was something about that girl. The sorceress had never been blessed with a child of her own, but if she had she'd want her to be just like Kida.

Qoal squinted through the smoke and barely made out the forms of the wyverns as they shrank into the distance. There was no use in going after them at this point, as much as he longed to. He had to find Kida. She was crawling directly beneath the mast which began to crumble as the flames ate away its structure. He ran to her and pulled her to himself just as the crow's nest fell and shattered a few feet away. Sailors both left and right leapt into the water to escape the fire. He'd lost sight of the others and hoped they made it to safety.

Kida grew limp and he scooped her into his arms. He caught sight of the pirate holding his side in pain and shot him a glare as sharp as knives. He had half a mind to finish the traitor then and there but decided against it when he noticed the pallor of Kida's face. The smoke thickened, and he coughed as it filled his lungs. It wasn't safe for him to transform now; he'd be too weak. Worse still, he'd be forced to eat whatever crossed his path. With no other option, he dropped Kida overboard and dove in after her. She stirred and gasped when she hit the water, only to again lose consciousness and sink before he reached her. He filled his lungs with breath and plunged beneath the surface until at last he grasped her arm. He strained to keep both of their heads above the water as he kicked to a crate that bobbed not too far away.

Liza and Xomax spotted them and paddled over, for they managed to escape in a small dinghy from the side of the ship. They pulled their friends into the boat and Liza exclaimed at Kida's state. She appeared lifeless apart from the slow rise and fall of her chest. They sat panting as they watched the flames roar and crackle. The ship soon collapsed causing steam to hiss and rise from the water when it met the smoldering embers. Something grabbed onto their boat, jolting them from their captivated stares. Liza screamed when she saw the hand. Xomax rushed to their aid and found Leo clinging to the side. They hesitated, casting nervous glances at one another before hoisting him into the dinghy. Qoal remained by Kida's side as they did. Leo paid no attention to Qoal's glare as he sat on the opposite side of the wobbly vessel. No one said a word when he removed his blood-stained hand from his side. A member of his crew, no doubt fueled by treachery, had stabbed him from behind during all the chaos.

No one had thought to gather supplies when fleeing the ship. All they had was Kida's satchel which she never removed and only she could open. The ship drifted many miles off course and they could no longer see the mainland, or any land for that matter. The group was stranded for hours. None said a word as night fell, for fear of bringing to reality the nightmarish events of the day. They slept in shifts, aside from Leo who soon passed out due to blood loss, and Qoal kept first watch.

When his turn ended, he couldn't find rest. He'd distrusted that pirate since he first laid eyes on him, but no one would listen. Kida wouldn't listen. His eyes traced the soft features of her face and lingered on her pale lips. She was so peaceful. He forced his eyes to the ocean's glittering surface. The moon shone brightly and Qoal trained his gaze on the horizon. A familiar sensation ebbed at the back of his mind as he scanned the waves. There in the distance, a red dorsal fin rose from the water.

He nudged Xomax's foot who woke with a start. Qoal motioned for him to remain silent and pointed to the fin. It was still miles away from them, but seemed to be approaching quickly. Xomax instantly panicked as the fin rose ever higher. He ignored Qoal's insisting to relax and shook Liza awake. She squealed and climbed in Xomax's lap who clung to her just as tightly. Before Qoal could explain, the leviathan was upon them.

Its gigantic head broke the water's surface and it opened its massive jaws. The group, boat and all, were gone in an instant.

CHAPTER XII

Fathoms Below

Morning greeted me with a splitting headache and my parched mouth filled with an unpleasant taste. Bright light seared through my foggy vision as I strained to sit up. The room resembled a sickbay with cots lined along its walls. Memories of my encounter with Martana came flooding back all at once and the difference between dreams and reality eluded me. Did it really happen? I sincerely hoped it was all a dream. Liza's voice rang in my mind until I realized she was sitting in front of me.

"What's going on?" I croaked, and she handed me a glass of water. A few cots were occupied by people I didn't recognize. Liza's explanation confirmed my worst fears; Martana stole my powers and Leo was her accomplice. They all felt the sting of his betrayal, but they saved him anyway. We'd been stranded on a small boat until we were rescued by a shifter clan off the coast of Xenoc. Qoal was acquainted with their leader who's second form was a colossal shark-like creature and I did my best to hide my shock. Too much was happening at once.

Her face brightened suddenly, "Come with me, the others will be so glad you're okay." She held my wrist and I followed her reluctantly. I was anything but 'okay' as she dragged me along. In a daze, I paid no attention to where she led me. Our footsteps echoed off the marble floors and walls until we reached an immense dining room. Its impressive size and marine décor were not what first caught my eye, however. Qoal stood at the opposite end of the hall. I rushed to him only to be intercepted by a giant of a man who encompassed me in a bear hug.

"Kida, it is the greatest honor to have ya in my humble domain. I am King Halvon, or Hal to ya," the burly man spoke with a booming voice as he returned me to my feet. A thick beard covered his chin and his blond hair flowed from his head like the mane of a lion. His joyful eyes grew serious as he patted my shoulder, "I know your situation and I give ya my deepest condolences. Y'are free to remain here as long as ya like."

"Surely, that won't be very long," a new voice piped up. I hadn't noticed the girl standing beside Qoal. She came forward and introduced herself as Gemina, the captain of Hal's guard. She was close to my size, only much more sturdily built. Her carrot colored hair was braided back in three long plaits and her steely eyes were as blue as the sky. "A pleasure, your majesty," she said as she nodded to me. When I asked what she meant by before, she scoffed, "I meant no offense, but you have your own kingdom to attend to; if in fact Lambart even exists anymore."

Hal held up his hand to silence her, "Captain, ya'd do well ta hold yer tongue and respect our esteemed guest."

Qoal then stepped forward, "She does have a point, your majesty. While we are eternally grateful for your hospitality, we will be staying no longer than necessary." His composure surprised me, and I stared at him. He avoided my gaze whenever possible and my chest tightened at the distance rising between us.

"Well, let me treat ya for the time I have yas," Hal said and bade us to take a seat at the far end of the dining hall as dozens of servants entered carrying heaping dishes of food. Hal sat me at his right hand and Liza took the other seat next to me. He then instructed for the curtains to be opened and what laid behind them took my breath away. Servants obediently pulled the curtains open with silver chords revealing a watery scene flourishing with ocean life. I had no idea water could be so clear, but I could see every detail of every fish and plant along the sandy ocean floor. That's when I learned we were in an underwater city called Darya.

I couldn't bring myself to eat and hardly touched my plate. Instead, I watched an octopus put on a show behind Hal. It changed colors as it moved and posed gracefully. I enjoyed the distraction as my friends ate. Qoal and Gemina were deep in conversation and a pang of jealousy rose in my chest. Liza often leaned over and encouraged me to eat something; each time I'd shake my head. Hal tried to engage me in conversation, but I never knew how to respond other than nodding my head when it seemed appropriate. All I could focus on were the dancing fish. If I let my mind slip for even a moment, tears would well up in my eyes and I'd have to choke them back.

"Kida," Qoal said softly, pulling me from my thoughts. He watched me intently with concern written all over his face. I couldn't fight it any longer. The tears burst forth without warning and I buried my face in my napkin. A sob escaped my aching throat as Liza placed her hand on my back. I'd never felt so embarrassed; so used; so unworthy. I trusted Leo with my life and my heart, and he played it. To top it all off, I had put my closest friends in danger. They must have thought I was a fool. I fell hard and dragged them along with me. I wanted to disappear, right then and there, never to be seen again. I secretly wished they had left me to die on that ship. They'd stand a better chance without me now that I had no powers. I stood to leave, but Hal stopped me.

Still chewing, he dismissed the others. I was still breathing heavily when they left the room. Qoal lingered at the door before he followed Gemina. My heart ached to see them go; I didn't really want to be alone. Hal guided me to a window. Upon closer inspection, I realized they weren't windows at all. There was no glass keeping the ocean from flooding into the room. To my amazement, the king reached his arm into the rippling waters and stroked the back of a manta ray. He motioned for me to do the same. The water was cold and refreshing. Tiny fish darted around my hand as I wiggled my fingers. Even Pearl was mesmerized by glinting scales as fish swam by.

My octopus friend came closer and resumed his dance before darting away when a large fish drew near. I retracted my hand and Hal laughed. The fish was as big as me with a mouthful of sharp teeth. Hal showed no fear as he patted its slimy head. The fish then whipped around, causing a splash of water to spray out of the wall onto us. Hal cursed loudly at the fish who paid him no mind as it swam away. My lips cracked a smile for a moment then relaxed. I wiped my face with my dry hand and looked to Hal. He eyed me in a strange way.

"Ya have much to be upset about, Kida," he finally spoke, "but not all is lost. Y'are alive, aren't ya? That's reason enough to keep yar chin up. And ya have yar friends. Now that's quite a bonus, I'll say." I nodded halfheartedly, and he crouched to be eye level with me, "Now I know anyone can tell ya there is much to be happy about. Anyone can go on about how good ya have it. In the end, though, yar happiness depends on one thing. It's yar choice."

My eyes met his at last and another wave of tears ran down my cheeks. There was great truth to what he said, but how could I choose to be happy when the whole world was crashing down around me? Hal stood and opened his arms. I accepted his embrace, mainly to hide the still flowing tears. His robes were soft and inviting and he smelled of a fresh ocean breeze, with the slightest hint of fish.

"Go on, now. Yar friends need ya just as ya need them," he said with one last smile before sending me into the hallway. I took a deep breath and left to look for them. They'd gathered in a small room not far off and I noticed Qoal standing in the doorway. He let me by and Liza ran to hug me. Xomax joined her, as did Qoal and we stood wrapped in each other's arms. I didn't want the moment to end and smiled to myself as yet another tear escaped.

Qoal was the first to break from our huddle when someone tapped his shoulder. It was a servant with a worried expression. He spoke softly, and I barely made out the word 'prisoner' before he abruptly stopped speaking. Xomax and Liza casted nervous glances at Qoal. He didn't look at me as he spoke, "It's the pirate."

Dread gripped my already weak heart. I wrung my hands as the others directed their attention to me. Liza cut the tension and said, "They don't think he's going to make it."

I struggled to breathe but managed to say, "Take me to him."

Qoal protested but Liza stopped him, "It's her choice." He was none too pleased when the servant led us into the hallway. He refused to accompany us and Xomax stayed behind with him. My head throbbed with suspense. What was I thinking? He was the last person I wanted to see in that moment. Time flew by and much too soon, we arrived in the dungeons. I hadn't paid attention to how close we were but by then it was too late to turn back. Liza held my arm, bringing me little comfort. The servant left us with the guard who took us to Leo's cell. My breath caught when I saw him lying motionless on his cot. His torso was bare apart from a bloodstained bandage wrapped around his waist.

"Is he…" I couldn't finish my sentence.

The guard answered patiently, "He's alive, but not for long. Our healers did all they could." Liza asked him to unlock the cell and we stepped inside. I reached the bedside and peered down at the man I once loved. A slew of emotions welled in me. I was furious with him and myself for my blind stupidity. Even still, my heart went out to him as he laid helpless and dying before me. But there was nothing I could do. I was powerless.

I started to walk away when Liza spoke, "The bottle…do you still have it?"

Of course! I'd completely forgotten about my practicing. I only ever managed to make three successful beads of healing light and never got the change to test them. There was no guarantee they'd even work. I rummaged through my satchel and found the bottle. Pearl flew out as I did and perched on my shoulder. I held the bottle to my chest and stared at Leo. For a fleeting moment, I considered leaving him to the mercy of his wound. No one would have blamed me. Yet, something wouldn't let me turn a blind eye.

My hands shook as I opened the bottle. I half expected the lights to fade as soon as I touched them, but, as soon as the lid was removed, one of the beads floated out and rested in the palm of my hand. With a trembling breath, I placed it over the injury and watched it drift into the bandage. Liza and I held our breath as the color returned to his scruffy face and his breathing strengthened. It worked! My excitement was dashed by dread when I realized he could wake at any moment. I removed his necklace and placed it on his hand then hurried out of the cell, dragging Liza along with me.

Xomax was waiting for us when we entered the corridor. We followed him to the others, all the while Liza held my arm. She once asked if I was feeling okay and I lied by answering positively. She didn't buy it for a second. King Halvon greeted me with a smile when we entered. Qoal asked how soon I'd be ready to go, but my mind refused to think clearly enough to answer. Darya was pleasant enough and it was a welcome feeling to be cut off from the rest of Ordenia. However, I knew the longer we stayed, the harder it would be to leave. Then there was the matter of Leo. Do we take him along? Or leave him in the dungeon?

They must have read my thoughts, for Xomax soon brought him up, "We should at least wait until Leo recovers."

"On the unlikely chance he does, he needs to stay right where he is," Qoal answered quickly.

"We can't condemn him for being controlled by Martana," Xomax argued, "You of all people should understand that."

Qoal hit the table and his voice rose, "That pirate acted in his own will. As you said, I understand such things. She may have been holding something over his head, but he very well could have fought her."

"How can you be so sure? You can't!" Xomax retaliated. He and Leo were close friends, but I could not deny the hurt I felt as his defending him.

"What say you, voyager? Have you seen a single future where the pirate brings us any benefit?"

Liza, who clearly wanted no part in the conversation, answered, "It's not that simple. But…he does have a role in our future."

Qoal rubbed his head in frustration, "I suppose that means he'll survive his wounds." That's when Liza mentioned my healing him. Qoal looked me dead in the eye and growled, "You did what?"

I gulped guiltily, "I couldn't just let him die."

"You did the right thing, Kida," Xomax encouraged.

Qoal stood abruptly, clearly exasperated, "This means nothing. He is still a traitor who deserves extreme punishment."

"If we had kept that mindset, you wouldn't be here, Qoal," Liza interjected.

"That was different," he started, but he knew she was right. He returned to his seat with a sigh.

"We all know why you're really so worked up," Xomax muttered under his breath.

"And what's that supposed to mean?" he demanded. Liza tried to stop him from explaining, but he cut her off saying I deserved to know. Nothing could have prepared me for what he said next. Leo and I were bound to one another. The ritual Martana made him perform united us, thus giving him the ability to open my box and extract my powers. Such ties could only be broken by two things; death and an unspeakable method. My mind couldn't fathom a fate worse than death, so I begged him to tell me the other way to break the bond. His eyes shifted, and he refused to comply, for even he didn't know the answer. After much debate and many objections from Qoal, we decided to bring Leo with us when we left in the morning.

We rose early, and Hal provided us with new satchels filled with provisions enough to last a lifetime. He and Gemina accompanied us to the edge of the city which was a vast wall of ocean. I craned my neck upward in effort to find the top to no avail. The wall seemed to be a dome that covered the entire kingdom. I asked Hal how in the world we were supposed to reach the surface without drowning.

He laughed, "You could always ride in my mouth again."

His response confused me, and my head ached as I tried to comprehend. "Relax," Gemina said rolling her eyes, "We have a portal to the mainland for non-aquatic folk." She then turned to Hal and requested to come with us.

Immediately, I wanted to protest, but the king refused for me, "You are needed in Darya, Captain. As you always will be."

She huffed and said, "Aren't you tired of being known as the coward of Xenoc? It is not I who says it, but if we don't return to the mainland and fight, we will waste away."

"Now, Gemina," Hal scolded, "We've been through this time and again. Have ya no pride in your ancestors?"

"If I may, my king, what good are ancestors of there are no future generations to remember them?"

"My answer stands," he replied, his anger rising, "No daughter of mine will set foot in Xenoc while war continues to rage." I hadn't known their relation until now, but things between them wear clearer upon the discovery. Her eyes narrowed as she spun away from him. She approached Qoal and they clasped hands in farewell. My eyes darted to my feet hoping he hadn't seen the redness of my face. With one final goodbye, Gemina plunged into the wall of water. As she did, her shape changed. Her legs fused into a long rust colored tail and the three braids atop her head grew into three green fins that ran along the length of her spine. Her skin became a shade of blue that matched the water almost perfectly. She took one last look at us before swimming away.

Upon Qoal's request, Leo was led to us by a prison guard with his hands restrained. His health had returned completely. I felt his eyes on me from the moment we spotted one another from a distance and I avoided looking as him with every fiber of my being. The portal was hidden within the wall and Hal showed us precisely where to walk through. I thanked him for everything and he welcomed me back any time. Without looking back, I stepped through the wall of water followed by Qoal, Liza, Xomax and finally, Leo. We reached the other side and found ourselves in a worn-down palace. The ruins smelled of foul brimstone. I tried in vain to push the stench from my nostrils as Xomax examined the map King Halvon gave us. Not soon enough, we started out in the direction of Xenoc's neighbor; Lambart.

We did our best to make good time and only stopped when we could walk no further. One night, as we neared the border, Liza panted that we should set up camp. I, too, was overcome by exhaustion. Leo was removed from the night watch shifts and Xomax took the first. I was instructed to sleep through the night, despite my eagerness to help keep watch. Rest would not come easily, though. Wheels turned incessantly in my mind as the hard ground reminded me just how wonderful beds were. After much tossing and turning and little comfort, I at last found sleep.

My dreams were filled with haunting images of darkness consuming me and Martana murdering each of my friends as I stood helplessly by. At the very center of my nightmares was Leo, holding my beating heart in his outstretched hand. I couldn't retrieve it from him before he let it fall from his grasp. I awoke gasping and clutched my chest. My hands were icy, and I held them to my burning face as I let out a sob. A low rumbling met my ears and I sat up slowly. Qoal sat a few feet away with his back to me. I remained frozen and slowed my breath as I contemplated going over to him. Something had changed between us and it drove me mad. After a short pep talk, I bucked up enough courage to sit beside him.

"You're supposed to be asleep," he whispered without even turning his head to look at me.

"I tried," was all I could say. We sat in silence and watched Pearl as she curled into a ball in the grass by my feet.

Qoal sighed and said, "I have to go."

My eyes darted to him, "What?"

He grunted as he stood, "I was going to leave after waking Liza to relieve my watch, but since you're awake…"

"What do you mean, leave," I asked incredulous, "you aren't abandoning us, are you?" He held up his hands and shushed me as my voice rose. We moved a few steps away from the group to keep from disturbing them.

"Please, don't do this," he said softly, "I thought helping you would make up for some of the pain I'd caused, but it's time for me to return to my people."

"Why- why are you doing this?" Tears burned behind my eyes threatening to spill at any moment and my voice cracked, "I need you here."

He heaved a heavy sigh, "You don't need me, Kida. You have them." He gestured to the others, but my eyes remained glued to his face. His gaze was unwavering, and I knew there'd be no convincing him. I removed a bead of light from my satchel and pressed it into his hand when he tried to refuse it.

"If you're going to leave, the least you can do is take it."

He accepted my gift then took my hand and laced his fingers through mine, bringing the back of my hand to his forehead as he had in times past. My tears escaped as I did the same.

"You have my trust," I felt his breath on my arm as he spoke. Thunder sounded in the distance as his hand left mine, and my skin grew cold where his touch once rested. I stared after his tall frame as he walked away, my stomach twisted in pain. My heart couldn't take much more. Despite my efforts to suppress my feelings, they could no longer be withheld. I ran to him and he turned just in time for me to fall into his embrace. His lips found mine and we stood entwined for what felt like ages. He held me so close, I felt as though I were melting into him. I longed to reside in that moment forevermore. I buried my face in his neck and my body flooded with his warmth. The oncoming storm had not yet reached us when he pulled away slowly. He held my face in his hands and gazed into me, the same way he had on the day we met. I searched his eyes for any sign that he'd changed his mind, but they showed nothing but sadness. I opened my mouth to beg him to stay once again, but he brushed his thumb across my lips to silence me.

He put his head down and turned away. This time, he ran. In mid step, he transformed until all I saw was the silhouette of a dragon disappearing into the dawning sky. Numbness overtook me, and I didn't feel the first drops of rain as they fell softly into my hair. The others stirred as the drops fell harder. We quickly packed up camp just before sunrise and hurried forward despite the unrelenting downpour. Liza asked about Qoal, but my silence was answer enough. I couldn't bear to give voice to his absence and pushed him from my thoughts. We entered Lambart a day and a half later and found it in no better state than Xenoc. Each and every town we passed through had been pillaged and left in utter disrepair. Hopes of finding my parents were all but dashed. Liza did her best to keep our spirits up by recanting her visions. Of course, not many involved us in any way, but she assured us that not all hope was lost.

I asked her why she couldn't just tell us everything that was to come, and her reply never wavered; that's not how things worked. My frustration grew when she refused to explain any further. All I could do was trust. As we walked, I ignored all attempts of Leo to talk to me. With Qoal gone, he found a new boost of self-esteem and convinced Xomax to unbind him. After countless cold shoulders, he eventually stopped pestering me.

We walked along a river which opened to a bay in which the capitol lied on an island not far off the coast. If my parents were alive, that's where they'd be. Upon Leo's suggestion, we entered a nearby village and salvaged enough materials to create a makeshift raft. As we worked, I was unable to shake an eerie feeling that we were being watched. Soon, the others noticed as well. There was no denying the occasional rustle or sound of footsteps which caused each of us to glance around in paranoia. Even still, our abduction was swift and effortless.

They came while the guys were busy dragging our raft and Liza and I were weighted down with the satchels. A mob of fifteen to twenty people ambushed us and carried us away after placing dark hoods over our heads. I kicked and flailed wildly, but it was no use. I hoped the others were faring better as I was pushed and shoved in all directions. Liza shouted as she was thrown into me. I tried to reach out and steady her, but my blindness hindered me. I heard the others cry out in confusion. My senses were bombarded by a multitude of voices shouting, hands guiding me forward and smells of herbs and body odor. My heartbeat pounded in my ears. In one swift motion, my blindfold was lifted to reveal a cavern jam packed with dirty faces who peered up at me in awe and wonder.

A voice called out from afar, "State your name and purpose in our province."

I looked to the others whose faces bore the same confusion as mine. Liza's eyes met mine and she shook her head in terror. Swallowing the lump in my throat, I replied, "I am Kida, and these are my friends. We mean no harm; we've just come to-"

My explanation was interrupted by a woman who yelled, "Wait!" Her voice came from behind and I slowly turned to face her. She had bright green eyes and light brown hair that darkened at the roots. Something about her was strangely familiar. Tears cascaded down her lined cheeks as she reached out to me. "My daughter," she said, "you've come home."

Made in the USA
Monee, IL
12 February 2020